Bones in the Nest

HELEN CADBURY

Allison & Busby Limited
12 Fitzroy Mews
London W1T 6DW
allisonandbusby.com

First published in Great Britain by Allison & Busby in 2015.

First Edition

ISBN 978-0-7490-1759-0

Typeset in 10.5/15.5 pt Sabon by
Allison & Busby Ltd.

The paper used for this Allison & Busby publication
has been produced from trees that have been legally sourced
from well-managed and credibly certified forests.

Printed and bound by
CPI Group (UK) Ltd, Croydon, CR0 4YY

HELEN CADBURY writes fiction, poetry and plays. She worked as an actor before becoming a teacher and recently spent five years teaching in prisons. She has an MA in Writing from Sheffield Hallam University. Helen grew up in Birmingham and Oldham. After living in London for many years, she came north and settled in York where she lives with her family. Her debut novel, *To Catch a Rabbit*, was winner of the inaugural Northern Crime Competition.

helencadbury.com

By Helen Cadbury

To Catch a Rabbit
Bones in the Nest

To Z, the girl on the train, and her dad

PROLOGUE

O, Allah,
help me through the hardship and agony of death

Glass crunches on the road. Pavement hammers up through ankles, knees. On to the grass. Too slippery to get a grip. Jump over a low fence. Playground. Feet whack down and it gives something back, speed, pace. Can hardly breathe. They're not far behind. Need to get under cover. There's someone there, by the community centre, moving my way. Don't go down there. Double back, past the swings. Now there's another one, crossing Darwin Road. Thick-necked fucker. Need to get to the flats, lose myself.

I'm not even tooled up, nothing, because I promised her I'd stop carrying. She's the best thing that ever happened to me and I told her, I'm in it for the long haul, girl, I'm going to change up for you. And I meant it. I mean it. Right now the last thing I need is some white boys on my tail. She wasn't at the library. The text said to come and pick her up. But there was nobody there. Door locked. Where did you go, princess? Saw the flicker of a reflection. Got out of there before a baseball bat whacked on my skull. Heard it crack on the glass. Been running since. There were three of them. The big one with the bat and two others. White boys, bad skin. Maybe smackheads, maybe not. Now there's two more. My chest's burning. Need to stop. Door open, corner of the block. Head for it. Head down. Don't know who they're with or what their beef is, except my face don't fit.

Cooler inside. Dark. Bleach on concrete hurts my throat. Grab the handrail and haul myself up the stairs. Something moves. A shape. Two shapes. Turn round and the door shuts below me.

This is it.

CHAPTER ONE

One Week Earlier
Doncaster

The marked police car slowed as it turned the corner behind the railway station. A row of terraced houses led away from the fenced-in track. From the passenger seat PC Sean Denton could see two hooded figures, silhouetted beneath a street light. It was hard to tell, but male and under twenty would be his best guess. There was a glimmer of skin as one hand reached out from a pocket into another hand; a split second as the two figures froze and one hooded face peered up at the approaching headlights of the car. Then they were gone.

'Down there,' PC Gavin Wentworth put his foot on the accelerator, without changing out of second gear, then slammed the brakes on at the opening of a narrow alleyway.

'I'm on it,' Sean said.

He jumped out and ran into the dark. Ahead of him a security light came on and the shadows flooded with colour. He clocked one red and one blue hooded top, one pair of grey tracksuit bottoms and one pair black. A car door slammed behind him, followed by Gav's footsteps. Sean was gaining on the suspects, but he had to make a choice. One was faster than the other, so he left the slow one for Gav. There was a risk the slower lad would make a swing for him and, for a split second, it was like running through the pages of the training manual: torch in his left hand to shield himself, while he grabbed the back of the red hoodie, twisted the fabric hard round and tucked his leg in front of the runner. The suspect fell sideways, folded under Sean's arm and went down. Out of the corner of his eye, Sean sensed the other lad look back, see Gavin and sprint off down the alley.

'Shit.'

He felt like he'd backed the wrong horse, but he didn't have time to dwell on it. His prisoner squirmed face down on the ground, kicking and swearing, as Sean reached for the cuffs.

'Oi! Calm down, son!'

He tried to grip the boy's wrists. They were bony and thin. Sean wondered how old he was. The boy turned his head and the hood fell back to reveal sharp cheekbones and dark eyes, which narrowed as they met Sean's. Then the boy lifted up his head and smacked it face down on the ground.

'What the hell?'

Sean had the cuffs on him now, but again the boy cracked his forehead against the stone sets of the alleyway.

'Oh, Jesus! Stop him doing that!' Gav shouted.

Sean tried to get the suspect up on his feet, but the boy pulled back, twisting and slippery like a fish. His forehead met the ground again and when he lifted it this time, there was blood above one eyebrow. The security light went out and the blood dimmed to a shiny purple in the gloom. Then Gav was there, grabbing the boy's shoulders, spinning him round. Sean pulled him up from behind, both hands on the cuffed wrists. It was like trying to control a puppet with a life of its own, but together they managed to propel him towards the car.

'What about the other one?' Sean said.

'He's gone.'

'You shouldn't have done that,' the young lad was saying. 'You're not allowed to batter the suspects.'

Sean felt sick.

'Take no notice,' Gav said. 'He's well known, this little shit. He tries it every time. Don't you Saleem? Well I think you've pushed your luck now. Let's see if we can have you for resisting arrest.'

At Doncaster Central Police Station, they handed Saleem Asaf over to the custody sergeant and went back to the car. It smelt of overripe apples, sweet and dying in trapped air.

'Mucky buggers,' Sean said. His foot found an apple core under the empty chocolate wrappers and it gave way under his heel. 'How come the day shift never clean the cars out? I've got a good mind to dump this lot in someone's boots.'

Gav belted up and put the car into reverse. Except it wasn't reverse, it was third. The car leapt forward and juddered as it stalled, inches away from the concrete wall of the police yard.

'Bollocks,' Gav said. 'Why does every car have reverse in a different place?'

'One of life's mysteries, Gav.'

'You're not wrong there.'

Sean loosened the seat belt that had tightened across his neck.

'Count to three and start again,' Gav muttered under his breath and reversed the car, smoothly this time, out of the tight space, avoiding the dented end of a van. He wiped something sticky off the steering wheel with his sleeve and indicated to pull onto the road.

'Living the dream, Sean, living the fucking dream.'

Sean didn't reply. He wanted to say it was all right. It's what he'd signed up for, worked hard for, harder than some when it came to it. He knew he was lucky to have Gav as a partner. There were plenty of officers who took the piss, still made the same jokes they did when he was a Police Community Support Officer, but Gav was all right: a time-served constable with a reputation for being fair, but firm. Sean just wished he didn't moan so much. It was taking the shine off.

Sean shifted his feet on the mound of thrown-away crap as Gav swung left around Market Place. They parked the car and watched and waited for the next call. This town didn't sleep and Sean wondered where people found the money. After half an hour a job came in around the corner, two men fighting outside the Ace Bonanza Amusement Arcade. When they arrived, neither assailant wanted to press charges.

'No worries, he's my best mate!' The apparent victim was wiping blood from his nose.

The two men locked together in a hug, but Sean thought they were just as likely to shift back to something uglier.

'If you say so,' Gav shrugged. Sean was reaching for a notebook, but Gav shook his head. 'Let it go, son. Less paperwork.'

A pub called in a handbag theft, so they dropped in to take statements, shouting to be heard above the karaoke. Then they were back in the car, trying not to collide with a woman weaving drunkenly across the road. She turned and flicked two fingers at them, before staggering on to the opposite pavement.

By 11 p.m. they were passing the railway station again. A British Transport Police van was parked up on the forecourt. Sean thought back to the first case he'd covered as a PCSO, and the vulnerable women who'd been befriended on the station platforms and ended up on the game. He wondered what their colleagues in the Transport Police were up to tonight. He hoped for their sake it was nothing more than fare dodgers.

'What's the difference between South Yorkshire Police and the BTP?' Gav said.

Sean shrugged.

'BTP do longer shifts.'

'That meant to be funny?'

'That's what they say!' Gav laughed but Sean just shook his head.

As they drove, they looked out for Saleem's associate and argued back and forth over what the two lads were doing, who was dealing and who was buying. The sky began to lighten. Sean opened the car window to let the clean, damp morning air drive out the stale smell. A blackbird sang a greeting from the skinny tree outside the law courts as Gav pulled into the police yard. It was 6.25 a.m. and their shift was almost over.

'What are you up to for the next couple of days?' Gav said as they walked down the corridor of the police station.

'Not a lot.' Sean did have a plan for his days off, but he wasn't ready to share it with Gav. 'You?'

'I've got a box set to catch up on and the usual domestic drudgery of DIY and sorting out the jungle we laughingly call a garden. Nothing special.'

Gav said goodbye and went off in the direction of the custody suite. Sean finished his paperwork and was handing in his radio, when Gav reappeared.

'They've let him go.'

'Saleem Asaf?'

'Aye, nothing on him. Little bastard.'

'What a waste of time,' Sean said.

'There's something else,' Gav said. 'He's filed an official complaint.'

'Against me?'

'That's right, son. You might be getting a call from Professional Standards.'

'Should I be worried?'

'Not necessarily.'

Back in his nan's kitchen, Sean sank his face into a cup of strong tea. It was eight o'clock in the morning and he needed to sleep.

'Busy night?' Maureen put a plate of toast in front of him.

Sean rolled his head to one side to release a crick in his neck from wrestling with the boy.

14

'You could say that.'

He chewed on the hot toast and picked up the local newspaper, trying to read the sport on the back page, but his eyes couldn't focus. He liked to read something every day, to keep up what he'd started at night classes. It's what his teacher had told him to do: that patient, mild-mannered man, who'd never called him thick or lazy, just gave him ways to see things differently. He put the paper down. It was exhausting sometimes. He would always be dyslexic, however good he became at finding ways around it.

A second piece of toast, and a third, filled his stomach. Sleep was overcoming him. There was something he needed to say to his nan, but it would have to wait.

'I'd better go up,' he pushed the plate away.

Maureen reached for the paper and opened it in the centre, hunting for her horoscope. He read the headline on the front page.

'"Chasebridge Killer . . . Released?" What's that about?' he said 'Have I missed something?'

'Hang on, I'm reading my stars: it's going to be a good week for money, but I need to be careful who I rely on and someone will bring me news about a change. What? Oh.'

Maureen looked over the headline and the short column underneath. Most of the page was taken up with a picture of a dark-haired girl in a school uniform, with a choppy fringe and a sharp chin.

'I can't believe they've let her out. Flipping nutter.'

Sean leant against the door frame, wanting so badly to go up to bed, but not moving. 'Who's that then?'

'It was while you were still living at your dad's, not long

after your mam died. Here it is: Marilyn Nelson, teenage killer. She pushed a lad of sixteen off the top of the flats. Says here he'd been abused and tortured before she pushed him. Nasty.'

'I think I remember.' The sound of a rusty swing and a shape falling. 'And she's out?'

'Says so here. Thought she could be living in Scotland or Devon. Well, that's not very precise. Served ten years. Doesn't seem much when his poor mother will never get him back.'

He hesitated, needing to say something to Maureen, but he couldn't find the words. *Someone will bring news about a change*. Not yet. It could wait.

Upstairs, he closed the curtains and kicked off his shoes, undid his belt and let his trousers fall. He peeled his shirt off over his head and climbed into the single bed. He set an alarm on his phone and turned his back to the light that was seeping through the pattern of footballs and trophies on his curtains. In the back pocket of his trousers was a piece of paper, folded into a tight, hard square. It was details of a flat to rent in town.

He was on the edge of sleep when it came back to him. He was eleven years old and swinging on the only swing that wasn't broken, listening to the grind and squeak of the rusty chain around the top bar. He saw something move on top of Eagle Mount Four, the block where the lift never worked. He thought it was a bird at first, then he thought it was a bundle that someone had dropped. And then he understood. It was the unmistakable shape of a person in a dark coat, a coat that billowed out like a pair of wings. The shape carried on falling and the wings didn't open. He knew it must have

16

landed in the square, in the middle of the four blocks that made up the Eagle Mount flats. He didn't want to see it. He stayed on the swing until the sound of metal on metal slowed down to nothing.

Long after it happened, after his own memories were messed up with other people's versions, he could still hear the quietness that followed, as if the four towers were holding their breath.

CHAPTER TWO

York

The telly's on in the corner of the lounge. There's a programme on about that spaceman. Years ago. First man on the moon. Chloe doesn't like the look of the other girls hogging the soft seats. She doesn't want to sit on the hard plastic chair with the wonky leg, so she stands for a while just inside the door. Nobody looks round. Eventually she goes back upstairs and lies down on her bed. There's no need to put the light on; the orange street light floods the thin cotton curtain. She can see the pattern of a stain. It's like the outline of an arm with a knobbly elbow. She narrows her eyes and it changes to a bird's-eye view of a cliff edge and a beach, the ins and outs of coves marked in orangey brown. The woman's voice on the spaceman programme is still with her.

'There were no challenges left. He'd flown higher and further than anyone had ever flown.'

The woman speaking was his wife. The second one. She was obviously prettier and younger than the first. The spacewife said it wasn't true that he was a recluse, just that he was a media recluse. Chloe smiles. She can relate to that, except he had a whole ranch to hide in, while she's only got these four yellow walls and a curtain between her and them. She wonders how long it will be before they find her. There's always someone who needs the money, who's willing to sell a story to a tabloid. The spaceman threw himself deeper into work. He went into the world of business. That sounds like a nice world, not open and empty like the moon, but a busy world, a world you could hide in; a whole planet of computers and desks and photocopiers. She closes her eyes and sees star-fighters flying at lightning speed through a landscape of filing cabinets. It's too hot in the room; she can't settle. She gets up to open the window. The hinge is fixed so that it only creates a five-centimetre gap, but it's better than nothing. She notices a car waiting on the kerb, engine running.

'He was true to himself. He was the man that you saw. That was him,' the spacewife said.

What you see is what you get. She closes the curtain again and gets back into bed. *That's me too*, she thinks, and turns on her side, pulling the quilt over her. She'd like to sleep now, it's been a long day, but someone is ringing the doorbell below. A man shouts into the intercom:

'You've got to talk to me!'

There's a silence and she hears the front door open. They shouldn't let a man in here, not at this time of night. She gets up and peers through a small gap where the curtains don't quite meet, not wanting to draw attention to herself. The man hasn't gone inside, he's standing on the path and the young woman who welcomed her this morning is standing close to him. Chloe can't hear what they're saying, but the woman is trying to calm the man. It looks like she knows him; they stand close but they don't touch. There is no violence between them and the man is pleading with his hands. Chloe is relieved that it's an officer he wants to speak to, not one of the women. Then she corrects herself. The Asian girl on duty isn't an officer, she's something else; Chloe can't remember the word. There will be new words, new jobs now she's on the outside. The 'us' and 'them' will have different labels. The young man is Asian too. He wears a suit, but his shirt is hanging out of his trousers and his tie loose around his open collar. Chloe thinks he must be the staff woman's boyfriend. Link worker. That's it. She's Chloe's link worker. She gets back into bed, thinking about links in a chain, links in a fence, the missing link.

The door closes and for a few moments there's quiet. Then someone's kicking the door from the outside, kicking it so hard Chloe can feel it coming up through the building, vibrating through her thin, spongy mattress. The front door opens again and another voice, male this time, clearly threatens that the police will be called. Chloe gets up and shuts the window. As she gets back into bed, she reaches for the radio she got this morning on the market. It plugs into the mains, so she can have it on all night.

Under the quilt a DJ's voice joins her. He introduces a guy called Jimmy Page and together they tell a story about Jimmy Page's mystery guitar. The DJ and Jimmy must know the story, but the DJ's asking questions to make sure Jimmy doesn't miss bits out. She listens carefully to see if Jimmy sounds like he means what he's saying, or whether he's just going through the motions. It's a special skill when someone's asking you about stuff you've said a thousand times before. She's an expert in it. Panels and boards and psychologists and governors. She's been over the same things again and again with them.

The guitar is in the house when Jimmy Page is growing up. It doesn't belong to anyone and he doesn't know how it got there. He sees someone playing a Lonnie Donegan tune at school, and he wants to be able to do that. He goes home to get the guitar and the rest . . .

She doesn't hear the rest. She wakes up later and there's a woman talking. The music is different. She switches the radio off and puts it on the floor, carefully. Behind her closed eyes, Jimmy Page and the spaceman dance together, silhouetted against a huge Hollywood moon.

Chloe wakes in a light-filled room. For a moment, she thinks she must have taken an extra tablet. She can't focus, can't snap out of the heavy, sweat-damp sleep of messy dreams. The sun is pouring through the glass, cooking up the air. She remembers closing the window to keep the noise out, but now it smells of the trapped odour of all the other women who have slept here before her. She pushes the quilt off and peels her damp T-shirt away from her belly, flapping it to cool her skin. The display on her phone reads ten-twenty. Confused, it takes a moment to sink in that this is ten-twenty in the morning; she's slept for eleven hours. She leans over and reaches for the bottle of water she filled from the tap last

21

night. It's blood heat, but she swills it around her mouth and swallows it anyway.

Finally she swings her legs round and sits up, dizzy for a moment. She takes the can of Icy Mist body spray from the top of the bedside locker and sprays a long burst, coughing as the droplets drift back towards her and sting her throat. She bought it yesterday in Boots. On her way to the till, she browsed the lipstick testers, inhaling the greasy sweetness that took her right back to her childhood, watching her mum get ready for work. *Don't touch me! You'll mess up my face.* She left the lipsticks on their stand and paid one ninety-nine for the own-brand body spray.

She moves on shaky legs to the window and opens it again, letting a puff of warm air into the room. A bus is pulling up outside. There's something she has to remember. Her link worker mentioned it yesterday. A trip out, did she want to come? A trip into the city centre, on the bus, or they could walk, it would depend on the weather. Meet at ten-thirty. She looks at her watch. Ten twenty-eight. Shit. She drops the curtain and pulls off the T-shirt, sprays her body all over and grovels in her bag for a clean pair of knickers. No time for socks. She pulls her canvas pumps over sticky feet. In two minutes she'll be ready.

The girl in the office is wearing a pale pink dress over black leggings. Her shoes are tiny sandals, covered in pink sequins, as if she's going to a party, not on a sightseeing trip. She tells Chloe that she's waiting for a couple more and then they'll set off, and she might as well sit in the garden until they're ready, since it's so hot. Chloe wishes she'd made more effort to remember the girl's name. She

22

can't ask her now. It will make her sound stupid.

The garden at Meredith House is more like a yard, surrounded by an old brick wall. Someone's filled a few pots with busy Lizzies and begonias. Chloe would have chosen something textured, like gazanias, whose petals she would like to press against her cheek to feel their softness. The back door of Meredith House opens and she senses someone watching her. She's not going to turn around; she's got stuff to look at. This is her time and her space. Let them cram in their sweaty TV room with the curtains closed, watching daytime chat shows, if they want to, but they should leave her alone.

'You Chloe?'

She nods.

'Not deaf then. Thought you might be.'

She turns then, thinking this woman is trying to wind her up, but she sees someone smiling through grey, broken teeth. The woman has a scar pulling her cheek up to the corner of one eye. Despite the damage, Chloe sees softness in her face. Maybe the smile is genuine. She does her best to return it.

'I'm Emma,' the other woman says. 'Taheera said you were coming on the trip into town. I think it's just the two of us. The others can't be bothered.'

Taheera. She'll try not to forget it again. Taheera. It sounds good, smooth and pretty like a stone on the beach. Emma heads back into the building and Chloe follows. It's too hot to walk, so they take the bus. A low single-decker carries them through streets of semi-detached houses and out on to a straighter road, before it dumps them opposite a dirty concrete building, with a Job Centre wedged in one corner.

When she heard she was coming to York on release, Chloe wasn't bothered either way. All she wanted was to go where nobody knew her. People told her it was a beautiful city, the sort of place you'd go on holiday, but that didn't help. The only holiday she remembers was a trip with her mum to Skegness, sitting on a donkey with a melted ice cream dripping down her arm, not daring to lick it in case letting go of the reins made the donkey gallop away.

'There's the Job Centre, Chloe,' Taheera's voice interrupts her thoughts. 'You've got your appointment tomorrow, so you'll know the way now, won't you?'

Chloe's not sure she'll remember anything. She took no note of street names or how many corners they turned. She just watched the people, the colours and shapes of them, the sheer variety of people. It shouldn't have been so sudden, her release, but her jail was closing and although the parole board asked the same questions they'd asked every year, this time she got them right. Now she's out, with a room in a bail hostel and Taheera as her link worker. It could be worse, she thinks, and lets herself smile.

'Good,' Taheera nods briskly. 'You'll be fine. Right, let's go sightseeing.'

As they wait to cross the road by the bus stop, Chloe watches a group of tourists, cameras slung round their necks, hunting for something to capture, but there's not much to see on this street. Minicabs and buses go past, looking like minicabs and buses. To Chloe the world looks the same as it always has done, as if ten years were a day, or an hour. A woman lifts her camera and Chloe turns her face away.

'Come on!' Emma takes hold of her arm.

24

They cross the road and pass the Job Centre. Immediately the streets become narrower and prettier. She dodges a school party, pressing its way along the pavement, and steps into the road. There are fewer cars now and the buildings begin to push in on them. Taheera rushes ahead, cutting between the clumps of people. Chloe and Emma nearly lose her.

'There!'

Taheera has rounded the end of a high wall. In front of them is an enormous old building. Chloe can't take it in. She steps back to get a better view.

'York Minster,' Taheera says. 'If you fancy it, we could go up the tower. You can see for miles.'

Chloe looks up. There's a figure, standing on the very top of the tower, like a statue on the battlements. He raises an arm and waves. She blinks hard and he's gone.

'Are there people up there?' Chloe says.

'I should think so,' Taheera says. 'There's a tour every half hour. Shall we?'

'I'll give it a go,' Emma shrugs, laughing, as if she's not sure she'll make it. 'I'll try anything once.'

Chloe shakes her head, rooted to the spot, trying to understand what she's seen.

'You coming?' Emma says.

The other two women are walking across the open space that surrounds the building. Taheera looks back, inviting, shaking out her straight black hair. Chloe looks up and sees someone falling from the tower, long hair streaming out behind. It can't be. She looks again and there's nothing. Taheera and Emma are walking away from her. She can't

25

stay here alone, so she forces herself to step forward, longing for the claustrophobia of the shopping street.

As they get closer to the building, Chloe thinks she might be sick, but she doesn't tell them that. They climb a wide flight of steps.

'I'll sit here, by the wall of the church,' she says, pressing her back into the warm stone and sliding down until she's cross-legged.

'They call it a minster, actually,' Emma says. 'Are you not coming in?'

Taheera glances at her watch and looks out across the open space as if she's expecting someone. A young man is working his way round a tour group towards them. He's taller and slimmer than the man who was shouting outside Meredith House last night.

He stops a few feet away and flicks a glance to Emma and Chloe, as if he's waiting for an introduction.

'Hey! You made it,' Taheera tucks a long strand of hair behind her ear. It makes her look instantly younger.

'Yes, I made it,' the young man says.

'Hiya! I'm Emma, pleased to meet you.'

Emma holds out her hand to shake his and Chloe thinks she sounds a bit forward, a bit desperate. Taheera doesn't introduce him, just suggests they go inside. That suits Chloe, the fewer people she has to talk to the better.

'I'll stay here,' she says, 'I've got a bit of a headache.'

'Are you sure?' Taheera looks concerned.

'I'll be fine.'

'You'll stay right here, on the steps?' Taheera says. 'I don't want you wandering around getting lost.'

'I won't budge. Promise.'

Chloe watches them go in, Emma leading the way. As the young man passes, Chloe catches a glimpse below the hem of his jeans. He's wearing an electronic tag round his ankle. His hand reaches for Taheera's and together they disappear inside the Minster.

CHAPTER THREE

Doncaster

After a run of night shifts, Sean slept until mid-afternoon. He'd got two nights off and was hoping to get into town before the estate agents' shop closed. He pulled the little square of paper out of his pocket and unfolded it. *Fabulous studio apartment to let in sought-after square, a few minutes' walk from Doncaster centre*. He dialled the number. Getting a place of his own had been on his mind for a while, but it had to be the right place, at the right time. When he had everything sorted, he would tell his nan. A woman answered the phone and invited him to come in right now, if he was in the area. She'd be happy to take his details and set up some viewings, including the flat he'd got his eye on, and there were others that might appeal. He thanked her and said he'd be there shortly.

The afternoon was beginning to cool as he rode his moped up the hill through the Chasebridge estate. He usually tried to avoid this route, but today he stopped near the top of the slope, beside the playground. It looked as if someone had lit a bonfire at the foot of the slide. A patch of asphalt had sunk into a hollow, its edges curled up, like burnt bacon. There was something about the girl in Maureen's newspaper that was pulling him back to where he'd sat on the swing, a witness to something he didn't understand at the time. He never told his dad what he'd seen that day. Jack Denton's moods had taught Sean to be wary of starting conversations for fear of them spiralling into arguments. Not long afterwards, one final row has driven him out of his father's home for good, down the hill to the quieter streets of The Groves and his nan's house. Gradually the story of the murder had faded from his consciousness.

He switched the engine into neutral and rested his foot on the kerb, trying to recall what he'd seen. While he was staring into the middle distance, he spotted an old man, shuffling along the pavement towards the entrance to Eagle Mount One, a white plastic bag dangling from one hand. It knocked against the side of the man's leg as he limped slowly along the pavement. Sean put the moped into gear and followed the road around the top of the playground. He watched the man put the bag down and fumble in his pocket for something, his free hand clenched awkwardly as he steadied his balance. Sean gripped the brake and came to a standstill.

'All right, Dad.'

Sean was struck by the fact that his father had shrunk since he last saw him. Folds of dry, bristled skin met round his mouth and his skin had a yellow tinge. A slow smile revealed more gaps than teeth. Jack Denton wasn't even sixty, and Sean had mistaken him for an old pensioner.

'Sean, lad! You coming in for a cuppa?'

There was still plenty of time to get to the estate agents' before they closed. Jack had been a bugger all his life, but he was still his dad. It wouldn't hurt to spend five minutes with him. As he followed his father up to the first floor flat, Sean told himself that Jack couldn't hurt him now. That was all a long time ago.

In Jack's hallway it looked like someone had tried to decorate. One wall was painted a muddy orange, which petered out before it reached the ceiling, and a new vacuum cleaner stood in the doorway of the lounge. It would take more than a vacuum cleaner, Sean thought, to find the pattern in that carpet; it was dark with grease.

'Nice colour paint.'

'That was Eileen's idea. Terracotta she says. Not finished yet. Needs someone with a stepladder to do that last bit.'

Jack headed for the kitchen.

'Who's Eileen?' Sean said.

His dad coughed and it caught in his throat so he couldn't answer for a moment.

'Lady friend. She stays over, keeps the place in shape.'

The kitchen was grubby and strewn with dirty plates, but someone had put a bunch of artificial flowers in a vase on the table.

'Good. That's good.'

Jack bent stiffly to put a carton of milk in the fridge and Sean noticed there wasn't much else in there. No food, but also a curious absence of beer cans, both in the fridge and on the side, and not a bottle of whisky in sight.

'Dad,' Sean asked carefully, 'have you packed in drinking?'

His father stood up straight and turned to face him.

'Doctor's orders, son. My body can't take it. I've been off four weeks and counting. They've even got me going to AA meetings.'

'That's great.'

'Aye, well, it was that or die and I'm not ready yet. Are you going to put that kettle on?'

Sean filled the kettle and considered this new information carefully while Jack shuffled off into the lounge; Sean heard him lighting a cigarette.

'Eileen's gone to her sister's,' Jack called through to Sean. 'Bit of fresh air, you know.'

'Right,' Sean said.

Any air would seem fresh compared to this flat. She must have been gone a few days and Jack wasn't keeping up her good work. Sean found a couple of clean mugs in a cupboard and made two cups of tea.

'Here you go.'

In the lounge, Jack was staring into space, the ash building up on the tip of his cigarette. He looked momentarily startled to see Sean standing there. He focused and reached for the mug.

'What are you going to eat for your tea?' Sean sat down next to him, carefully checking the settee for anything that might stick to his jeans. 'Was Eileen doing your cooking?'

Jack shrugged. 'Not that hungry.'

'But you've got to eat. Do you want me to ring for a pizza before I go?'

'Don't be bloody daft,' Jack snapped. 'They don't deliver in the blocks any more. Haven't done for ages. Where have you been?'

Sean felt like telling him exactly where he'd been. He'd kept his head down and got himself a good job.

'I didn't know.'

'Too many delivery boys getting robbed. Drugs mind, you can get them any time, delivered to the door. Not my thing, but there you go.'

'Dad, be careful what you're telling me.'

'You still a frigging copper? You want to give that up, get a proper job.' Jack Denton started to sing. 'Maggie Thatcher's boot boys, Maggie Thatcher's boot boys, tra-laa la la, tra-laa la la!'

He cackled himself into a coughing fit and Sean was saved from having to justify himself by his phone vibrating in his pocket. He got up and went through to the kitchen.

'Hello?'

'PC Denton?'

Sean didn't recognise the voice.

'Yes.'

'This is Wendy Gore from Professional Standards. We're looking into a complaint that's been filed.'

'Right.'

'Can you come in for a meeting tomorrow, first thing, with myself and your divisional inspector? Nine o'clock.'

'Yes, ma'am.'

It wasn't a question; it was a command. He looked through the half open door into the lounge. His father drank from the mug, missed his mouth and wiped his face on his sleeve. Wendy Gore ended the call.

'I'll nip out and get you some chips, if you like,' Sean said.

The estate agents' would be closing soon, but the studio

apartment could wait, at least until after his meeting in the morning.

Jack winced. 'I have to be careful what I eat. Can't handle most things, if I'm honest. Bit of white bread. Or the fish out of the middle of the batter. Everything else, you know, just goes straight through. Chips are no good.'

Sean didn't think he was putting on the self-pity. He really was ill.

'What does the doctor say?'

'They do tests. I have some pills, but my liver's had it. It's only a matter of time, then I'm finished. There, that'll put a smile on your soft face!'

'Don't be daft.'

But was it daft? Hadn't he wished him dead every time he'd run out of the flat to Maureen's or hidden in the woods around the quarry? His mum had died from a brain haemorrhage when he was ten, and for years he'd held onto the idea that Jack Denton was in some way responsible. His temper was horrible in those days, but looking at him now, it was hard to believe he could hurt a fly.

'Why don't I go out and get you a can of soup, eh? Could you manage chicken? And a bit of toast?'

Jack's faced creased in a smile.

'You've got such a look of your mam,' he said, 'standing there. Get us mushroom, will you? I prefer mushroom.'

Sean suppressed a shiver and headed for the front door.

On the way back from the shop, Sean saw a group of men coming out of Eagle Mount Two, heading for Eagle Mount One. By the time he got to the entrance hallway, they were going up in the lift. Sean took the stairs and was at Jack's door in time to see a man in a white T-shirt shoving a leaflet through the letter box. He bent down and called through the slot.

'Jack! Will we be seeing you at the meeting?'

'Is it my dad you're after?' Sean said.

The man stood up and looked at him.

'Your dad? I didn't realise he had a son.'

Sean let it go.

'Just seeing if he's coming to the meeting,' the man continued, fixing Sean with surprisingly blue eyes.

'AA?' Sean said.

'You what?'

'Is it an Alcoholics Anonymous meeting?'

Sean wondered whether he'd breached a code of confidentiality as the man frowned and the muscles in his neck tightened. He was a little over six foot, early thirties at a guess, with a tattoo on his neck that read: *Made in England.* Sean instinctively took a step back.

'No, mate, it's the CUC.'

He thrust a leaflet at Sean. The title was in large black letters: *Clean Up Chasebridge – Public Meeting. Thursday June 2nd 6.30 p.m.*

'It's at the community centre. Getting everyone involved in improving the estate.'

'Right,' Sean said.

'I haven't seen you before, have I?'

The other man didn't appear to be in a hurry to go, although the rest of his group could be heard clattering up the concrete stairs to the next floor. Sean shrugged and shook his head.

'I've been living . . . away.'

He wasn't sure why he said it like that, but something told him that he needed to be cautious.

'Working?'

'Something like that.'

'Right,' the man smiled and the eyes lit up. 'Give my regards to Jack. Tell him Terry was asking after him.'

Sean let himself in with Jack's key. He took the shopping into the kitchen. As he passed the lounge he could see Jack fast asleep on the settee. He stood at the kitchen window and looked out across the dual carriageway to the rough edge of the fields and the woods beyond. Tomorrow's meeting with Wendy Gore filled him with dread. The little boy inside him wished he could run away and hide in the woods until it was all over.

'Is that you, Terry?'

Sean jumped at his father's voice.

'It's Sean, Dad.'

He put his head round the door of the lounge where Jack was trying to sit up straight on the settee, wincing at some nameless pain nagging at his insides.

'There was a feller here called Terry,' Sean said. 'He left this.'

'Right, right.'

Jack was blinking, trying to read the writing on the leaflet Sean was showing him.

'You might be able to help him,' Jack said.

'With this clean up campaign?'

'No, your inside knowledge,' Jack tapped his swollen nose. 'You might be some use after all, being a copper.'

'What are you on about? Anyway,' he said, to himself as much as to his dad, 'after tomorrow I might not even be a copper.'

He wasn't sure how much damage Saleem's accusation could do him and although he knew Gav would stand by him, what if the lad really had hurt himself, got brain damage or something, and was pinning it all on Sean?

'What did you get for my tea?'

Jack's mind flicked from one thing to another at random, but Sean was happy he was thinking of food. He went back into the kitchen and warmed up some mushroom soup while the toast cooked.

'I'll have to be getting back home.' Sean settled a warped tray on his dad's knees and handed him the spoon.

'Home?'

'To Nan's. She still fusses over me.'

'Oh, aye. Will I see you tomorrow? You could take me to this.' Jack waved the spoon at the leaflet, spraying it with soup.

'Aye, why not. I'll come over later in the day and give you a hand cleaning up.' Sean said. 'We'll give Eileen a surprise when she comes back from her sister's. See you, Dad.'

As Sean was letting himself out of the flat, Jack called after him.

'Terry wants to find who killed his brother.'

'You what?'

'He wants to find who did it.'

Sean went back into the living room.

'He needs to go through the proper channels then. Look,

Dad, if it's easier for you, you don't have to tell anyone I'm a police officer.'

'No, good plan!' Jack wheezed a bitter laugh, 'I never do!'

Sean wasn't sure how well this Terry knew his dad, but it sounded like Jack didn't even admit to having a son, never mind one in the police force.

CHAPTER FOUR

York

When the York Minster clock strikes the hour, the bell vibrates through the stone steps, up into the bones of Chloe's chest. Compared to this huge building she is nothing, just a bundle of twigs that can be rattled apart by the sound. She hugs her arms around her knees even though it isn't cold. The sun is overhead and she feels it pressing through her thin hair. She needs to move before her skin burns. She gets up and looks around. To one side she sees a road full of people and bicycles, but to her right there's a sort of garden. If she stays close to the building there might be some shade.

She walks through a gate onto a lawn, slips her shoes off and enjoys the grass, cool and soft under her feet. There's an ice cream van, but she can't afford anything on their price list. She's bought food, toiletries and her radio. She's paid her hostel charge for the first week and now she's down to her last few pounds. There are some children at the ice cream van, speaking another language, laughing, so she turns away from them and heads for the shade of the building where the grass is longer, more protected. There is something there, where the wall meets the ground, and she thinks at first she's looking at the broken pieces of a wafer or a cornet, but as her eyes adjust to the shadows, she sees they're little bones, cradled in a dry brown nest. She kneels down to get a closer look. Two skulls, with perfect beaks, tiny ribs and fine white legs, tucked up where they lay, hungry perhaps, or their hearts stopping as the nest fell. She looks up and sees a line of guttering, and beyond it a glimpse of the square edge of the Minster tower. It seems to be falling towards her. Her stomach lurches and she drops down on all fours. She's crouching, staring at the skeletons of the young birds in the nest, when she hears a voice.

'Are you all right?'

A woman is watching her from the path with two children, a boy of about eight and a teenage girl. The woman hesitates, while the children look embarrassed, the boy tugging at his mother's hand.

'I'm fine,' she says. 'Just found something, a nest. The baby birds are dead.'

The girl pulls a face, but the boy lets go of his mother's hand and darts forward.

'Cool! Can I see?'

Chloe sits back on her heels and he comes close.

'Amazing! They're sparrows' skeletons, I think. Can I pick the nest up?'

She nods.

'How do you know they're sparrows?' she asks him.

'From the beaks.' He cradles the nest in his small hands

and peers into it. 'It's hard to be exactly sure; they could be coal tits. I'd need my book.'

'Do you want it? The nest?'

'Would you mind? Brilliant! Thanks.' He looks back to check. 'Mum, this lady says I can have it. Can I?'

The teenage girl rolls her eyes.

'It's not very clean,' the mother says.

'It's fine, Mum. They're just dry bones.'

'Well, all right,' she smiles at Chloe as if to say, this is what he's like, this curious little boy. 'Say thank you to the lady.'

'Thanks.'

Chloe shrugs. She doesn't have anything to say. It's only when she watches them walk away down the path, the boy holding the nest up to eye level to scrutinise its contents, that she thinks how easy it was to give a gift of something that wasn't hers to begin with. She shivers, her skin cooling in the shade. She lets her fingers play over the grass, thinking back to the first time she was allowed to work outside, in the prison grounds, and how strange the grass felt to her then. It was as if she had misremembered it. Each blade seemed stronger and thicker than she expected. Another chiming bell startles her and she checks her watch. Quarter to twelve. She stands up and decides to explore further round the building. She runs her fingers along the stone mass of wall until she reaches an iron fence and a gate. A cobbled street curves round to the right and she picks her way over the uncomfortable bumps until she feels smooth stone slabs under her feet again.

She half-laughs inside her mouth. Laughs at herself. They said at one of her parole hearings that she hadn't grown up yet and she'd have to grow up if she was ever going to settle back into society. They wouldn't think talking to little boys about dead birds and walking barefoot was proper grown-up behaviour, but who cares? They're not watching her now. She takes a step, which is half a skip. For the first time in ages she thinks she might be happy. She skips again, two, three times, until her toe catches the edge of a paving slab and she swears. She looks around to check if anybody saw and puts her shoes back on.

They're coming out of the door when she gets back to the entrance. Emma is rubbing one of her knees and moaning about how many steps there were.

'Oh my God, Chloe, I wish I'd stayed out here. You go round and round this horrible little staircase and the top's all fenced in, like a cage. I wanted to go back down, but they said I couldn't.'

Emma scowls at Taheera and the young man. Chloe isn't sure what the situation is, but she saw them hold each other's hands as they went in and she thinks they might want to be alone for a bit. Her mum trained her from an early age to be discreet around all the boyfriends she brought home from the pub.

'Come on, Emma, there's some nice shops we went past before. Wouldn't mind having a look in the windows.'

She links her arm in Emma's and half expects her to pull away, but she doesn't. She clamps Chloe closer to her and they start to walk back across the open square towards the narrow streets.

'Wait a minute!' Taheera calls after them. 'I thought we might all go for a coffee.'

Emma hesitates.

'OK, if you're buying,' she says.

Chloe thinks she's shameless, after having moaned so much, but all the same she wouldn't mind one herself. It's only her second day on the out and she fancies sitting in a café, sipping a nice coffee. They end up in a little place, not much more than a shop front, with two soft untidy sofas in the window. Chloe would rather sit further back where it's more private and there are proper chairs and tables, but Emma has steered her towards one of the sofas and sits down heavily.

'I'm knackered!' she says. 'Do they do cake?'

Taheera ignores her and asks Chloe what she'd like first. Then she takes Emma's order and tells the young guy, whose name turns out to be Mo, that he'll have to get his own. The budget doesn't stretch to him. She doesn't sound mean when she says it, just playful and then Chloe gets it. This trip is meant to be about her. That's why Taheera has got money to spend. That's why she didn't want her and Emma to go off together and why she clucked like a mother hen when Chloe said she wanted to stay outside the Minster. Chloe sits back on the sofa and decides she doesn't mind being fussed over. She's sure it won't last.

Taheera goes up to the counter and Mo leans forward.

'Do you want to see a magic trick?' he says.

'Do you make yourself disappear in a puff of smoke?' Emma laughs, her scar tugging at her skin. 'Only joking!'

But Mo looks annoyed. He turns to Chloe.

'What about you?'

She shrugs.

'You don't say much, do you?'

No, she thinks. But that's probably just as well because if she was a talker she'd be asking questions; what she really wants to know is why he's on tag, what he's done and where he's been. She's sure he's been inside, and he must know she and Emma have too. What she really she wants to know is why Taheera has got a criminal for a boyfriend. It's probably a sackable offence if you work in a bail hostel.

Emma goes off to find the ladies' toilet as Taheera comes back to the table.

'It's a shame you didn't have your camera up the tower, Mo.'

'I left it at home. I didn't think you'd want . . .' he doesn't finish.

Chloe sips the froth on her coffee and pretends he's not looking at her. She sits back in the depths of the sofa and soon it's as if they've forgotten she's there.

'Have you been doing much photography?'

'Not much time,' he says. 'Been helping my cousin in the shop.'

'How is she?'

'Ghazala? She's OK. Yeah, she's good. She gave me the train fare to get up here. Her little brother Saleem's being a pain in the arse, though.'

Taheera nods.

'My brother was here last night,' she says quietly.

Chloe tries to look interested in the tassels on one of the sofa cushions, spinning the purple and gold threads and watching them unravel. When you don't say much, people tend to think you don't hear much either.

'Kamran?' Mo says. 'What was he doing in York?'

'He'd been to York Races and he wanted to borrow some money to get into a club. He'd been drinking. My parents would go mad if they knew.'

So that was her brother. Chloe's almost forgotten the scene she witnessed from her window last night, but now it comes back to her.

'Had he come up here on his own?' Mo says.

'Someone was driving his car, a white guy. At least he wasn't stupid enough to drive himself.'

Mo looks worried.

'This guy, what did he look like?'

'I didn't really see, it was dark. Why? Does it matter?'

'No, probably not.'

'Mo?'

'Nothing. It's nothing. Look!' And he touches Taheera's ear and pulls out a pound coin.

CHAPTER FIVE

Doncaster

The low ceiling of the corridor outside the Divisional Inspector's office had a fluorescent light which flickered as Sean waited, like a schoolboy outside the headteacher's office. Maureen had ironed every inch of his uniform. She'd even offered him one of her sleeping pills to make sure he got some rest, but he said no. He needed a clear head. When he got in from his dad's he went for a run to tire himself out and, by some miracle, fell asleep not long after midnight. He'd had five or six hours, but his right eye was twitching. Or was it the light? He couldn't tell.

The door opened.

'Come in PC Denton.'

He phoned Gav as soon as he came out.

'Well?'

'It was OK,' Sean said, still not quite believing it himself. 'What I said, how I described it, tallied with what you told them and as there were no independent witnesses. Basically, that was it.'

'Good lad. Right, let's celebrate!'

'I'm not sure . . .' He was thinking of his dad and the promise he'd made to help clean up the flat.

'They've got a nice guest ale on at the Red Lion,' Gav said.

'Sorry, mate, I've got stuff on.'

Sean didn't tell him the other part of what they'd said, Wendy Gore grinning at him through over-done lipstick that had smeared on the lip of her coffee mug, the bit about young eyes seeing things that others might overlook, that his previous work as a PCSO, especially in the investigation of a senior officer, hadn't gone unnoticed. He had the feeling that they were asking him to spy for them. The only bit that made any sense was the warning to stay away from Saleem Asaf.

'That shouldn't be difficult,' Sean said.

'Except that he lives at an address on the edge of the Chasebridge estate, Denton, where I believe you have family.'

The Divisional Inspector couldn't have made it sound worse if he'd actually come out and said 'a drunk for a father,' but Sean let it pass.

Sean sat on the side of his bed and unfolded the crumpled page with the estate agents' logo and the colour photo of the 'fabulous studio apartment'. He would be back on the night shift tomorrow and by the time he got round to viewing it, it was sure to have been let out. He screwed the details into a ball and threw it in a neat arc, straight into the wastepaper basket by the door.

'Goal!'

He could hear the television. Maureen must be watching a comedy because the canned laughter came up through the floor at regular intervals. When he went downstairs, one place was laid at the table and a cup of tea was waiting for him.

'I was at my dad's yesterday.' He let it sound casual, as if it was the most normal thing in the world.

'Oh.' She was at the cooker, stirring a pan of baked beans. She didn't look at him.

'He's packed in drinking.'

'Why would he bother doing that? It's like air to him.'

'Because he had to.'

Maureen tipped baked beans onto two waiting slices of toast and scraped angrily at the saucepan with a wooden spoon.

'Bloody idiot. He's ruined everyone else's life and been killing himself for years, so why give up now?'

'It's serious. His liver's packing up.'

She turned to him for a moment before flipping a piece of bacon out of the frying pan onto the mountain of beans and putting the plate on the table in front of him.

'I really should eat a proper vegetable once in a while, shouldn't I?' Sean said, trying to change the subject.

'You going to see him again?' she said.

He didn't reply.

'Sean, love, it's none of my business, and he is your father, but what good's going to come of it?'

Sean shrugged and poked at the beans with his fork. Maureen went through to the front room and the sound of a game show filled the silence.

When he'd finished eating, Sean found a carrier bag under the sink and helped himself to a bottle of anti-bacterial cleaner and a couple of cloths. This wasn't going to cut very deep into the built-up grime of Jack Denton's home, but it was a start. He put his head round the door of the living room to say goodbye to Maureen. She waved her cigarette but kept her eyes fixed on the screen. He could tell she was annoyed, but it wouldn't last long.

Behind the house, he looked at his moped and thought better of it. He'd rather walk than leave it up at the flats. Along the road, a group of teenagers was hanging around the front gate of one of the gardens. Sean wasn't a fighter, never had been. As a kid, he'd learnt to dodge rolled up newspapers, swinging belts, fists and feet, and he'd learnt to run. As a police officer, running away wasn't an option any more, so he'd joined a gym to build muscles he hoped he wouldn't have to use. Sean clenched his fists and felt his biceps harden but the teenagers didn't even look round as he passed.

At Eagle Mount One Jack opened his front door cautiously.

'Who's that?'

'Me. I thought I'd have a go at a bit of cleaning,' Sean held up the carrier bag.

'Come on in.'

Sean looked round the kitchen. He wished he'd bought some rubber gloves. Yesterday's mugs and soup bowl had been added to a sink that was full of thick grey water, where the edges of crockery stuck up like the tips of icebergs. He held his breath and plunged his hand into the chilly slime to find the plug. A memory of his mother came to him. He must have been very little, standing on tiptoes to get his hands over the edge of the sink. She was wearing pink Marigolds.

Her fingers looked long and elegant, as if they were dressed up for a party. She let him put the gloves on and he danced round the room. It made her laugh.

He ran the tap and waited for some hot water, but none came. He filled the kettle and put it on to boil. Jack was lingering in the doorway watching him.

'How are you feeling today?' Sean said.

'Like shit.'

'Sorry to hear it.'

Jack sighed. 'I've been a bugger. I know it.'

'Leave it, Dad.'

'I should have been there for you, after your mam died.'

Sean rubbed at the murky window with his thumb. The view from this side of the block was away from town. Cars streamed by on the ring road, and beyond was the dark outline of the woods. He could see himself, a boy of ten or eleven, sitting against a tree, head back, mesmerised by the leaves of the upper branches waving against a blue sky, the rush of the wind drowning out the sounds of the road and the estate beyond it. He sometimes fell asleep and woke up shivering, dry-mouthed, with the light beginning to fade. He always went home in the end, not because he was afraid of the woods, but because he feared what his father would do if he stayed out any later.

'I should have taken you to football and that,' Jack said.

'I don't think so.'

There'd been occasions when Jack was in a good mood, the right side of drunk for a joke and a laugh, but Sean never really understood what the jokes were about and just laughed along to keep things sweet. Then there were the times he'd had to help his father home, paralytic and covered in vomit.

'We should do something together, father and son, while . . .'

The cough caught his words and Sean was left to finish the sentence in his own head. He didn't want to turn round and be reminded that Jack was only a man, not a monster. The kettle rattled to the boil and he poured a splash of boiling water onto a cloth and scrubbed away at the sink.

'You said you might come to the meeting, what's-their-name? They've got this thing, this group,' Jack said.

Sean put the plates and cups back into the sink, squeezed in the washing up liquid and poured the rest of the kettle water on top.

'Clean Up Chasebridge?'

'Aye, that's what they call it. They've got a bit of fire in their bellies, these lads. Haven't seen much of that since Arthur Scargill.'

Sean rubbed away at a stubborn deposit of greenish-white mould at the bottom of a mug.

'CUC. Clean Up Chasebridge. Good name, in't it?' Jack said. 'Brings all the issues together.'

'Right.' The bottom of the mug was gradually turning white again and Jack was staring into space.

'Aye.' It was like a motor starting up. Jack nodded, blinked and licked a bit of spittle from the corner of his mouth. 'Good lads, getting this place in order. Chasing out the undesirables. Chasing them out of Chasebridge! D'you get it? I should write the bloody slogans, me!'

He laughed and coughed his way into the next room where he collapsed back on the settee and lit up a cigarette, hands trembling. Sean stood in the doorway of the living room and watched him struggling to catch his breath. When Sean turned back to the kitchen, he half expected to see it how it was before, when his mum was alive, and the floor tiles were still bright green. Through the window he watched a blue light flashing down the dual carriageway. It looked like an ambulance. If it was an RTA, who'd be attending? Maybe it was an attack. Every case started somewhere. Suddenly, a wave of relief flooded over him. The Saleem Asaf business was over, as quickly as that, and tomorrow night he'd back in uniform with Gavin telling his rubbish jokes in the battered squad car. Fuck it, he thought, it wouldn't hurt to spend one evening with Jack.

'When's the meeting, Dad?'

CHAPTER SIX

York

Chloe follows Taheera's instructions: right out of the hostel, down a street of terraced houses, punctuated by the dark eye sockets of bin alleys. The mid-morning streets are quiet and she tells herself that nobody's watching her, but still she feels exposed out there on her own. She could have taken the bus but she needs to save her money. When she turns onto the main road, she can see she's going in the right direction. The tower of York Minster is ahead of her, its sandy-grey bulk against a dark purple sky, long windows like the eyes of a bloodhound. There's a flicker and she blinks. She's seen it again: a human shape, from this distance no bigger than a feather, falling through the air.

She picks up speed, the blood pulsing in her temples and tries to concentrate on something else, to wipe the image from her mind. There's a row of shops ahead. As she gets closer, she sees that there are two charity shops and a dry-cleaners. In the window of the first charity shop there's a set of crockery: white with a pattern of blue irises around the rim of each plate and cup. She won't be at Meredith House forever. Taheera keeps reminding her they'll be moving her on to a place of her own in a few weeks. Then she'll come back and buy these plates and cups. She'll invite Taheera round for tea to show her how well she's settling in. She'll invite Emma too, but not the others. Only people she can trust will see her new home.

She needs to hurry now, walking is taking longer than she thought. The sky's threatening rain and she wishes it would get on with it. Her skin is sticky with sweat. She pulls the appointment letter out of her pocket. Mrs Hildred, 11.45 a.m. She's going to have to run to get there in time.

She arrives out of breath and waits on a hard chair by a reception desk. A fan turns slowly on its stand, like the head of a sunflower, turning towards her and away, towards and away. She's so mesmerised she doesn't hear her name being called. A woman with a badge announcing 'Specialist Advisor' is standing in the doorway, her wide hips filling its frame.

'Pleased to meet you, call me Sally.'

She's not sure she'll be able to do that. There's something about her that reminds Chloe of a teacher she had in primary school, soft-edged and cardigan-clad. She definitely looks more like a Mrs than a Sally. They go through to a small room in the back of the building where faded prints of flowers hang on magnolia walls. The armchairs are meant to be comfortable, but Sally Hildred has some difficulty lowering herself into one. She picks up a pen in chapped fingers and smoothes the paper of the notebook on her knee. She's an eczema sufferer. It's on the back of her hands and disappears inside her sleeves. Chloe looks at her pen poised above the clean sheet of paper. Her heart sinks at the thought of another test. There will be right and wrong answers and she will have to guess which is which.

'How are you settling in to Meredith House?'

'Fine. Yeah, I feel right at home.' She doesn't say she can't bring herself to sit in the TV room, or that most of her possessions are still in her bag.

'Good,' Sally Hildred says. 'I expect you're looking forward to getting into work.'

Smile. Meet her eyes. Don't fiddle with your hands. Sound convincing.

'Yes.'

It's warm in the room and Mrs Hildred takes her cardigan off. The eczema on her hands has reached up her arms and formed livid patches on the insides of her elbows. It must be so tempting to scratch at it and exhausting not to give in. She must be the queen of self-control.

'Now, I'm sure Taheera has explained; I'm here to help you with your job search.' Sally is frowning. Chloe pulls her gaze away from the sore skin and tries to look as if she's been listening. 'It's not always possible to get exactly what you want, not straight away. You may have to compromise.'

'I want to work in a garden.'

'What I'm saying is, you may have to cut your cloth.'

It's a phrase she's heard so many times before. It goes along with *you've made your bed, now you have to lie in it*. Those were her mum's words. Cut. Don't go there. Rewind. *You may have to cut your cloth*. The truth is, Chloe is forever cutting her cloth. There are great holes cut out of the fabric of her life. Chloe unfolds the CV she's had in her back pocket and hands it over.

'Oh, how lovely,' Mrs Hildred opens it on her lap. 'You have got a lot of gardening experience.'

'And qualifications.' She begins to list them, but Sally holds up a hand to stop her. Her fingers are soft and one of them is pinched by a gold wedding ring. Chloe wonders what Mr Hildred looks like and whether he minds the eczema.

'Great, yes, great,' Mrs Hildred says. 'It's all on here. You don't have to, you know, prove yourself. Don't worry, Chloe, I'm on your side.'

On her side of the fence, her side of the wall. She's still getting used to being on the same side as people like Mrs Hildred. Would Mr Hildred think they were all on the same side? She wonders if they talk in bed at night about the special clients his wife sees at work.

I met a girl today. Interesting case. She'd been away a long time, I was wondering if she's that one who . . .

Sally Hildred is reaching into a folder and shuffling through sheets of paper. Chloe's CV slides off her lap and lands on the carpet. She hesitates to pick it up in case she collides with Mrs Hildred's knees.

'Perhaps, as you're a little further along the journey than some of our clients, if there's something available . . . Yes, here we are. Right up your street.'

Chloe reads the page upside down.

Halsworth Grange, Trainee Gardener, full-time.

She's looking for a pound sign and some numbers to go with it. She can't wait to be earning her own money, but Mrs Hildred has moved on to an application form and is telling her that the closing date is very soon, so if she's interested they'll need to be quick.

'How much are they paying?' she asks.

'It's an apprenticeship, Chloe. It's just £2.73 an hour while you're training.'

'That's not even minimum wage. And I'm already trained. I've got . . .'

'Yes. No. Ah, well, I mean, I know you have your certificates but with you being' – she runs a finger up the inside of her arm and pulls it away – 'out of the job market for such a long time.'

The eczema rash has deepened to a livid scarlet and the rest of her skin is pink. Chloe wonders why Mrs Hildred is so embarrassed. She might as well say it. It's clear she knows exactly where Chloe's been.

'It's OK,' Chloe says. She can't watch the poor woman suffer any longer. She dodges the knees to pick up her CV and gives it back to Mrs Hildred. 'I'll apply.'

'Wonderful! I'll go and scan this and we can get an email off to them straight away.'

The next morning Chloe stands under the shower. She's been awake since six, to be sure of getting in the bathroom first. Mrs Hildred phoned the hostel shortly after Chloe got back and said she needed to be at Halsworth Grange the next day for an interview. Taheera has offered to take her in the car. It's tiny, like a creamy white toy car with a burgundy roof and seats to match. It's beautiful and Chloe doesn't want to stink it out, so she scrubs herself hard and when she's dry, she sprays herself all over with Icy Mist.

She stands in the lobby of Meredith House waiting for Taheera to finish her handover to Darren, the assistant residential officer. Taheera's got a few days' leave and is going to see her family. She says Halsworth Grange is on her way and at least Chloe won't have to worry about being late. She's helped her to look up her return journey: bus, train, bus. It's going to take a while, but it's OK. Chloe is looking forward to the ride. The times and numbers are all printed out and she's grateful for that. She's no good with computers.

The office door opens and Taheera's there. There's no sign that she's done a night shift. Her make-up is perfect. The black kohl around her eyes rings the green like pools of water. She's wearing pale pink leggings and a green tunic with a pattern of peacock feathers. Chloe can't get over how beautiful she looks.

'Come on, then!' Taheera laughs as she speaks. 'Are we going?'

Chloe nods. She holds her carrier bag tightly in her hands. Inside is a folder with all her documents, including a letter sealed in a brown envelope, which she must not lose. As they head towards the door, Emma comes out of the TV room.

'Good luck, pet. Knock 'em dead!'

Chloe manages half a smile but she can't speak.

CHAPTER SEVEN

Halsworth Grange

Halsworth Grange is up a long drive. She asks Taheera to drop her at the gate. She wants the last few moments to clear her head, to think a little. In the car they listened to the radio. Taheera was happy to be going home and Chloe tried to be happy for her. There's a mum and a dad and a brother there, Taheera said, and an older sister who's left home but who comes back all the time with her baby son. Every now and then, Taheera gave her little pieces of advice about how to answer questions and to remember to smile and look interested.

Chloe practises the smile as she walks up the hill, but it feels strained. She is wondering if Taheera will be seeing Mo, the young man with the tag on his ankle. It's none of her business, she knows that, but it doesn't seem right. She stops at the top of the drive where a car park drops away to her left. There's a grey-haired woman in a little hut selling tickets and brochures. Chloe looks back at the way she's come taking in the sweep of lawns, dotted with trees, like something from a TV drama.

Her appointment is with a Mr William Coldacre. He's a big man, both tall and wide. He looks old, but she can see he's still strong. They sit opposite one another across a table. There's not much to look at in the small brick potting shed, except a newspaper with a crossword half done and a screwed up paper bag. Someone has scattered flaky crumbs on the table. Mr Coldacre doesn't meet her eye and she realises that he's almost as nervous as she is.

'So, um, Miss Toms,' he looks at her CV and her application form. She has taken her folder out of the carrier bag and fingers the envelope on her lap, waiting for the right time to hand it over, to practise the lines she's been learning for this moment.

'I don't usually do the interviews. I'm more of a plantsman myself, but Giles, he's the land manager, he's off with the flu, so he's left it up to me.' He runs a large forefinger round the top of his ear. 'Tell you what, Miss, uh – can I call you Chloe?'

'Yes, that's fine. Yes.'

'Right, well, why don't we have a look around the garden and we can talk about what you've done before and I can see what's what? That would be the best way, I reckon.'

'OK.' She's still holding the letter, not sure how to do this if they're walking about outside. 'I have to give you this,' she says. 'In case, well if you were to offer me the job, I have to— I mean, you have to read it.'

He nods towards the sealed envelope with a grunt and puts it in his pocket.

'Aye. I know the score. You're not the first from the Probation, so don't worry about that. I'll pass it on to the boss.'

She silently prays that he'll keep it safe and deliver it to Giles, or whoever's in charge. It's her disclosure letter, explaining about her criminal record. She pictures him pulling out a hanky and the letter flying free, blowing along the paths between the clipped edges of the lawns, being picked up by a visitor and opened. That person would get straight on the phone to the tabloids and then the whole pack would appear.

'If you're lucky,' Taheera said to her in the car, 'people won't remember.'

Chloe hopes she's right. She's sure she looks quite different. Her hair's lighter and longer and she'll never go back to where it happened; she's not allowed to anyway. But the law says she has to tell her employer and, even though it's supposed to be confidential, she knows that confidential isn't a wall or a fence that keeps you safe. It's just a word, and it's not a word that Chloe sets much store by.

An hour later, William Coldacre (call me Bill) says they'll let her know and wishes her a safe journey. He didn't ask her much, except some plant names and about what tools she'd used before. She walks back down the drive. There's a monkey-puzzle tree, its geometric branches standing out among the softer shapes of beech and ash. She stands still and listens to the birds. She can't quite believe she's here and she hopes, she prays, she'll get the job and she'll soon be coming back.

At the bus stop she doesn't have to wait long before she's on a little single-decker, winding through a succession of old pit villages towards the station. When she gets off there are no proper station buildings, only a shelter on each side of the track and a narrow footbridge over it. The sign says: 'Trains to Goole, Hull and York: Platform 1' and 'Trains to Doncaster: Platform 2'. She stares at the sign. She can't understand how she missed it on the way here in the car, how she's got this close without realising. She wonders how many miles it is to Doncaster. She looks around her, like a child who's wandered into a room where she's been forbidden to go, then hurries towards Platform 1.

A woman with a sticky toddler in a buggy is fanning herself with a free paper. Chloe shrinks back into the shadow of the metal fence. When she was released from prison, her licence clearly stated that she must not go within ten miles of where it happened. She waits for the York train, willing it to hurry up, while she imagines what she'll say to Darren back at the hostel. If she's breached her licence, she'll go straight back to prison and she won't see Taheera or Halsworth Grange again.

The road map is on the table between them. Darren purses his lips and traces his finger along the road that leads from Doncaster to Halsworth Grange.

'It looks OK to me,' he says and shrugs.

Darren mostly shrugs. Chloe reckons he comes to work half-stoned. She wishes Taheera was here, but she's still on leave.

'Mr Coldacre says I can start on Monday, but I'm not going down there just to be pulled by the police and end up back in jail for breaching my licence.'

It comes out in one breath and Chloe hears her voice leap up to a high-pitched whine. Control. Get it under control.

Darren doesn't notice. He twists his fingers into his hair and plucks a long, greying strand.

'Here.'

He tightens the hair between his fingers and lays it on the map, curving it round each bend in the road. It straightens on a stretch of the A1(M), and bends off again into the town.

'Not the centre,' Chloe says. She points to a mass of dark shapes towards the M18. 'There.'

Darren stretches the hair to where Chloe's pointing and lifts it carefully, keeping the measurement precise. He lays it along the scale rule in the corner of the map and folds it back on itself three times.

'Fifteen miles,' he looks up at Chloe and smiles. 'Your licence says you must stay ten miles outside the location of your offence, so you're fine. Just make sure you don't get on the wrong train home.'

'No chance.'

Chloe sits back and lets herself relax. Her stomach's been so tight it aches to let go. She thinks of the lawns at Halsworth Grange and the monkey-puzzle tree zigzagging across the view. Soon she'll be going there every day.

'Does Taheera know you've got the job?'

Chloe shakes her head.

'Phone her from here if you like. She'll be pleased.'

He dials from the office phone, hands her the receiver and soon Taheera's voice is whooping in her ear, congratulating her.

'Amazing! Oh my God, I love that place. I knew you'd get it.'

Chloe holds the phone a little distance away to protect her eardrum.

'The trees are lovely in the spring. We used to go for picnics when we were kids.'

'Oh,' Chloe manages. 'That's nice.'

Of course it's a place that means something to someone else. It hasn't been magicked up just for her benefit, and it's cool that Taheera loves it too.

'If you're starting Monday, then maybe I could pick you up and give you a lift back to York on your first day,' Taheera says. 'I'm back at work on Tuesday.'

'If you're sure it's not out of your way,' Chloe says.

'Not at all. I go past the door and it'll my make my mum happy if I stay on another night. She wants to cook a family meal on Sunday night and my sister's coming over with my baby nephew, he's so sweet!'

Chloe pictures Taheera's family as a mass of colour, with a mum in a bright pink and gold sari, their home like a Bollywood film set, everyone dancing and laughing. She hands the phone back to Darren and beyond the soundtrack in her head, she hears him telling Taheera that everything's fine at the hostel, there are no problems and she should enjoy her time off.

'Stay safe, Miss T,' he says and puts the phone down.

CHAPTER EIGHT

Doncaster

Sean worked for three solid hours. The kitchen floor was two shades lighter and Jack was standing by the door, jingling his keys. It was time to go to the Clean up Chasebridge meeting. Sean pulled his father's baseball hat low over his eyes. Its greasy band felt cool on his forehead and he tried not to think about how seldom Jack washed his hair. He folded his arms over a grey-green anorak he'd found hanging on the back of the front door. The zip was broken and he didn't dare put his hands in the pockets, but it was a good disguise. Even his dad agreed.

'I wouldn't know you in that lot,' Jack Denton peered through his cigarette smoke. 'Ah, I get it. You fancy yourself as an undercover spy, now you've given up policing.'

'Eh?'

'Aye, you said, yesterday. You'd soon be out of a job, you said. Her Majesty's Secret Service is it now? Eh? Nice one, lad!'

Sean shook his head. Let Jack have his mad fantasy; he wasn't going to admit that staying unnoticed was deliberate.

The estate had been on Sean's beat when he was a PCSO and it was impossible to be off-duty where people still remembered you.

They set off in the stinking lift to the ground floor and left the building. The low sun cast a glow over the estate and a bank of dark clouds was stacking up in the east. It was one of those pent-up summer evenings when something is bound to break. Sean noticed several people heading towards the community centre. Groups of middle-aged men, whole families, one or two couples and an elderly pair making slow progress with their wheeled walking frames. It could have been a summer fête, except no one was smiling. Sean pulled the peak of the cap lower.

The community hall was even shabbier than Sean remembered it. The rain had come in through the roof and left a dark stain across the mural: *Chasebridge Kids: Peace and Love!* The result of a summer scheme a decade ago.

'We can go near the door so I can get out for a fag,' Jack said.

The hall filled up slowly. At the front, a man in a white T-shirt was adjusting the microphone. He bent down to check a cable. When he stood up, Sean could see it was the guy with the sharp blue eyes who'd put the leaflet through the door. Terry.

'What were you saying yesterday? About his brother?'

'Eh?' Jack looked blank. 'What?'

'Nothing.'

Sean shuffled lower in his seat. The chairs began to fill and a tall man sat in front of him. It was enough to block his direct view of the stage, but that suited him fine. He looked around at who else was here. Rain had started tapping on the skylights in the roof. A couple of teenage girls ran in, shaking water from their hair and giggling. The next arrival was better prepared. He saw her from the back as she threw the butt of her cigarette outside the door. The smoke was still escaping through her lips as she came into the room, fingers struggling to un-knot the plastic rain hood protecting her neatly set hair. It was Nan. Sean dipped his head but not quick enough. She caught his eye and started towards them.

'Now then, Jack Denton,' she greeted Jack, who looked at her, confused, not recognising the mother-in-law he hadn't spoken to for years. Sean stared at his feet and she hesitated, nodded at them both and veered off down the side aisle to find a seat nearer the front.

A man with a bald head and a thick neck, squeezed into a tight shirt collar, stood up at the front. He welcomed the residents of Chasebridge with a warning that these were dangerous times and it had never been more important for people to stand shoulder to shoulder. Communities of like-minded people were forged in times of adversity, he said, and this was one of those times.

'The foreigners who claim to be part of our community have no respect, even as they're making their money out of us.'

There was a murmur that sounded like a suppressed laugh.

'There's a shop on the corner there, and where you're seeing ciggies, newspapers and birthday cards, I'm seeing something else. The younger generation are drawing undesirable elements into the area, folk who are causing trouble, bringing drugs onto this estate. Our parents stood by and let those people come in. Now the gates are open to all the Asians, Polish, Bulgarians and so-called asylum seekers. And what protection is there for our own youth? The police don't care. Look, this campaign may have started with litter picking, but now we've got to get rid of the rest of the rubbish, so our own people can walk the streets without fear.'

A few people clapped and there was a cheer from the front row.

'We're organising a torchlit march next week, to reclaim our estate, to keep it safe.'

Applause broke out as Sean sank deeper into his seat.

'Friends!' The voice changed. It was Terry. 'I've been away, but you've welcomed me home, like the prodigal son. But what do I find? I find my home has been spoilt and I want it back; I want it how it used to be. Is that too much to ask? I don't want foreigners bringing their drugs round here. So, listen to me, if you want to keep your estate clean, you need to keep it English.'

More applause broke out at the front and a woman punched the air with a big bare arm. The rain started to knock harder against the skylights. Terry handed the microphone over to the man with the tight shirt collar. He was saying something about the torchlit parade, but it was no use, the rain was too loud. Talking was breaking out among the back rows and only the loyal supporters at the front were able to pick up their cue to clap and cheer at the right moments.

The rain turned to hail. Jack was twitching and Sean saw he was chuckling with laughter.

'What is it?' he mouthed.

Jack pressed his mouth to Sean's ear. 'I hope they get better weather. I'd like to see 'em try a torchlit march in this.'

'I'm going, Dad. I've heard enough.'

He stood up but a hand grabbed his sleeve. Jack was pointing at the coat. His father was only wearing a thin shirt. The air had been warm when they'd left the flat. Sean quickly dropped the coat on the chair and pulled the brim of the baseball cap lower. He'd drawn more attention to himself than he'd wanted and it hadn't been missed by the speaker.

'This is not the time to leave! This is the time to stand with your own people!' The voice from the front boomed above the rain.

Sean headed for the door and had his hand on the handle, when the drumming on the roof stopped as sharply as it had started. In the quiet that followed he sensed everyone staring at him.

'Are you with us, or against us, lad?' A voice from the front spoke calmly in the silence.

Sean didn't look back. He pushed the door open and walked out into the clean, damp air. The ground shone with water and the sky ahead was brilliant blue. A rainbow arched over the four tower blocks. He could hear a muffled voice from the hall, rising to a crescendo, followed by a burst of applause. It grew louder for a moment before being muted again, as if the door had opened and closed behind him.

'Now then,' Terry was standing on the rough concrete ramp in front of the hall. It gave him a couple more inches of height over Sean. 'Want a smoke?'

'I'm OK.'

'So you're Jack's lad.'

Sean nodded.

'He's been good to me,' Terry said.

'Really?' Sean didn't mean to sound surprised, but he hadn't realised that being good to other people was in his dad's repertoire.

'That bother you, does it?'

'No, no. It's up to him.'

Sean mentally logged all the details in front of him: height, hair colour – a browny-red already peppered with grey – a spotless clean T-shirt, new-looking jeans pressed to a crease and an expensive pair of trainers. The 'Made in England' tattoo was rougher than the rest of his outfit, the sort of amateur job that might have been done in prison.

'Terry . . . sorry, I didn't catch your other name—'

'And I didn't catch yours, can't call you young Denton, can I? So we're both at a disadvantage with only half a name each.'

Terry smiled as he dragged on his cigarette and the light caught his eyes. Sean had an odd feeling, like he was being flirted with.

'The name's Sean,' he said and wondered if he should offer a handshake, but he held back; there was too much energy around Terry that he didn't like. Trust your instincts, Gav was always telling him.

'Terry Starkey.' Another long slow drag on his cigarette. 'Good to meet you.'

'Likewise.'

'You don't want to come back in?' Terry flicked the spent

69

butt onto the grass. 'It's a good bunch of lads. We look out for one another.'

'I'm OK, thanks, I—' Sean struggled to think of a reason apart from the obvious truth. 'I don't like so many people, crowds, you know, I get freaked out.'

'I hear you, bro!' Terry lurched forward and Sean winced as he gave him a manly clap on the shoulder. 'Take care, I'll see you around.'

Another chattering round of applause burst out of the opening door as Terry went back inside and Sean let out the breath he'd been holding. He pulled his phone out and scrolled through his contacts.

'Gav? Is it too late to change my mind about that pint?'

CHAPTER NINE

Halsworth Grange

At nine-thirty on Monday morning, Chloe walks up the drive for her first day of work at Halsworth Grange. She feels sick. She thought it was the motion of the bus, but it's still with her. Something moves on one of the chimneys of the house. She holds her breath, but it's just a bird, taking off and circling above the trees. It's a warm day, but dark grey clouds hang about to the east. They have a strange effect on the light, deepening the colours around her. She hurries on; Bill Coldacre is waiting for her in the potting shed.

'Height of summer,' Bill says. 'The garden's at its best, especially the borders. Now we've had a bit of rain, even the lawns are recovering.'

He keeps up a running commentary: the weather, the rain last night and the forecast of another heatwave on its way. They go outside and he shows her where she'll be working today. She leans forward to touch the soft leaves of a plant with purple flowers.

'Lamb's ears,' he says, 'because, well, you can see why.'

They're a dusty pale green but they feel like velvet. She strokes one of the leaves with her fingertips.

She spends the rest of the day deadheading roses and pulling up cleavers where they've started to encroach on the beds. Bill has given her a pair of gloves. They're not like the tough cotton ones she's used before. He says these are made of pigskin in China. They're too nice to get dirty, but they stop the cleavers giving her a rash. It's a quiet day; Bill says Mondays usually are. The few visitors look at the plants and ignore her. That suits her fine. She's happy to be invisible.

She works hard and by four o'clock she's stacking the tools according to Bill's tidy system, when she hears a familiar voice outside the potting shed.

'Ouch! Ow, ow!'

She looks out to see Taheera, wearing a huge pair of film-star sunglasses, hopping on one leg, trying to take one of her sandals off.

'Got a stone right under the ball of my foot.'

She hops onto a strip of lawn and puts her foot down, shaking the offending sandal to check the gravel isn't stuck inside it. A tiny pink sequin falls out onto the grass.

Bill follows Chloe outside and wipes his hands on an old rag. His arm twitches as if he wants to offer Taheera a hand. She hops on one leg again, trying to put her sandal back on, and he hesitates. Chloe can tell he sees what she sees: Taheera is beautiful, and here, in the garden, she looks more beautiful than ever.

'Hi,' Chloe breaks the silence. 'Is it all right if I go now, Bill? This is Taheera. She's going to give me a lift home.'

'Aye,' he clears his throat and rubs at an oil spot on the

palm of his hand. 'You get off. You've worked hard.'

They walk to the car park where the little cream car is parked. They get in and Taheera pulls away fast, spinning the wheels on the gravel. The car swings round the corner of the drive and Chloe reaches for something to hold on to. She wonders if they'll chat, but Taheera turns Radio 1 on loud. Chloe sits back in her seat and settles down to enjoy the ride.

At the far side of the village, Taheera pulls up to a junction and indicates right. The sign says Doncaster, twelve miles. Chloe feels the sweat rising in her armpits and hopes Taheera can't smell her fear.

'Hope you don't mind, I need to nip back to my parents' house, I've left something,' Taheera shouts over the music. 'It won't take a minute.'

'OK,' Chloe says, reading every signpost carefully.

Taheera slows at a crossroads and turns into a leafy narrow lane overhung with beech trees.

'Sleepy hollow!' Taheera says. 'That's what I call it. Mum and Dad think it makes them more English to live in a village like this.'

Chloe isn't sure what she should say, so she says nothing. The house is at the end of a pretty lane. It's detached, with a big garden. Along the side of the house there's a row of apple trees heavy with leaves and the tiny nubs of fruit waiting to fill and grow.

Taheera drives between two large stone pillars and stops in front of the garage, next to a dark blue BMW.

'You OK to stay here?' Taheera says, opening the door and getting out.

'Sure,' Chloe feels a crush of disappointment that she's

not been invited in, but she tries not to show it.

'Won't be a minute.'

Taheera slams the door shut and Chloe watches her pick her way across the gravel drive. As she reaches the front door, it opens. Taheera stands aside for a white guy in jeans and a denim jacket. There is a younger man standing in the doorway. Chloe recognises the brother, the one who shouted under her window the first night she slept at Meredith House. She can't hear what's said, but the guy in the denim shakes the brother's hand and turns to get into the BMW. He doesn't notice Chloe, a few feet away, as he ducks into the driver's seat. He adjusts the rear-view mirror and starts the engine. It's only when he begins to reverse that he looks across at her, but she lets her hair fall in front of her face and turns away. When the BMW has gone she looks up to see Taheera gesturing angrily to her brother, who simply smiles and stands aside to let her in.

She's gone for a few minutes and when she comes back she's carrying a bag and a paper plate.

'My mum thought we might be hungry. Do you want some sweets?'

The plate is crammed with brightly-coloured cakes; one of them is oozing orange jam. Chloe takes the plate on her knee and puts one in her mouth. She's hungry and the sugar is wonderful.

'Who was that guy?' she says, when she's swallowed most of it.

'Who?' Taheera starts the engine.

'In the BMW.'

'No idea, one of my brother's cronies, I guess.'

'Oh.' Chloe says.

There was something about his eyes, but she tells herself lots of people have blue eyes.

'Kamran must think pretty highly of him: he's lent him his car.'

Taheera turns the radio back on and turns it up loud, skids into reverse and backs out of the driveway.

Chloe doesn't recognise these roads. They're nowhere near the local station where she got the train home after her interview.

'Are we heading back to York?' Chloe shouts over the drum and bass.

Taheera turns the music down a couple of notches.

'Just need to see someone,' she says. 'It won't take long.'

They pull up to a 'give way' sign and wait. Halsworth is to the left, Doncaster to the right. A gap opens on the main road and she swings right.

'But where are we going?' Chloe says.

'I'm going to try his uncle's shop. He's probably working.'

Chloe stares out of the window, pressing her fingernails into her palms.

'The guy who came to the Minster?'

'Oh, yeah, of course, you've met him. I forgot.'

Chloe sits tight. They're on a stretch of dual carriageway now and there's no chance of turning round. She shifts in her seat, the backs of her legs stick to the leather. Taheera fiddles with the control for the air-conditioning and the temperature starts falling.

The road feeds onto the M18 motorway and a sign reads: *Doncaster - four miles*. They pass an exit but Taheera keeps going. They swing out into the middle lane to pass an Asda lorry. Maybe it will be all right. Maybe they're headed beyond the town. The car is swamped on either side by lorries that will surely crush them. She looks at Taheera's hands on the wheel, gripping so tightly her knuckles peak in little mountains of hard bone. They sway back into the left-hand lane.

It's hard to tell what direction you're going on a motorway. Everything looks the same, except the sun. It was on their right when they started but now it's behind them. Taheera is indicating onto a slip road and the next sign leaves Chloe in no doubt. She feels like she's going to be sick.

'I can't go this way,' Chloe says. 'I'm not allowed to go to Doncaster.'

'It's just on the edge,' Taheera says. 'It's OK. We're not going into the town or anything.'

They slow down for the roundabout at the top of the slip road and Chloe feels for the catch on the door.

'What the hell are you doing?' Taheera turns to look at her.

'I can't be here. It's part of my licence. I thought you knew. Didn't you read my file?' Her fingers pull at the catch, but Taheera is faster and clicks a switch on her door.

'Calm down! You can't get out here. Where would you go?'

Chloe slumps back. The nausea is real now. She takes deep breaths to keep the sticky sweets down but acid creeps into her throat. Taheera's right. If she got out here she'd be wandering along a road she doesn't know, a road where a police car could pull up at any moment.

'Look, sorry, Chloe, I had no idea this is where . . . where

76

you're from. Hang tight. You can stay in the car. No one will see you. Here, wear these. You can be in disguise, like in a movie.'

She's laughs and hands Chloe her sunglasses.

'I need to check if Mo's at work. It's just a shop. I promise I won't take a second.'

They pass rows of new houses and a supermarket, more fields and a stretch of dual carriageway. Chloe knows this road. The new houses confused her for a moment, but the line of hedges and trees hasn't changed. They're slowing down, turning in along the side of the playground. Chloe catches a glimpse of the four Eagle Mount tower blocks and closes her eyes.

When the car stops, they're in front of the shops. Library at one end, Health Centre at the other, with the bookies and AK News and Convenience Store sandwiched in between. It's a bit shabbier than she remembers it, but otherwise nothing has changed. She shouldn't be here. She shouldn't have trusted Taheera. While she waits in the car the sunglasses keep sliding down her nose. She daren't open the door. A group of teenage girls shriek past in too-tight shorts. She tells herself that they won't recognise her; they would have been toddlers the last time she was here. The older women scare her more. She's torn between wanting to scrutinise their faces and trying to keep her own face turned away. There's a glossy magazine in the footwell of Taheera's car, so she stares hard at a C-list celebrity's wedding photos, and lets the people outside blur in her peripheral vision.

Finally the driver's door opens and Taheera puts her head in.

'You have to get me out of here,' Chloe says but it comes out as a whisper.

'Here, have a couple of quid and get yourself a cold drink. I've got to nip into the library.'

She drops two pound coins on the seat and shuts the door again. Chloe picks them up and holds them in her damp palm. She turns to see Taheera disappear through the double glass doors of the library. She's thirsty, incredibly thirsty. Rows of cold drinks will be lined up in the fridge in the newsagent's. She looks around her and opens the door, pushes the sunglasses back up her slippery nose.

He's coming out of an alleyway between the buildings, Mo, the bloke she saw at York Minster. He's carrying a big folder and heading for the library. He walks straight past her and if he sees her, he doesn't acknowledge it. That's good: if the huge sunglasses that cover half her face have hidden her from someone she's seen recently, then perhaps she's safe from being recognised by people who haven't seen her for ten years. She decides she'll be all right, if she's quick, and walks the few yards to the shop without turning round.

Inside it's cool and gloomy. She finds her way to the fridge, but it's hard to see with the glasses on, so pushes them on top of her head. She lifts out a small bottle of the cheapest lemonade and goes to the till. There's a girl in a headscarf who takes her money and gives her the change. Chloe turns away quickly, back towards the door, passing a low shelf of newspapers on her left. Heavy black headlines and the face of a teenage girl in school uniform stare up at her.

She doesn't break her stride as she leaves the shop. The sunglasses thump against the bridge of her nose as she runs to the car. She gets in, slams the door shut and presses the cold plastic bottle against her neck. Her hands are trembling.

When Taheera comes back, Chloe says nothing. She barely notices the young man slipping back up the alleyway. They move off and soon a blast of air from the fans chills the sweat on her legs.

'Thanks for waiting,' Taheera says cheerfully, as she drives towards the top of the estate, where the road opens out onto the dual carriageway.

Chloe just wants to get out of there. She doesn't look at the flats this time, keeps her eyes fixed on the label of her lemonade bottle, scratching it away with her thumbnail. When they reach the motorway, she snatches a look at the speedometer, creeping up past sixty, seventy, still rising as the tiny car hurtles along the inside lane, getting her away from the estate and its towers, the shop, the local paper with the headline she's been dreading. She wishes they could go even faster.

'Look, um, I hope you don't think I put you in a difficult position,' Taheera says, twirling a section of her long black hair in her fingers. 'I should have explained. It's a bit difficult between me and my boyfriend. I'd rather you kept it to yourself, do you know what I'm saying?'

Chloe doesn't reply.

'I've said I'm sorry, Chloe. But nobody needs to know about you being in Doncaster, or about me and him, do they?'

It sounds like a deal. A deal in which she has no choice. The kind of trade she's got used to over the years. Another debt to honour and obey.

'OK,' she says. It sounds hollow in her mouth.

The little car drifts towards the hard shoulder, until it runs over the catseyes and the tyres set off the ratchet sound designed to wake up sleeping drivers.

'Oops!' Taheera laughs and straightens up the car.

'He's on tag, isn't he?' Chloe says. She doesn't care all that much, but she'd like to know the terms of their deal, to work out how much it's worth.

A truck swings too close to them. It tries to overtake, gives up and slides back in behind them, as the road rises up over a long bridge. Yellow fields are spread out on each side of a river far below. Chloe feels the nausea of vertigo rising in her throat. She tries not to look over the side.

'He was,' Taheera finally says. 'But he's just had it taken off. How did you know?'

A sign to York causes them to swerve onto a slip road, a lorry horn blaring behind them. On the smaller road, they drive some way in silence, careful now, taking the bends at a speed that the little Fiat can manage.

'I saw it. His tag,' Chloe finally says. 'He was going up the steps at the Minster.'

'I see,' it comes out very quietly. 'Did Emma see it?'

Chloe can't decide what to tell her. 'Don't know.'

'I'm going to pull over, I need to think.'

She swerves into a gap on the grass verge. They come to a standstill with the bonnet of the car inches from the gate to an empty field. Taheera turns off the ignition and they sit listening to the ticking fans cooling the engine.

'I met him when I was teaching in a prison,' she says slowly, as if each word must be selected and checked before she uses

80

it. 'Nothing happened, I mean, nothing then. I decided to leave my job after he was released. The hostel job came up and I had the right skills, the right background. I mean, it's not like he's one of our residents,' she hesitates. 'I don't think it's against the law, but . . . Oh God, it's really messy. I could be sacked if anyone found out and my parents—' Taheera's voice wavers and Chloe can see she's trying not to cry. 'I haven't been able to talk to anyone about it.'

Chloe decides to leave her to it. She can't believe she cared for this silly girl, with her shiny new car and wealthy parents. Someone who has all that, a degree and a job, and risks it all for a boy; it's ridiculous. She gets out and walks to the centre of road. They are in the middle of nowhere, on a country lane raised up from the flat fields either side. Heat shimmers off the road. She feels the huge space all around her and holds out her arms, as if she could touch it. Someone knows she's out. It was there on the front cover of the newspaper. If she's lucky it's just one local paper, not the nationals. But she doesn't feel very lucky. Her arms fall by her sides.

Across the fields, the cooling towers of a power station fill the sky, soft cotton wool clouds of steam, hanging in the air around them. She looks up and sees a figure, balancing on the rim and falling into the steam cloud. She wants to call out to him. *Jay!* But her ears are filled with the roar of the wind, as if she's the one who's falling. Someone grabs her arm and pulls her back.

'Chloe!' Taheera screams above the sound. They thud against the side of the little cream car and Chloe feels her elbow crack on the metal. 'That truck nearly hit you.'

Dust clouds billow around the rear wheels of an empty skip lorry, chains clang against its frame and the sound of an air horn hangs in the air, as it disappears out of sight.

'What the fuck were you doing?'

Trying to die, Chloe thinks, but she says nothing. She closes her eyes for a few seconds and when she opens them again, she thinks she sees a blue BMW following the skip lorry, disappearing in its tail-cloud of dust. She blinks and it's gone, as if it was never there.

They sit in the car outside Meredith House. Neither of them speaks. Chloe feels a bead of sweat run down between her shoulder blades. It was cooler when the car was moving but now the heat is rising. Taheera breaks the silence first.

'Don't tell anyone.'

Her tone has changed. She's not confiding in Chloe any more, it's an instruction.

'I won't,' Chloe says.

'And I won't tell anyone where we went.'

That's the final deal on the table. Chloe watches her own hand reach for the door catch. Thin and white like the bones of dead birds.

'See you,' she says.

'Yeah, see you,' Taheera replies without looking at her. She starts the car before Chloe has shut the door.

Chloe tries to go straight to her room, but Emma is coming down the stairs.

'Hiya! Tough day?'

Chloe wonders how she can possibly know about her day.

'Takes a bit of getting used to, doesn't it?' Emma carries

on. 'I know I was on my knees after my first day at work. Got used to it, mind.'

'Yeah.'

'There's an IT course starting tonight. In the dining room.' Emma says. 'Do you fancy it? It's on three nights this week and it's good if you're not used to doing emails and going online and all that. I can show you how to get on Facebook, if you like.'

Chloe stands still, scanning Emma's face, trying to work out what she knows. Is it obvious she was away for so long? That the Internet will be so different now? She never had a computer at home, just at school, and she wasn't often there.

'We get a certificate if we finish it. Some woman from the council,' Emma says and her scar twitches in expectation. 'Summat to do, anyhow.'

'Go on then,' Chloe says and watches the scar on Emma's face pull back into a smile.

CHAPTER TEN

Doncaster

'I've got a feeling in my waters. And still waters run deep,' Gav said, resting his head back and drumming on the steering wheel with his thumbs.

'What are you on about?' Sean stifled a yawn.

'It's going to be a pleasantly uneventful night. That's my prediction.'

'Hope you're right. I'm knackered. I can't wait for the weekend.'

Even though his weekend came midweek, it was still something to look forward to. They would be back on the day shift after that, at least for the next fortnight, until the pattern switched again.

Sean hadn't been back to his dad's since the Clean Up Chasebridge meeting. Another run of nights had left him too tired to face it. He was annoyed with himself for not visiting the estate agent either. He'd settled back into a pattern of sleeping into the early afternoon and watching chat shows with his nan. Today's offering was slightly more challenging than most: a discussion about the death penalty for child abusers.

'What d'you reckon to the death penalty, Gav?'

'Don't fancy it myself.'

'On principle?'

'No, just rather die in my sleep.'

'Right.'

Sean flicked down the sun visor and checked his hair in the mirror. He was trying to grow it at the front, but it wouldn't do what he wanted.

'It's a relief they're not doing anything with that lad's complaint,' he said.

'Saleem Asaf? Don't worry about him. It's his favourite game.'

Sean got his phone out and opened up a game of Tetris. 'Keep him in our sights, though.'

'Oh, aye. We'll stick him with something one of these days. I can guarantee that.'

Sean wondered if Gav meant something legitimate, or maybe this was the sort of thing Wendy Gore had wanted him to listen out for. He didn't have the energy, to be honest, although he couldn't imagine himself telling her that. He was vaguely aware that the car was moving and stopping, moving and stopping. He tried to keep his eyes open, but it was so quiet, he couldn't help himself. He was fast asleep by the time the call came through on the radio and he missed the beginning of what was being said.

'The caller is on the first floor of Eagle Mount Two, top end of the Chasebridge estate. She says there's been some sort of fight on the stairwell and someone's been hurt. Ambulance is on its way. We couldn't get much else out of her, so can you go and take a look? There's something not quite right about this one and we need a safe pair of hands. Tread carefully.'

'I don't like the sound of this,' Gav said.

'Do you think it's a trap?'

Gav ground the gear stick around until he found first and put his foot down. 'Fuck knows. Told you we were in for a quiet night.'

'Funny.'

'No, seriously, it's gone five o'clock. It's technically morning.'

Sean sat back and watched the town unfold around them. His heart sank at the thought of being pulled back to the Chasebridge estate in uniform. They skipped another amber light and were soon on the dual carriageway. Gav hit seventy, seventy-five. Sean wondered if they should have a blue light on, but he kept his mouth shut. They swung round one final roundabout and approached the estate along its west side where the four matching blocks of ten-storey flats were arranged round the square, like the upturned legs of a table. Beyond the blocks were the low-rises, with concrete walkways traversing them like shelves. They were empty for now, but the arrival of the squad car would soon bring an audience out to watch.

Gav lurched to the left without changing gear. Sean grabbed the door to stay upright.

'It's the second block from the main road, opposite the playground,' Sean said.

The ambulance was already there; its crew got out of their vehicle as Gav pulled up on the pavement.

'Gav, mate, the service door.' Sean nodded towards the sheet metal door in the corner of the block. It hung a few inches open. 'That's where the stairs are.'

'After you.' The ambulance driver stood back.

Gav gave Sean the nod to go first. He peered into the gloom. There was no sound. He elbowed the door far enough open to get his head and shoulders through and switched on his torch. The beam picked out a pattern of brown marks on the concrete floor. He leant in further and saw the knees first: black jeans, narrow cut, and a pair of black Converse All Stars. He let the light play over the legs and up the torso. At first he thought the man was wearing a brown T-shirt, but as he held the torch steady, he saw he was covered in blood.

'Gav!' His voice resonated in the space and he heard a quiver of fear echo back at him. 'Get the ambo crew in here.'

Sean flicked the beam up the stairwell to where the dawn was filtering through a murky window. Nothing moved. He edged closer, picking his way round the marks on the floor. There were three steps before the staircase turned and where the body lay, curled up like a sleeping child, one hand holding his stomach, the other resting on the concrete. There was blood everywhere, all over his hands and across the floor. His face was pale, but the underside of his cheek and neck were a dark purple.

'Forget it, Gav. We're too late. Way too late.'

He heard shuffling in the doorway and Gav telling the ambulance crew to stand down.

'At least six hours,' Sean said. 'His skin . . .'

Post-mortem hypostasis, he'd learned about it at police college, even though he could never spell it. Gav was breathing heavily in the doorway, holding out a pair of latex gloves.

'Put these on. I'll put the call in and get the place secure.'

Sean had been leaning forward, not daring to touch the handrail or the wall, hoping for some sign of life, which was never going to come. As he straightened up, a wave of light fluttered behind his eyes and he wanted to grab the metal banister and hold on, but the rules kicked in: don't contaminate the scene or get any blood on your skin. He blinked to focus and looked about him. Wedging his torch between his knees, he fumbled with the gloves. Light danced across the victim's shoes, where remnants of mud and grass were wedged in the pattern of the tread. From beyond the door, Gav's voice was urgent on the radio, but inside nothing stirred.

It felt like a long time that he stood there, three steps below the body. He didn't need the torch now. The light was getting stronger through the upper windows. A door banged somewhere in the block and occasionally the lift mechanism ground into action. He dared himself to go nearer, to see the wound that had produced so much blood, but as he peered over the hunched up legs, he wished he hadn't. The man's jeans were open at the fly and his crotch was dark with a mess of deep-red flesh.

'Christ!' Sean looked away.

A fire door from one of the upper landings opened and Gav put his head out.

'I've taped up every door to this staircase. Thank fuck the lift works. No one here yet?'

'No one,' Sean said.

88

'It's all right, mate,' Gav called down. 'Stay where you are. I think I can hear the sweet sound of backup. I'm on my way down.'

Sean could hear it too, far away but getting nearer, several sets of sirens, out of sync, harmonising for a few seconds, then splitting again. For those last few moments before the mayhem began, Sean forced himself to look at the man's face, trying to get a clear picture in his mind of him as a person, not just a slaughtered animal. He had Asian features, or maybe Turkish. He was slim and, although it was hard to tell, Sean guessed he was nearly six foot. He wore a thin gold chain which fell inside his T-shirt and although, the curve of his cheek was already swollen in death, Sean could see he'd been a good-looking lad.

CHAPTER ELEVEN

York

'Has anyone seen my phone?'

The laptops are set up in the dining room for the second night of the computer course. Taheera is standing in the doorway, her hands on her hips and her face like thunder. She's looking directly at Chloe.

'Has anyone seen my phone?' she says again.

'Um, I'm Kath, from the council,' says the teacher. 'IT trainer? I'm sorry, I don't think we've met.'

'Taheera Ahmed, residential officer. My phone's gone missing and I was wondering if anyone had seen it.'

Emma leans back in her chair, arms folded. 'What you saying, T? That someone's nicked it? We've been in here for the last hour. Haven't we, Chlo?'

Chloe nods. She thinks about being in the car last night, tries to remember if the phone was there. She knows she didn't pick it up.

Taheera is still staring at her. Seconds have passed.

'I haven't got your phone,' she says.

She remembers Taheera texting before they got to her parents' house, but not afterwards. There was a plate of Indian sweets, but no mobile phone. Chloe needs to tell her but they have a deal. A deal which says they can't talk about yesterday.

'Can I have a word,' Chloe says, 'in private?'

As she gets up, the other girls watch her. Perhaps they think she's going to snitch on someone. Taheera is waiting in the hall.

'So?'

Chloe is taken aback by her hostility, but she understands. They were not meant to get to know one another, step out of the roles they'd been assigned. Taheera has let herself be seen, shared a confidence, and now she's closing herself in, trying to build up the wall between them again.

'I haven't got your phone,' Chloe says. 'I'm not a thief.'

'Really? So where is it? I had it yesterday.'

'I've never taken anything.'

'How can you say that?'

It hangs between them. A life. She was convicted of taking a life. His name comes to her again. Jay. She doesn't usually let it in, but yesterday she got so close. He's whispering something to her now. Telling her to stick up for herself.

'I didn't see it after we left your mum and dad's house. Maybe you left it there.'

'Do you think I haven't thought of that? I rang my mum and she's looked everywhere. It's not there.'

'You can search my room if you want to.'

She turns and starts towards the stairs. Taheera doesn't move at first, as if she's deciding whether to give up, but then she follows.

Chloe opens her door and puts the light on. Her bed is made. Her clothes are folded in the drawers. She pulls the top one open and moves the few items of underwear to one side.

'Look, here, look for yourself.'

Taheera shrinks back in the doorway. 'It's OK. I believe you.'

Chloe wants Taheera to say sorry, but she says nothing, just turns and lets the door snap shut on its spring. Chloe stands for a moment in the middle of her room and sees it as it is: bare and empty, no pictures of family on the walls, nothing to hint at a past and or a future. She feels weightless, like something untethered in zero gravity. Not zero gravity, Jay's voice is saying, you know better than that. There is some gravity on the moon, otherwise they wouldn't have been able to stand there. They would have floated off into space for good. He's right, she thinks. That's not going to happen. The sound when the truck screamed past, every hair on her body raised, the feeling when Taheera slammed her against the side of the car, the knowledge that she hadn't died, that she'd lived again; that's what she has to hold on to. She looks at her face in the mirror on the back of the door and slaps her cheeks, hard. It hurts. It's going to be OK. She'll go back down to the IT class. She will listen. She might even take notes.

When she gets back, she's missed something about Internet safety, but the teacher says she'll fill her in later, right now she wants them all to look at the BBC weather site – it will remain hot for the next few days but some areas will receive occasional heavy showers – then the news. Chloe's not interested in the national news. The website is the same as the TV news, but with more writing and even more boring.

The tutor's telling them how to search for local news. Chloe senses Emma watching her.

'Type in a place, and you'll get the local news,' Kath from the council says. She suggests they all type in 'York'. 'What can you see?'

'Town centre development unveeled,' Emma reads out.

'Unveiled. Good.'

Kath is oblivious to the fact that she's embarrassed Emma by correcting her. Chloe understands now how this works. While Emma is busy digging some imaginary dirt from under her nail, Chloe types 'Doncaster' into the box. She waits, expecting the headline from the newspaper in the shop and her younger face staring back at her, but the picture on the screen is all greens and browns and the bright colours of racing silks: *Residents' Raceday and Family Fun Activities*. She clicks on a triangle and the picture comes to life with the sound of horses' hooves and a man's voice rattling out the commentary. The tutor is flapping her hands.

'Not just yet, Chloe, we'll get on to the video content next session. Can you mute that? Can you?'

Emma leans over and grabs the mouse. The BBC news screen disappears, but in Chloe's mind the horses are still rushing by on the track, as if she were a little girl again, holding on to her mum's skirt, and her mum leaning into a man, both drunk, the man ruffling Chloe's hair, calling her 'sweetie'. The lesson is over. The tutor is saying that she'll be back next week. She's forgotten all about Chloe's Internet safety.

CHAPTER TWELVE

Doncaster

Gav offered to finish off filling out the paperwork, while Sean drove round to the twenty-four-hour garage on the dual carriageway to fetch a couple of coffees. He needed the sugar more than the coffee, but it was the best way he knew to digest four sachets. The full circus had arrived by the time he got back: three squad cars, with their lights still going, and the Crime Scene Incident van, all parked up at the foot of Eagle Mount Two. An audience of women and children, still in nighties and pyjamas, was scattered along the walkways of the low-rise flats.

One end of the tower block was cordoned off behind blue and white tape and there were three uniforms stationed at each corner. One of them was PCSO Carly Jayson, Sean's partner on his old beat. She was chatting with two little girls in rabbit onesies. As he watched, she lifted up her hat and ruffled her short, spiky hair. The girls laughed. He was surprised these children were up and about so early, but it had been a warm night and promised to be an even hotter day. The kids said something and Carly shook her head. He wondered if she'd told them what was behind the cordon.

Gav got into the car and helped himself to a coffee.

'Cheers!' He peeled back the lid, inhaling the steam. 'Forty minutes to go: then we can down tools. I've given the tear off sheets to CID, but the sergeant wants us to stay put until the end of the shift, just in case, so I suggest we sit back and enjoy the show.'

Sean lowered the electric windows and the smell of bacon frying and a faint of whiff of dog shit competed with the aroma of the coffee. A black Range Rover pulled up and a man and a woman in suits got out. They headed for the service door, where a uniformed constable was guarding the entrance.

'Reinforcements,' Gav said. 'They've brought them in from Sheffield. DCI Sam Nasir Khan and . . . I don't remember her name. But he's the one you have to watch.'

'Oh,' Sean said. He watched DCI Khan stride ahead, long legs like a cricketer.

The door opened and the two detectives stopped in the doorway, talking to someone inside. The woman said something to the constable on guard, who looked over to where Sean and Gav were waiting in the car.

'What d'you reckon, Gav?' Sean said.

Gav shrugged. 'Drugs probably. There's a load of gear coming in from Sheffield. No really big players round here, just these kids, getting in over their heads.'

'You PC Denton?' The constable who'd been guarding the service door was leaning in at Sean's window.

'Yeah.'

'CID wants to talk to you. Sergeant says you know the building. The Indian one wants to look at the access points.'

'I think you'll find he's Pakistani, of Kashmiri heritage,' Gav muttered under his breath.

Sean's legs were shaking, as if his body didn't want to go back inside the building, while his brain was telling him it was all part of the job. He looked in through the door. An arc light flooded the stairwell and a white-suited forensic investigator was standing over the body, back turned.

'Hang on a minute! Stay where you are. We haven't got all the prints from the lower steps.'

He knew the voice immediately. Lizzie Morrison had worked the case that inspired him to take the leap from community support to constable. He hadn't seen her since. She'd gone down to London, he'd heard, shacked up with some bloke, but here she was, back on his patch. His stomach flipped.

'If we take the lift, sir, we can come in above the stairwell,' he addressed DCI Khan. He kept his voice low, not wanting Lizzie Morrison to hear him. Not yet.

'All right with you ma'am, if we cut round and come in above you?' Khan's voice boomed off the concrete.

'Yep. Fine. Keep your eyes open, just in case I've missed something.'

She was staring intently at the ground as she spoke. Sean couldn't imagine that Lizzie Morrison would miss anything at all.

One of the Crime Scene Investigators passed them some plastic shoe covers. Sean backed out of the service door and led Khan around the building to the main entrance.

The battered stainless steel lift didn't look promising. Sean pressed the call button and they put the shoe covers on. At first nothing happened, then a rattling whine from above them announced its arrival. It was cleaner than he'd expected, as if someone had recently scrubbed the floor with bleach. The smell of disinfectant intensified once the doors were closed and he was glad when they reached the second floor landing. There were four front doors leading off it. The fifth was a fire door.

'Here,' Sean said, and pushed it open.

They ducked under the incident tape and the voices of the CSI team came up from below to meet them.

'Slowly. Eyes open,' Khan led the way.

The stairs, like the lift, were surprisingly well looked after. The usual dusty corners of fag ends, crushed cans and old crisp packets had been swept up. Eagle Mount One, where his dad lived, never smelt this fresh, but here it looked as if a mop had been passed over the concrete and the handrail was smooth and clean. Something caught his eye. He stopped and bent down to get a closer look.

'There's a thread, some sort of cotton I think.'

It was hooked in a gap where one piece of the metal handrail had been soldered onto the next. Khan passed him a specimen bag without speaking. Sean's heart was racing and he hoped his fingers weren't going to shake. He could see which way the thread had snagged, so he used the open bag like a glove, pulled the thread back on itself and freed it from the jagged metal. Then he turned the bag round and trapped it like a tiny, precious snake. A gift for Lizzie Morrison; he hoped she'd like it.

They'd reached the last few steps before the first floor landing. On the next section of the staircase, another CSI was taking footprint patterns. It was Donald Chaplin. Sean heard him humming something that sounded like the tune from a car advert. Chaplin looked up and read his expression perfectly.

'Verdi's "Requiem". The *Agnus Dei.* "Lamb of God" to you,' Donald said.

Khan cleared his throat and Donald didn't say any more, just went back to what he was doing and carried on humming his tune, as if he'd never broken off. Sean looked beyond him to the victim below, the body curled like a baby, a white plastic sheet placed across to hide the worst of the wounds. Sean could see how the blood had pooled in front of him like an oil slick.

'Someone's going to have his DNA all over their feet. They didn't even try not to step in it,' Khan said.

A trail of marks led towards the first floor landing. It was clear in the bright glare of the arc light that they were footprints. Each was labelled with a little white flag. The door to the first floor flats was propped open and he could see where the prints stopped abruptly at the doorway. Beyond the floor was clean.

'How long has he been here?' DCI Khan said.

Lizzie looked up and Sean instinctively stepped into the shadows behind the detective. This wasn't exactly the right atmosphere for a reunion, but he still had the thread sample to hand over.

'The pathologist reckons about eight or nine hours,' Lizzie said. 'There's no ID on the body. The call came shortly after five this morning from the woman at flat three. A Mrs Armley. It's not clear what took her so long to call it in.'

'I think we'll pay her a visit,' Khan said, picking his way around the prints. 'I'll take the constable, he's got a friendly face.'

Sean held up his plastic bag for Lizzie. Those familiar eyes were looking right at him. Her hair was tucked inside her white hood and he wondered how she'd got it cut under there, whether she still had the long dark bob that used to curl over the collar of her blouse.

'Found this,' he said. 'Could be something. Looks like denim, maybe?' He fought the urge to grin at her.

'Sean?'

'Police Constable Denton, if you don't mind.'

'Bloody hell. You did it! I knew you would.'

She had been the first to encourage him to apply for police college, to move up from PCSO to fully badged officer, but by the time he'd qualified, she'd disappeared to London. Khan turned round at the doorway to the first floor landing and Sean thought he saw the flicker of a smile, but it didn't last.

'Are you coming? We've got a statement to take.'

'Thanks,' Lizzie said. She took the bag and held it up to the light. 'I see what you mean. It's not quite white, more like a very pale blue. We'll get it sent off. Check out Mrs Armley's coat hooks while you're in there. See if she's got a denim jacket she does her cleaning in.'

Inside Mrs Armley's flat, it was clear she wasn't the denim jacket type and it seemed unlikely she'd leave a single thread of anything where it wasn't supposed to be. All her furniture was in perfect condition; spotless as the day she'd bought it. Mrs Armley herself was about five foot tall and looked like she was in her early sixties. She was wearing a brown, nylon housecoat buttoned over her thin frame.

'I told the young lady to let me know when they've finished,' she said. 'I'll give it a good going over.' Her voice was soft, Irish underneath, but as if she'd been in Yorkshire for a long time. 'I'll have to get started soon, if I'm to get it all done today.'

'There's no need Mrs Armley,' Khan said. 'We'll send out a specialist cleaning team. It's very unpleasant.'

'I quite agree. But I can't be waiting around. If the day warms up any more, we'll have bluebottles before we know it. And you know what that leads to, don't you?'

The two men shook their heads.

'Maggots.'

DCI Khan looked around the room, taking in every detail. The walls were white, the woodwork even whiter. There were no paintings or ornaments on display, except in a glass-fronted cabinet where a set of ornate, crystal glasses stood next to a pair of school photos. Two young boys, slim and freckled, with red hair and blue eyes. Sean knew the uniform. It was the Catholic high school that his own school used to fight on a regular basis.

Khan cleared his throat.

'Is that what you're worried about? Maggots? Now, I have an idea. Why don't you come with us, and we can take some information down at the station? Then you don't have to worry about the mess and it'll all be cleared up by the time you get back.'

'Oh no. That's not what you do. That's most irregular. I've seen it on the television. You'd only do that if I was a suspect, and I'm not a suspect am I?'

'We just want a statement, and we want to do things properly. Our cleaning team will come, but they can't come yet, because we're not ready for them.'

'Is it still there?'

'It?'

'The corpse.'

'Yes. The victim's body will be removed soon.'

'The sooner it gets cleaned up the better. Disgusting . . .' her legs folded under her as she sank down onto a brown velour settee.

'Are you all right?' Sean instinctively bent towards her. She was staring into space.

'I don't like to go out. I stay in, you see. It's my nerves.'

'Don't worry, Mrs Armley . . .'

'I know you. Don't I?' She looked at him sharply.

'It's possible, I . . .'

Khan cleared his throat, as if warning him to say nothing.

'I know,' she smiled. 'You look like that one off the telly. I don't go out much. I'm phobic. But I like my programmes.'

'Mrs Armley. We need to talk about the man out there on the stairs, about what's happened.' DCI Khan was pacing now, not that the room gave him much scope to pace.

'Was it a man?' she said. 'Or a boy, do you think?' She looked straight at Sean.

'Sorry?'

'I saw someone running. And I wouldn't say he was much more than a boy. A fast runner.'

'Can you describe him?' Sean asked.

'Dark.' She dropped her voice to a stage whisper and nodded in Khan's direction. 'Like him.'

Sean winced.

'When was this?' Khan said.

'Last night.'

'But you only called us this morning.'

'I saw him running. And I said, there's someone up to no good. Then I couldn't see him any more. I lost sight of him. This morning there was all this mess, footprints outside. I always wake up early, wake with the dawn. Anyway, I thought it was mud so I started to clean it up, then I stopped, when I saw . . .' She fanned her face with her hand.

'But what about last night?' Khan said.

'I didn't hear a thing.'

'And what did you see, Mrs Armley?' Khan said, looking out of her window, as if it would all replay in front of him and tell him what he needed to know.

'I've told you. I saw the boy running and then I lost sight of him.'

'Who was he running from? Did you see anyone else?'

'No. There was nothing else.'

When they got back outside, Gav was standing by the squad car looking at his watch, but Khan took no notice. He turned to Sean.

'Do you think Mrs Armley was telling the truth?'

Sean was surprised the DCI was asking his opinion.

'About what, sir?'

'Any of it.'

102

'Something odd about the way she described the body. She said "it". Then she talked about seeing a boy running.'

'But only after I'd told her it was male.' DCI Sam Nasir Khan sighed and rubbed at a crease between his eyebrows. 'I think we might need to get her in for a proper chat, which is going to be a nightmare if she really is agoraphobic.'

'There's not much soundproofing from the stairwells to the landings,' Sean said, recalling the sound of footsteps running up and down, voices calling out in the night, which had punctuated his dreams as a child. 'Unless they've done some improvements in the last few years, she must have heard something.'

'Is that so? Let's test that idea.' Khan started to walk towards Eagle Mount One. 'Come on, you know your way around. Let's get out of the SOCOs way and find a flat in one of the other blocks. They must be pretty much the same. We'll see just how soundproofed they are.'

Sean looked back at Gav.

'I'll be right here, son,' Gav said quietly. 'Just remind him there's no budget for overtime.'

Khan was already heading up the path to the block.

'I'll go inside,' he said, 'you imagine someone's stabbing you in the privates and we'll see if anyone comes to save you.'

Sean thought he knew the answer to that. He also thought the chances of anyone willingly opening their front door to two police officers was slim. There was one option he could try.

'Hang on a minute, sir. I've got an idea.'

He took out his phone and dialled. There was no reply. He rang again. This time the phone was picked up. A rasping breath and finally the familiar cracked voice.

'Hello, who's this?'

'Dad? It's Sean.'

'Who?'

'Sean. I'm round the corner. Thought I'd come in and see you.'

'What for? It's the middle of the fucking night.'

'It's the morning and I'm right here on the estate.' He hesitated. Khan was looking at him, waiting. 'Thought I might see if you needed anything getting in.'

'Don't bother, I'm skint.'

'Well, I can sub you.'

'I wouldn't mind,' Jack cleared his throat. 'You know what? Eileen's not coming back.'

'Sorry to hear that,' Sean could feel Khan's impatience. 'So shall I come up?'

There was a pause, punctuated by his father's laboured breathing, and the sound of him lighting up.

'Mm. OK then,' he mumbled through the cigarette in his mouth. 'But don't go expecting a cup of tea. I've no milk.'

Eagle Mount One was in desperate need of a Mrs Armley. The inside of the lift stank. The two men watched as the doors closed and two halves of a swastika came together in front of them. On the right-hand door someone had written 'EDL' and on the left, 'NO SURRENDER'.

'Is that how you spell surrender?' Sean wondered out loud. Khan said nothing.

Sean rattled the letterbox on the front door. He ran two

fingers under his collar in an attempt to loosen it. A trickle of sweat was running into the armpits of his shirt.

'Maybe you should wait on the stairs, sir. Do the scream as soon as I get inside, then we can go.'

'You don't want me to meet your father?' The challenge in Khan's voice was undisguised. His eyes were fixed on a sticker on the door, all that was left of a St. George's cross, peeling around the edges.

Sean looked at his feet. Regulation kit, steel toecaps hidden under the black leather. He'd come a long way from the little boy whose mother was dead and whose telly was broken because his dad had kicked it in.

'No. It's fine.'

Although it wasn't fine. It wasn't fine at all. If this was a bright idea to impress DCI Khan, it was one he wished he hadn't had.

At that moment the door opened.

'Now then, lad. Look at yer! Trussed up like a wanker. I thought you'd packed it in.'

'Hi Dad.'

'Who's this? Your business partner? Fancy suit, that. What's he up to? Loan sharking? You've come to the right place. I'm flat broke.' His laugh broke into a fit of coughing. 'Eh, that'd be right, a loan shark hiring a bent copper for a bit of muscle.'

'I'll go to the staircase. Count to twenty?' Khan sounded embarrassed.

Sean followed Jack into the narrow hallway and closed the door, trapping them together in a flat full of stale air and bad memories. The sympathy he'd started to feel for his dad was evaporating fast. He put his hand in his inside pocket for his wallet.

'How much d'you need?'

Jack licked his lips with sticky spittle. Sean stared at a pile of dirty clothes lying on the floor.

'What happened to Eileen?'

'We've split up. Artistic differences!'

Jack laughed, hacking his way through a chest full of phlegm. Then Sean heard it: the high-pitched scream of a man in pain.

'Did you hear that?'

'If you say so.'

'But did you?'

'Hear what?'

'Nothing. It doesn't matter.' He pressed a twenty-pound note into his father's hand. 'Buy some food with that. You look like you need it.'

'As if you bloody care. I can hardly manage the walk to the shop, you said—'

But Sean had opened the door.

'See you, Dad.'

He shut the door as Khan came through from the stairwell.

'Well?' Khan said.

'I heard you. He didn't.'

'What's that supposed to mean?'

Sean jabbed his finger at the lift button. He couldn't wait to be out of there.

'People hear what they want to.'

CHAPTER THIRTEEN

York

The early morning music show is playing a song her mum used to like. Chloe leans out of bed and turns it off. That DJ is way too chirpy anyway. She sits up and swings her legs over the side of the bed, rubbing the grit of sleep out of her eyes. There's a couple of slices of bread in a plastic bag by her bed. It's all she's got left until the first payment for her apprenticeship comes through. The mealtimes in the hostel are too late for her early morning starts and too early in the evening. It's all cleared up by the time she gets back. She owes money for her hostel charge, but now she's getting nothing for it. She'll take the bread with her and eat it on her journey.

The whole building is quiet. She tiptoes downstairs, her work boots in her hand. Bill had them waiting for her yesterday. There was a sale on at the garden centre, he said, and they happened to have her size. She'll pay him back when she can. The office door is ajar, but she doesn't want to see Taheera. They didn't speak again last night after the accusation over the mobile phone. Chloe thinks there should have been an apology; you can't speak to people like that and decide it doesn't matter. It does matter. With any luck, Taheera will still be asleep in the little staff bedroom, beyond the office.

As Chloe reaches the bottom of the stairs, the office phone starts to ring. The light is switched on. She heads for the front door and hears Taheera answer.

'Hello? Yes. Ghazala? What's wrong?'

Chloe has her hand on the exit switch to unlock the door.

'I can't hear you properly. What are you saying?' Taheera says. 'Which tower? He's what?'

The catch clicks and Chloe opens the door to the street.

'Dead? Mo's dead? What d'you mean?'

Chloe hesitates.

'No! Oh, God, no! No!'

Something crashes to the floor in the office. Another door opens and a sleepy voice from upstairs asks if everything is all right. Chloe slips out into the cool morning air and walks quickly to the bus stop.

CHAPTER FOURTEEN

Doncaster

The words on the menu in Val's Café danced in front of Sean's eyes and he didn't have the energy to work it all out. He pretended to be too tired to choose and let Gav order.

'Uncle Gavin knows best, sunshine, and you need to eat. You've had a shock and your blood sugar will be on the floor.'

In minutes a full English breakfast was put in front of Sean. He stuck his fork into his fried egg and watched the yolk pour out and merge with the juice from the baked beans. He shuddered, trying to blank out an unbidden image of blood pooled on concrete, and shoved a forkful of food into his mouth.

'Back in the day, we'd have been in the pub by now,' Gav was saying, pouring sugar into his tea. 'A couple of double whiskies to get over ourselves. Now they offer you counselling.'

'Food,' Sean said through his mouthful, 'is just as good. You were right.'

They ate in silence until they were mopping up the last juices from their plates with slabs of Val's white sliced bread. She replaced their mugs of tea without asking. Sean wasn't even sure if she was actually called Val, or whether she was a successor to the original owner, but she'd been running the café round the corner from the police station for years.

'He's taken a shine to you, that DCI Khan,' Gav said, wiping his mouth on the back of his hand.

Sean shrugged. 'Useful that I know the territory, nothing more than that.' In the pocket of his trousers, the corner of Khan's business card pressed almost imperceptibly against his thigh.

'He's a tricky bugger,' Gav said, 'so watch yourself.'

'How d'you mean?'

'Bit of a reputation for running to the bosses at the first sniff of things not going his way. Plays the race card if anyone crosses him, so I've heard.'

Sean shrugged. He hadn't had much time to form an impression, but he thought the detective was all right. Serious, but all right.

'He's not got a lot of friends in the Sheffield force. That's probably why he's been sent over here,' Gav said.

'I thought it was the cuts. We can't even get a Major Incident Team together on our own.'

Sean drained his tea. He was so full of food he thought he might fall asleep, face down in his empty plate, but he still had to pick up his moped and get back to his nan's.

By 10 a.m. he was riding along Winston Grove, the curved crescent that ran along the lower end of the Chasebridge estate. The community centre masked his view of the base of the towers, but he could see the first floor windows and above. He wondered how good Mrs Armley's eyesight was and what she could see from her window.

His nan had texted him to say she needed a packet of fags and he thought he might pick her up some nice biscuits as a surprise. He parked in front of the parade of shops and rocked his ped onto the kickstand. AK News appeared deserted, but the jangling bell must have alerted someone because when he reached the counter, the plastic strips parted and a young woman in a hijab appeared from the back of the shop. Her nose was red and she had bloodshot eyes. He recognised her slightly as one of the family who ran the shop, but he didn't know her name. There were several daughters or sons or cousins; they were interchangeable. He thanked her but she didn't say anything. Not even a smile. Pretty rude, Sean thought. A smile didn't cost anything.

As he was about to leave the shop, he saw through the glass door that there was someone by his moped, fiddling with the mirrors. He rushed out, slamming the door behind him, as the small figure darted away up the side of the library. The packet of biscuits slipped out of Sean's hand and hit the pavement. Shit. A last drop of energy surged through his legs and he shouted something as he ran round the corner. It was meant to be *come here you little bastard*, but only the last word was intelligible.

Saleem Asaf was waiting for him behind the shops, a scabbed bruise fading on his forehead.

'I need to talk to you,' Saleem said.

'You've got a cheek. What were you doing to my bike?'

'Nothing. Just waiting for you.'

'Well I don't want to talk to you,' Sean said.

'You going to catch who did it?'

'What are we talking about here?'

'You going to catch who killed Mocat?'

'Sorry?'

'My cousin, Mohammad?'

Sean's hand went to his pocket and he held Khan's business card tightly between his finger and thumb. He was off duty now and his radio was back at the station, but he had his phone.

'Are you saying you can identify the casualty found at Eagle Mount Two this morning?'

'That ain't no casualty, man. That's a dead body. And he's my cousin. It's gone too far now. They take one of ours, if it don't stop, we'll have to take one of theirs. You get me?'

'Who's "they"?'

'Chase Boys. White boys. Working off the Chasebridge estate.'

'And you? Where do you work?'

He looked like he might be about to run again. Sean reached for his arm but Saleem didn't move. He went limp under Sean's grip and for a moment he was just a frightened young boy.

'I'm going to call someone,' Sean said. 'He's a senior detective. He'll want to meet you. We're going to stay here until he comes and if you try to run, I will stop you in whatever way I have to, God help me. Got that?'

The boy nodded.

* * *

They were in Khan's black Range Rover. Sean had a pain in his head that was spreading from behind his eyes, right round the back of his ears and up over his forehead. He should be asleep in bed, but he was sitting in the back of the car with Saleem, who squirmed under the seatbelt, his face turned away from the window, as if he feared being recognised.

All spare manpower was on the estate doing house-to-house under the female detective's orders. DS Simkins, Khan said her name was. He said he'd rather not bother her for any more officers and Sean heard himself offering to come along with the boy. He must be mad. He wasn't even getting paid overtime and technically he was off duty. None of this seemed to concern DCI Khan.

'Who were you talking about, Saleem?' Khan said quietly. 'Who was involved in your cousin's death?'

Saleem was still for a moment before he replied.

'*Haram zathey*. Just scum. Don't know any names. But he was clean, man, you won't find nothing on him. Gone all straight-edged for some girl. I'll take you to his mum, but that's it. That's all I know.'

'How did you know it was your cousin who was the victim?' Sean asked, then wondered if he should keep quiet but the thought was out of his mouth as soon as it had formed in his head.

'Word gets out.'

'Not from us, son,' Khan eyed him for a moment in the rear-view mirror. 'So who?'

The boy shrugged and focused on picking the skin off the side of his thumb. He didn't say any more, beyond directions to turn right or left, until they were on Nether Hall Road, where they pulled off into a street of red-brick terraced houses. There was nothing remarkable about the house where Saleem told Khan to stop. Net curtains hid its occupants; the short front path was swept clean and a row of potted geraniums filled the space between the bay window and a low wall to the street.

'We going in or what?' Saleem was anxious to get out of the car now that there was a possibility of being spotted.

'I'm waiting for a female officer,' Khan said.

'What for? Come on man. You got bad news to tell my auntie, you better get on with it.'

A car was turning into the road behind them. Sean recognised PCSO Carly Jayson behind the wheel. As she got out and walked over to them, it was clear that her uniform and the Range Rover had caught the attention of the people in the house. A net curtain lifted and dropped. A few seconds later, the door opened and a girl of about twelve, in purple shalwar kameez, peered out. She saw Saleem, but as he stepped forward, she frowned and ran back inside.

'Look, this is the house,' he said. 'You don't need me now.'

'We don't,' Khan came closer to him and spoke gently, 'but your auntie might.'

The boy's shoulders dropped and he seemed to grow younger still with this new level of responsibility. Khan led the way, followed by the boy, Sean and Carly. The house was quiet.

'Hello?' Khan called.

The girl appeared from the kitchen and mutely beckoned

them into the front room where a woman was sitting, her hair covered by a pale green, embroidered shawl, which matched her dress and trousers. She looked surprisingly young, but her face was tired and shadowed with dark circles under her eyes.

'*As-salamu alaykum.* My name is Detective Chief Inspector Khan.'

She looked up at him for a second before saying something which Sean didn't catch, then she fixed her eyes on the carpet. Khan spoke to her in Urdu and Sean was able to pick out a few English words: *Chasebridge, police.* The girl sat next to her mother and held her hand. The woman remained still, nodding gently. She hadn't acknowledged Saleem, but when Khan stopped speaking she looked at the boy with fire in her eyes. She spoke in rapid Urdu and her fury was undisguised.

'No, auntie, it's not my fault,' he replied. '*Allah dey Kassam.* What d'you blame me for?'

Khan turned to the boy. 'Is there a father? We need someone to identify the body.'

'His dad and mine,' Saleem said, 'they're both away in Pakistan.'

'She'll have to do it. You should come too.'

'OK. I'll come.' The woman's voice was quiet and thick with the effort of holding back tears. 'But not the boy, he stays here.'

There was a sound in the hall and Sean realised the house was filling with people. The vehicles outside, messages flying between phones, from young to old, had confirmed what until now had been a rumour.

'We'll wait outside,' Khan said. 'PCSO Jayson will accompany you to the car when you're ready.'

A press of bodies in the hallway moved aside as they passed and two women pushed forward into the living room. As Sean and DCI Khan stepped out into the daylight, a sound like a wounded animal rose from inside the house.

CHAPTER FIFTEEN

Halsworth Grange

There are too many people in the garden, stopping and staring. Chloe tells herself they're looking at the plants, not her, but it does nothing to calm her nerves. A sticky-faced toddler kicks a ball into one of the herbaceous borders and it thwacks against the stem of one of Bill's best hollyhocks. She wants to tell the parents to get out and take the little brat with them, but instead she goes inside the shed to get some twine and a cane. While she's staking it back up, hoping the damage isn't too severe, she turns round to see a man taking photographs. He has the camera pointed right at her. She turns away and pulls the elastic out of her hair, letting the dyed blonde strands cover her face.

'*Alcea rosea*,' he says.

'Sorry?'

'Latin name for hollyhocks. I wish I could get the ones on my allotment to grow like that.'

'Oh.'

She busies herself with a knot. She doesn't want to hear

about his allotment. She can picture it without him having to tell her. It will have neat rows of military cabbages and a 'Keep Out' sign on the gate. He wears white socks and beige lace-up shoes and he's probably a leading light on his allotment committee.

There were allotments near where she grew up. She used to go there when she bunked off school with Jay, or after dark when her mum was working in the pub. Some of the plots looked like the gardens of real homes, with paved paths and chalet-style sheds. She and Jay broke into one once and found deckchairs. They pretended it was their own garden and called themselves Mr and Mrs Clutterbuck. He smoked and laughed at nothing on earth. She laughed too, but she didn't know why. Then suddenly he was crying and she crossed over to his deckchair and sat on his lap. The striped cotton ripped and they ended up on the ground, laughing again.

'These are a fine bunch of specimens,' the man with the camera says.

She ties another length of twine lower down the stem of the plant, her face brushing the blousy flower head, and breathes in to see if they have any particular smell. The air's full of the roses in the neighbouring bed, so she almost feels sorry for the hollyhocks; they smell of nothing. She looks past the allotment man and realises she's staring at the spot on the strip of lawn where Taheera hopped on one foot, trying to get the stone out of her shoe. It seems like months ago, not Monday. She sounded very upset on the phone this morning. If Chloe was dead, Taheera would carry on as normal, she's pretty sure about that. She could die now, fade away among the hollyhocks and disappear; Taheera wouldn't even notice.

A voice in her head says, *you can't die just to make people feel sorry for you.* She knows that voice, she used to hear it all the time. It was the voice of a bird that flew past her window and told her the truth – or lies – she never really knew. The bird was a jay, which laughed like a crackle of static and flashed her a blue tattoo on its red-pink feathers. The bird and the boy, they shared the same name, the same voice.

'You look ready for a break.' Bill's huge frame casts a shadow over her.

The man with the camera has gone and she wonders how long she's been standing in the border, half hidden behind the hollyhocks, winding a piece of twine in and out of her fingers. Bill's voice is reassuringly solid.

'Why don't you sit in the shade behind the shed and have your lunch?'

She nods and makes her way back onto the path, not wanting to tell him that she hasn't brought any lunch. She'll get a glass of water from the tap and make do with that. If Bill offers her a coffee she'll put extra milk and sugar in it, but she has no money left for bread or sandwiches until she gets paid. She leans against the shed and lets the water cool her cracked lips. She closes her eyes and sees the face of Taheera's young man, walking towards them outside the Minster, smiling at Taheera because he loved her. Like a delayed reaction, she feels a shock rip through her. It twists her stomach and forces her forward. She's vomiting water and bits of bread, then dry retching until she's crying, sobbing silently, tears stinging her cheeks.

CHAPTER SIXTEEN

Doncaster

Sean took the bus back from the town centre and went straight to where he'd hidden his moped behind the library. He motored slowly out onto Winston Grove and followed the streets to his nan's. It felt like the moped knew where it was going, like an old horse. He struggled to keep his eyes open and felt himself leaning forward and jerking back, as sleep tried to catch him.

There was nobody home. Just a note on the table to say Maureen had gone shopping. He went straight upstairs, got undressed and fell into bed, the cool sheets against his skin. It could have been several hours later, or a few minutes, when the dreams started. A newspaper was rolling out, unfurling, like a red carpet, then blowing down the street in the wind. The words were everywhere, but he couldn't make sense of them. The papers gathered together and blew into a ball like tumbleweed, knocking a young man to the ground. The figure lay, holding a wound in his groin, then he stood up and it was Saleem, brushing the papers off, telling

Sean it was all right, he wasn't dead after all; it had been a mistake. Then the young man had Mohammad's face and the newspapers were soaked in blood.

Sean woke, drenched in sweat. He shook the dream away, sat up and took a drink of water from the glass by his bed. The glass hadn't been there when he went to sleep. Nan must be home. He turned over on his back and stared at the ceiling. He'd painted it himself and he could see an annoying bit where he'd got yellow paint on the white plastic light fitting.

He stood no chance of getting that little studio flat now. It was a shame because he liked the road it was on, South Parade, tree-lined and full of old houses from the days when rich merchants lived along there. Most of them were broken up into offices and flats, but it was still a cut above. All the clubs and bars were a short walk away and it would be convenient if he ever wanted to bring a girlfriend home. That was a big 'if'. He rolled back on his side and stared at the wall. A single bed, with his grandmother popping in with a cup of tea in the morning, was nobody's dream. The last girl he'd dated would have died laughing if he'd brought her back here. Not that things ever got to that stage with her. It crossed his mind that Lizzie Morrison might be impressed with a studio flat on South Parade. Sean sighed. Don't go there again. She was so far out of reach, she might as well be on another planet.

There was a soft knock on the door and it opened a crack.

'All right, Nan. I'm awake.'

'I didn't want to bother you, love. But your phone's been ringing. You left it on the kitchen table. I've brought it up.'

'Oh. Right.' He sat up as she came in. 'What time is it?'

'It's coming up to five-fifteen. Shall I open the curtains?'

'Aye, go on.'

He took the phone from her and looked through the missed calls. One blocked number, then one from Carly and one from DI Rick Houghton, a drug squad detective he'd known since his first case as a PCSO. Sean selected voicemail and listened. They came in reverse order, so the last two didn't make much sense until he got to the first message. Carly and Rick were both checking if he wanted to meet up in the pub later. They appeared to know something he didn't about his shift pattern changing and were offering to buy him a drink. The first message explained why.

It was his unit sergeant, telling him there was good news, or bad news, whichever way he wanted to look at it. For the duration of this inquiry, Sean was being seconded to CID. DCI Khan had asked for him by name. He was to report at 8 a.m. the next morning for a briefing, which meant he had the night off and could he phone him back to confirm he'd got the message?

'Everything all right?' Maureen was still hovering by the window, pretending to be interested in something in the street.

'Yeah, great.'

'You don't sound great, you sound a bit worried, love.'

Sean tried to make sense of everything that had happened since he and Gav got the call to attend the flats earlier that morning. Sleeping in the day had an odd way of shuffling time and memory, so he could no longer tell what was today and what was yesterday.

Maureen didn't wait for an explanation. She went downstairs to the kitchen and soon the smell of bacon was drifting upstairs. Having another breakfast at teatime wasn't going to help his sense of disorientation, but his stomach was rumbling. He got out of bed and pulled on his clothes.

In the kitchen, one place was laid at the table, and a cup of tea was waiting for him.

'They're saying there's been a murder up at the flats.'

She was wiping down the surfaces, her back to him so he couldn't read her expression.

'Who's they?' Sean said through a mouthful of toast.

'I know you're not meant to say, but did you . . . was it on your shift?'

'Did I see him?' Sean nodded. 'I found him.'

'Are you all right?' She turned and gave him a look that demanded a truthful answer. She knew him too well.

He was all right, or at least he would be if he didn't have to talk about it. The body curled on the stairs wasn't the worst of it; the thing he couldn't get out of his head was the mother's cry of grief.

'If I can nail the bastard that did it, then I'll be all right.'

He told her about being seconded to work on Khan's team and a beaming smile lit up her face.

'I'm so proud of you. You know that, don't you, love?'

That evening, he found Carly, Rick and a couple of others in the corner of the pub.

'Well, well, if it isn't Acting Detective Constable Denton, the fastest promotion in the west, or make that the north,

or shall we just call him, "South Yorkshire's finest recruit!"'
Carly stood up and gave him a huge hug.

'Steady on,' he could feel his ears going hot. 'Not until tomorrow morning, technically. And it's only a secondment, I'm hardly . . .'

'Ah, leave it out! You've done well, and I, for one, am going to buy you a pint to celebrate.' She went over to the bar followed by calls from a couple of others to get one in for them.

Rick leant forward and spoke quietly.

'Keep me in the loop, mate. Khan's not known for being a team player, but the victim was part of an old case of mine.'

'Oh?'

'Mohammad Asaf seems to have been keeping his hands clean, but some of his associates are still on our radar, including the cousin.'

'Saleem?'

'You know him?'

'We've met.'

'Yeah? Well I hope you've still got your wallet, he's a light fingered little bastard.'

'To be honest, Rick,' he looked round to check nobody was listening, 'it's all a bit over my head. I'll do what I can, but I don't really know what's going on. There must have been someone more experienced available, so why did DCI Khan ask for me?'

Rick took a sip of beer and wiped his mouth on the back of his hand.

'Because you're young and impressionable,' Rick said, 'and because he's got no mates.'

'Funny!' Although Sean wasn't sure Rick was joking. 'Saleem Asaf thinks it's a turf war. His boys versus the white boys off the Chasebridge estate.'

Rick grinned. 'That's your real answer.'

'To what?'

'Why Khan wants you on his team. People trust you. They tell you stuff. Wish I'd thought of it first, you could have come along with me.'

'We're all in it together, mate.'

'Are we?'

Carly approached the table with their drinks and the conversation drifted away from the case and on to the scandal of the Doncaster Belles being relegated, simply because the dressing rooms at the stadium weren't up to standard.

'It's bloody typical, just because the men's game is shit, the women have to suffer,' said Carly, slamming a swiftly emptied pint glass on the table.

The jukebox was playing David Bowie's 'Fashion' and Sean's mind was focusing on what the hell he was going to wear tomorrow. Khan and Simkins wore suits. He'd have to dig his own out, and pray he hadn't put on any weight since the last time he went to a funeral.

CHAPTER SEVENTEEN

Halsworth Grange

Bill lets Chloe ride the mower. It's not the same model she used at her last place, so he takes her through its attributes one by one, as if he's selling it to her.

'Best thing, in my opinion, is this safety feature. Soon as you're not in contact with the seat, it cuts out. On these slopes, that could save your life if it topples over.'

He offers her a Halsworth Grange baseball hat to keep the sun out of her eyes and she pulls it low, hiding her face.

'There you go, much better!' He laughs a big belly laugh, but she doesn't see why. 'Only kidding,' he adds, holding up his big hands in supplication. 'Don't mind my sense of humour, no one else does.'

He explains where he wants her to go, behind the house to the orchard.

'Leave the grass long around the base of the trees,' he tells her, 'it's good for the bees. You'll have the place to yourself. Closed to the public.'

She nods and wonders if he knows that she wants to

hide. Perhaps he read her disclosure letter before handing it over to his boss, or he's seen the same headline that she saw in the local paper. All he needs to do is put two and two together. A quick search on the Internet will do that for him in a matter of seconds. She wonders what pictures they've got of her, and whether she'll need to change her hair again.

A pair of magpies spring up as she drives the mower into the orchard. She takes off the ear defenders and listens to their shouts. But they're not like her Jay, they don't have any message for her. She smiles to herself. If people knew what was going on in my head, she thinks, they'd lock me up again for sure. Birds don't talk; everyone knows that.

She puts the ear defenders back on and muffles the noise of the engine as she starts the mower. She guides the machine carefully around each tree trunk just as Bill asked. In her muted world her mind wanders back to the bird with the blue tattoo, laughing like static. The boy and the bird, the bird and the boy, one in the same.

Damn. She's mown too close to a tree. The circle of long grass and wildflowers is lopsided, more like a half-moon. She hopes Bill won't be annoyed. Her mind is messing her around; it might be because she's not eating enough. She's been trying to ignore the hunger, telling herself she can manage, but other people have noticed, so it's becoming more difficult. Emma kept some shepherds's pie for her last night. She wolfed it down cold while her friend stood watching her.

'You need to get something in,' Emma said. 'Some Pot

Noodles or something. I'll lend you if you're strapped for cash.'

Chloe said she would, but she knows if she starts borrowing, she'll have to pay it back with interest. She's not getting into all that again, not now she's out of prison. A debt is a dangerous thing. Another protected circle of long grass is cut in half, too close to the tree. She needs to concentrate, but a thought is hanging on, the thread of a thought, pulling her back to sitting in Taheera's car, outside the smart house that appeared to have been built in an orchard. While Taheera was talking to her brother, there was a man getting into a dark blue car, and the eyes of the man in the car were eyes she thought she knew.

'Chloe!' Bill is shouting from the orchard gateway. 'Lunch break! Kettle's on, d'you want a brew?'

She snaps back to the present and cuts the engine. When she gets back to the potting shed, ready to confess to making a mess of the mowing, a woman is there. It's Brenda from the ticket office, Bill's wife. She's broad, like him, but not as tall. Chloe feels the other woman sizing her up and not looking too impressed with what she sees.

'I see what you mean, Bill; there's nothing to her.'

Chloe is frozen to the spot. Brenda Coldacre must have seen the newspaper reports and she's come looking for a killer, a monster, but she's just found a woman with no strength at all, a woman with bones like a bird who can be snapped in two with one hand.

'I brought you this.'

Brenda Coldacre is holding something out to Chloe.

She expects it to be a newspaper or a printout from the Internet. She's sure Mrs Coldacre will say, *I know who you are*. Maybe it's a noose to hang herself with. Someone sent her one once in prison, but it got intercepted.

'Go on, open it,' says Mrs Coldacre.

Chloe shivers and makes herself look at the object. She sees a brown paper bag.

'Cheese and pickle, in case you were a vegetarian.'

Chloe walks slowly back into the orchard, not wanting to gobble down the sandwich in front of them. She still has some dignity. At the furthest row of trees she chooses one where she mowed too close to the trunk. At least she can sit on the short grass without fear of disturbing any wild bees. She leans against the tree, letting it press into the centre of her back.

The smell of the pickle starts her salivating. The cheese is sharp, strong enough to make her suck her cheeks in, but wonderful, and the bread tastes better than any she's ever experienced. There's something nutty and clean about it. She's sure it's home-made. Her throat tightens, but she fights the urge to cry. She should be happy. Surely this is as good as it gets. Live in the moment. Who said that? Jay was fond of saying it, but she was sure he got it out of a book. She remembers sitting like this in one of the allotment sheds with the sound of rain on the corrugated roof. They were safe inside. There was no need to talk.

Jay had a packet of orange Club biscuits from his mum's cupboard. He said she would only buy biscuits in wrappers, so she could be sure they were clean. Chloe thought that was daft because how could she know the people in the factory hadn't picked their noses before they wrapped them? The biscuits could last them all day if they were careful. They sat against the wall of the shed in a corner by an old filing cabinet. Its drawers were marked 'Top Secret', 'Middle Secret' and 'Bottom Secret'. They found a bottle of whisky in 'Top Secret', but she didn't want any; she thought the smell was disgusting.

She thought this might be the time that Jay would kiss her, but they weren't touching. They'd held each other once, hugged, sort of, but she wasn't sure if it meant anything. Jay was upset. He wouldn't tell her what about, but he cried for ages. She felt like a mum with a little child, not like a girl with a boyfriend. It wasn't really certain that he was her boyfriend, even though everybody thought they were going out and it was written on the back of the toilet door at school.

That day in the shed he was very quiet, quieter than his normal quiet self. She shuffled a bit nearer to him so that their thighs, where they sat with their knees drawn up, were close enough that they could be touching by accident. He flinched and wrapped his arms tighter round his knees. The space opened up between them again.

'What's up?' she said.

'Nothing.'

'D'you want another biscuit?'

'I'm all right,' he said. 'Have one if you want one.'

'I'm all right.'

The rain pattered harder above them and it was a while before he spoke again.

'I wish I could fly.'

'Yeah?' she said. 'Yeah. That would be cool.'

'Any time I wanted to, just up and out. I do it sometimes, in my head.'

She laughed and wished she hadn't, because he folded over his knees and hid his face. She thought he might be crying again, but there wasn't any sound. His curly red hair fell forward and she wanted to stroke it. On the back of his hand, where it clasped his leg, there was a mark she hadn't noticed before: a red disc of blistered skin. She looked more closely and realised the same marks were on his knuckles.

'Who's done that?'

'No one.' He didn't lift his head, but she sensed he was watching her from under his hair.

'Did you do it to yourself? That's flipping stupid, that is.'

'Why would I do that?'

She didn't know. Other people did stuff to themselves, she'd seen marks on girls' arms. She didn't think lads did it though.

He raised his head and looked at her. His eyes were dry, but there was something different, as if the light had gone out of them. She was looking at him, but it was like she didn't know him any more.

'Chloe?' Bill is standing in front of her, blocking out the light. 'You were fast on.'

'Was I? I'm sorry, I'm not sleeping so well at night.'

'Aye, well. Brenda's got the kettle on. Come and have a cuppa.'

She pulls herself up to her feet and follows him.

'You know what they say, don't you?' He calls over his shoulder. 'Them that lie awake at night have a guilty conscience.'

He'd no sooner said it than he hesitated, missed a step and mumbled to himself.

'Brain before mouth, Bill, brain before mouth.'

CHAPTER EIGHTEEN

Doncaster

Meeting room four was laid out with rows of grey plastic chairs. One of the IT guys was setting up the laptop. Khan handed Sean a marker pen.

'Time, date, location on the whiteboard, please. And leave some space to add anything important that comes up.'

'Hope I don't cock up any spellings. At least I know how to write "Chasebridge".'

'You're not kidding, are you?' Khan said. 'You worry about that a lot. In the lift you said. . .'

'Dyslexic.' Sean said. 'Thought I was thick until I became a PCSO, got a test and there it is. Doesn't cure it, knowing what it's called, just means you can't discriminate against me.'

Khan looked at him sharply, then a smile flickered across his lips.

'You were Community Support? So you're working your way up. Nice one. I like that.'

Quietly and carefully, Khan spelt out the victim's name

for him as the seats started to fill up. The room looked different this way round, Sean thought, standing up front with a cluster of faces looking at him. The new District Commander, Chief Superintendent Laine, was sitting in the front row. Not a crease in his uniform or his face. Sean wondered how many anti-ageing products he kept on his bathroom shelf. The community support officers at the back didn't even have chairs. He couldn't see Carly, but as Commander Laine started the introductions, Sean spotted her spiky hair edging round the door.

'I'd like to welcome DCI Khan, joining us from Sheffield. He's heading up the investigation. Sheffield has also kindly leant us Detective Sergeant Dawn Simkins, who'll be managing the incident room here and coordinating the house-to-house inquiries. I'm told she's the queen of spreadsheets, so she'll keep everyone organised.'

The woman in the grey suit, who Sean had seen yesterday, stood up in the front row, turned to the audience, nodded without smiling and sat down again.

'The current climate has left us shorter staffed than normal, so I'm sure we'll all benefit from the collaboration.' There was an unhappy murmur from the audience, which stopped dead when Laine raised his pale, unblinking eyes and scanned the room. 'From our side we've got DI Rick Houghton from drugs and I'm pleased to confirm that PC Denton will be seconded to CID for the time being.' He paused, offered Sean a brief glance of recognition and then his face softened into a smile. 'And it's a great pleasure to welcome Lizzie Morrison back to Doncaster. She'll be the operational Crime Scene Manager for this case.'

Her hair was different. She said something to the person sitting next to her and when she turned her head, Sean could see she'd had it cut short at the back of her neck. It looked like it would be soft and fuzzy to touch.

'We've got an IC4 male,' Khan launched straight in, 'positively identified by the family as Mohammad Asaf, aged twenty. No wallet on the body, but there was a Blackberry phone. That's gone to IT to see what we can get from it. Stab wounds to the shoulder, direct hit to the heart and then, hold on to your lunch people, but there's a particularly nasty knife wound to the genitals. Over to you, Miss Morrison.'

Khan stepped back and Lizzie stood up and took his place.

'It was a small, sharp blade, very clean wounds. The path lab is having a really good look, but it seems someone tried to remove his testicles. It's not clear yet whether this was pre- or post-mortem.'

A mumbled response from the audience was curtailed by Khan.

'Thank you. That'll do.' He gestured to Sean to start the slideshow.

The image of the young man appeared on the screen, lying as Sean had seen him, curled up, head resting on the step.

'We were at the scene at 05:30 hours,' Lizzie said. 'The way the blood had coagulated, and the general odour, suggests very early stage decay. Dr Huggins has put the time of death at between 21:30 and 23:00 hours. Next slide.'

Sean brought up a photograph of the bloody footprints with their little white flags, enlarged to show the landscape of the tread patterns.

'Four main sets,' Lizzie pointed to the screen. 'They came

135

and went in different directions, one from above, three different treads below. And . . . next slide please . . . a fifth set, much fainter, that came up when we dusted. These might be unrelated but they're quite fresh and carry traces of soil from outside. Looks like this one may have come in and gone out again. Potentially a witness. Next slide, please. Sean, can you zoom in a bit?'

She said his name as if they were old friends.

'That's far enough.'

The image on the screen was surprising. The head of a large ant was staring at them. Someone laughed.

'*Lasius Niger*, or the common black ant. He's fresh, his head and thorax were squashed on the concrete in these fainter footprints. The other half of him will be in the space between the treads, possibly still attached to the shoe. It sounds a bit Cinderella, but if we can find out whose feet fit these muddy shoe prints, we may have a witness. The others will know they're covered in blood and will probably have destroyed their clothes by now, but this one kept his feet out of the blood. He, or she, wears a size seven trainer, so could be a small male or a large female, and they came in and went out with soil on their feet, and possibly half an ant, but that's all.'

Khan was drawing something on the whiteboard, a zigzag of steps, populated by stick people.

'Recovering the weapon is a priority,' Khan said. 'So far, a local fingertip search has drawn a blank: playground, grass, bins, you name it. DS Simkins will draw up a grid of a wider area and assign officers to sections.'

He mentioned Mrs Armley and questioned her statement about hearing nothing.

'She said she saw someone running, so it must have still been light. If it's our vic, then that puts his arrival at the block at before 9 p.m. And if she saw him, did she see someone else that she's not telling us about? We'll see if we can have another chat with Mrs Armley, but she's vulnerable, sounds like she may have agoraphobia, so we don't bring her in unless we have to.'

DS Dawn Simkins was sitting on the front row making notes. She wore a permanent frown.

'Meanwhile,' Khan was saying, 'we need as much manpower as we can afford going house-to-house in the tower block. Did anyone else see a young man running? Was anyone following him? Again, Dawn, can you draw up a list of blocks on the estate and assign officers. We've got Mohammad Asaf on the PNC with form for drugs offences, and he's served a stint on the young offenders' wing at Doncaster Prison. Out early on tag for good behaviour. He's gone back to college recently, his mother says. So, Denton, I want you to go over to the college and ask some questions, then get yourself back up to the Chasebridge estate and join DS Simkins on the house-to-house inquiries.'

'Do we have a motive?' Rick Houghton spoke from the front row.

'Too early to say,' Khan said. 'He served nine months of an eighteen-month stretch for possession with intent to supply, but we need some intelligence on what he's been up to since he got out. He wasn't carrying a weapon when we found him. His clothes are being tested for traces of narcotics, but there's nothing visible.'

Rick nodded and jotted something down. At the back

Carly Jayson had her hand up. Khan called her to speak.

'There's a young woman recently been released, sir. She killed a lad on the estate exactly ten years ago. Marilyn Nelson. She's known as the Chasebridge Killer.'

'Thank you. Worth checking. Anything else?'

A few shrugs but no one spoke.

'When the tech guys have cracked the pin code on the Blackberry,' Khan continued, 'we should be able to find his contacts and track his last movements. By the way, no press release. I want media silence on this for as long as we can manage, please. I understand from DI Houghton that there might be a connection to a larger dealer, but there's something else I want you to be aware of: in my opinion, the nature of the area we're working in points to the possibility of a hate crime.'

Sean heard a ripple of muttering spread across the room. Khan paused, waiting for quiet.

'We need to see people's reactions when we talk to them directly, and when the time comes, I want the right kind of headline on this. OK. That's all for now.'

The mumbling was audible as everyone got up from their seats. Sean heard 'drug war' and 'Pakis' before he looked over to Khan to check his reaction. The detective was stacking his papers, cracking them down hard on the table. Sean wished him well on the media silence. If his nan knew there had been a murder, then half of Doncaster knew by now.

'Enjoying being back on home turf?'

Sean looked up, but District Commander Laine wasn't looking at him.

'Absolutely.'

Despite the scraping of chairs and general hum of voices in the room, Lizzie Morrison's private school accent was unmistakable. Sean had been hoping to have a word with her but he'd have to wait in line.

'Penny for your thoughts?' Carly Jayson made her way through the departing officers towards the front. 'Or are they valued at the upper end of the price range these days?' She fingered the fabric on his cuff playfully, giving a nod to where Lizzie was sharing a joke with Laine.

'Don't touch what you can't afford,' Sean said and slapped her away gently.

'Don't be mean. And I was just thinking if I might quite fancy you with all that power, if I wasn't a dyke.'

'Funny. Look, I've got to go over to the college. Fancy coming along for the ride?'

'The detective seems to have taken you under his wing. Are you sure he can spare you?'

'He's sent me on a mission.'

'Go on then, Captain Scarlet, if it means I can get a lift back to the estate when we're done. I've got to check in with DS Stalag Luft at ten-fifteen.'

'Rick says she's known as "The Rottweiler" back in Sheffield.'

'Suits her,' said Carly. 'Come on; let's see if we can find something zippy in the car pool.'

Lizzie was still deep in conversation with Laine and Sean didn't like the way the Commander leant over her, as if he was hoping for a better view down her top.

'Are you coming?' Carly said.

He followed Carly out of the room and down the corridor,

the words 'Police Community Support Officer' rippling in silver across the back of her jacket.

She was disappointed that the only car left in the yard was a Vauxhall Astra hatchback with luminous green and blue checks.

'We're not going to creep up on the baddies in this.'

'That's not the plan.'

'Pity. Might be a laugh. Have you got your magnifying glass and your sleuth's hat?'

'Give it a rest,' Sean said. 'Be thankful we've got a vehicle, otherwise you'd be on the back of my moped.'

The huge glass walls of the college reflected a cloud-filled sky. Carly pulled up in the disabled bay by the front entrance.

'Looks like a massive car showroom.' She peered up at the building.

'Don't knock it,' Sean said. 'About time this town had something to be proud of.'

He had his own reasons for feeling loyal. He'd spent months doing evening classes here, working his way through the exams he'd never got at school. His teacher was probably in there now, bribing his students with Werther's Originals and coaxing them through the minefield of Functional Skills English.

They planned to go straight to student services, but when the receptionist clocked Carly's uniform, she offered them a cup of coffee and asked them to wait until the principal was available. Carly peered into the rooms along the carpeted corridor.

'They've got better kit in there than we've got down at the station. Look at those computers!'

'Try and look just a little bit professional, Carly.'

She walked back and slouched down on the seat next to him. He was beginning to wish he'd brought someone else. Carly was several years older than him and she'd looked out for him in the past, but they were experiencing some kind of role reversal. Maybe it was his suit.

'What made you bring up that girl?' Sean said.

'In the briefing? Well she's called the Chasebridge Killer, isn't she?'

'Right. I think there would have to be a bit more of a connection than that, don't you?'

'Maybe.' She leant back in her seat and looked up at the glass atrium above them. 'I feel like a naughty kid sitting here,' she said.

'Yeah, and you're behaving like one. It's all about PR, I reckon. They want to make sure nothing reflects badly on them.'

'"College Student – Victim of Castration". They can hardly be blamed for that.'

'Don't be giving the press ideas,' Sean said.

'Get lost. Those wankers won't get anything out of me and you know it.'

At which point the principal, Dr Angus Balement, was standing in front of them.

'Detective Denton?'

Dr Balement was wearing one of those collarless granddad shirts which are meant to recall a glorious working class past, but Sean could see that the fabric was well-cut, top quality linen, stretched over too many lunches. Sean was about to correct the principal's mistake, but Balement was ushering them into his office and gesturing for Sean and Carly to sit. They remained standing, told him what they'd come for and watched him slump into a leather chair with a deep sigh. He ran his hand through his hair and turned to his computer.

'Yes. Mohammad Asaf. Name rings a bell. He's technically on roll here. We've been trying to engage with him.'

'Meaning?'

'Meaning that he's enrolled in a course of study. I don't wish to breach any data protection issues, of course. Suffice to say that it appears from his attendance record that we haven't seen very much of him. Here we go. He was on a second warning, so technically on his way out.'

'I don't suppose you could tell us who his associates were?' Carly said, through a poor pretence at a smile. 'I don't mean to pressurise you, but technically, I think we're a bit late for data protection.'

Dr Balement said nothing.

'He must have had some friends,' Sean said. 'Is there anyone here who knew him, from his course?'

'As I said, he was rarely here, so I think that's unlikely.'

'What did he study?'

Balement looked at the screen again and smiled. 'Foundation Diploma in Media. Does that help?'

'Might do,' Sean said.

'Hold fire on putting out a statement, if you don't mind,' Carly chipped in. 'We don't want anything in the press yet.'

'A statement? I can't see why we'd want to make a statement.'

'Yes, "the college regrets" etcetera. Usual thing.' She

smiled. 'We'll make sure the press know he was one of yours, but not yet.'

Sean wondered if he could kick her without Balement noticing. 'We'll be in touch if we have any more questions.' He shook the principal's hand and headed for the exit.

'Is it me or is that guy a slippery freak?' Carly said.

'It's not you. I wonder why Mohammad was on a second warning?'

'Maybe this fine young gentleman can help us.'

Outside, the squad car had a visitor. Saleem Asaf was testing the doors and windows.

'Now then,' Sean said. He was sure they were well covered by CCTV if Saleem tried his police brutality trick.

'I need protection,' Saleem said.

'I'm sorry?'

The boy's fingers played over the wing mirrors of the car.

'Mistaken identity, innit.'

'You've lost me.'

'They were after me and they got my cousin.'

'If you're worried,' Sean said, 'you're welcome to a lift home. I'm sure we could fit you in.'

Saleem jumped back as if the car had stung him. 'I'm not getting in that voluntarily.'

'We can cuff you, if you'd prefer,' Carly said.

For the second time, Sean fought the urge to kick Carly, but Saleem was looking at her, as if a new idea was forming in his mind.

'Can you tell me,' Sean said, 'why Mohammad was on a warning from the college?'

'They didn't like him doing business here,' he shrugged.

'This is where he got nicked. And even after he came back and was more sorted, they've been trying to find ways of getting rid of him.'

'What was he selling?'

'Whatever people wanted: skunk, sweets for the gym boys, a bit of miaow. Coke and old school ganja for the teachers. But nothing lately. That's what I'm saying. They got the wrong guy. I'm the one in danger now.'

'I don't know what you expect us to do,' Sean looked at his watch. He and Carly needed to be back on the estate or the Rottweiler would be on their case. 'Unless you're confessing to a crime.'

'Yeah, maybe I am. OK, you better bundle me in the car now. Knock us about a bit, in case anyone's watching. Then drop us off at the Cash and Carry on Christ Church Road, will you? I promised Ghazala, my sister, that I'd get some stock.'

Carly shook her head. 'Forget it.'

Sean watched the boy run his fingernail along the black rubber trim on the windows. It started to lift. 'Leave it out, Saleem, or you'll be nicked for damaging police property.'

The boy looked up and grinned. 'Suits me.'

'Go home, Saleem.'

They got in the car and left him in the car park, staring after them like a kid whose mates have taken the ball and left him with nothing and no one to play with.

'Just a wind-up merchant,' Carly said, as she opened the glove compartment and rooted around among the old tissues and sweet wrappers.

'What you looking for?'

144

'Dunno, peppermints. Whatever. Seeing if anyone's left us anything nice.'

'We should be so lucky,' Sean said.

At which point, Carly launched into an impression of Kylie Minogue that lasted all the way to the Chasebridge estate. Sean couldn't be bothered to tell her to shut up; he was still trying to make sense of Saleem Asaf. Carly was probably right. He was a wind-up merchant and an attention-seeker too. Sean thought back to the other night in the alleyway. He and Gav were sure they'd seen money or drugs change hands, but all the boy had on him, when he'd been searched at the station, was chewing gum and cigarettes. Saleem wasn't as gangster as he made out. His cousin, on the other hand, had been playing with the big boys, and it had cost him his life.

CHAPTER NINETEEN

Doncaster

Sean found DS Dawn Simkins sitting in an unmarked car on the access road alongside Eagle Mount One. He knocked on the window. She gestured that he should come round to the passenger side and get in.

'God,' she sighed. 'This place is a right shithole.'

He said nothing. It might be a shithole, but it was his shithole.

'I'd rather be in Sheffield,' she said. 'I was only put on this case so he could prove he could work with a woman.'

'Excuse me?'

'He's had complaints, that's why he's been sent over here. But then he's not shy of chucking his own complaints about, so be careful.'

'Right. Thanks. D'you mind if we talk about the job? Anything from the house-to-house?'

'Nothing much. I was going to start on this block when the uniformed constables get back. But you can do it if you like.'

Sean stared up at Eagle Mount One.

'Might be a slight conflict of interest if I take this one,' he said. 'Maybe I could do Attlee Avenue?'

'I think you'll find I'm in charge of allocating manpower, Acting DC Denton.' The emphasis was heavy on the 'acting'.

'I understand. But the thing is, I grew up in that block. My dad still lives there.'

He waited to see if she was going to apologise for calling his former home a shithole, but she didn't. She just shrugged and unclipped a list of house numbers and handed it to him.

'All right. Attlee Avenue. Be back here in half an hour and you can come with me to see Mrs Armley again. She might relate to someone local. And if we can't get any sense out of her, we'll have to bring her in and do it on video. The paperwork's underneath. Make sure you fill in the forms correctly, otherwise it's a waste of everyone's time.'

He decided not to take it personally and was glad to be out of the car. She was like a negative-energy black hole, pulling everyone in range of her force field down with her. He took his jacket off, slung it over his shoulder and loosened his tie. On Attlee Avenue, a few people were sitting out in their front gardens and there was a smell of freshly lit barbecues. Two uniformed officers were walking over the grass of the recreation ground, heads down, checking to see if anything had been missed.

'Gav!'

'Now then. Look at you!' Gavin Wentworth stood up straight and rubbed the small of his back.

'You off nights as well?' Sean called over to him.

'Aye, made sense to swap me too, and put me on this unit. Thanks for the night off, sunshine, though I'm not sure I've acclimatised yet. I could fall asleep on my feet, to be honest.'

Gavin's new partner kept going towards DS Simkins's car, while Gav offered to carry on down Attlee Avenue with Sean. In the first house, a nervous Polish woman shook her head and said 'sorry' to everything they asked. At the next, a tired woman with numerous children running around, said she'd had the telly on all evening in the back room, and didn't know a thing until the police arrived this morning.

'It'll be to do with all the immigrants,' she added as they turned to go.

'Sorry?' Sean said.

'It never used to be like this here.'

'Thank you for your time,' Gav said. 'Come on, son,' he said quietly to Sean, 'it's not worth it.'

Sean was wondering what glorious part of Chasebridge's past she was harking back to. Certainly not one that had existed in his lifetime. The names of the people doing the fighting might have changed, but that was all. The next few houses gave them nothing and one man just told them to f-off, he was having a sleep. Gav suggested they break off for ten minutes and pick up a bar of chocolate to give them the strength to face the other end of the street.

They followed Attlee Avenue down to below the primary school and walked round Winston Grove to the shops. Sean glanced up towards the flats at the top of the hill and picked out Mrs Armley's window, mentally marking the distance again. Inside the newsagents, the same young woman in a hijab was serving behind the counter. They waited behind an elderly lady buying scratch cards.

'Tax on the daft, that lottery,' PC Wentworth muttered. 'If she saved that up, she'd have a nice nest egg for Christmas.'

When their turn came, the girl looked at them warily.

'Look, I've already told the other officer, Mo was here until about eight that evening, helping me.' She looked around the shop, as if she was checking that they wouldn't be overheard. When she was sure they were alone, she spoke quietly. 'He was really happy. Checking his hair and all that in the mirror, I thought . . . no, it doesn't matter.'

The shop door opened behind them and the bell chimed. Sean was about to say something, when PC Wentworth cleared his throat.

'Thank you, young lady. Now, can I have a large bar of milk chocolate, please? And if there is anything else, just get in touch.'

Outside Gav snapped the end off the chocolate and looked up at the names above the door.

'The licensees are called A Asaf and K Asaf, so is she family too?'

'Yeah, I reckon she's the victim's cousin, Saleem's sister,' Sean said. 'Ghazala, I think he called her.'

Gav gave him a friendly pat on the back. 'Nice piece of deduction, Mr Watson.'

'Don't you start. I've had enough stick from Carly.'

'We're all made up for you, lad, truly. Anyway, that's something for you to give your new boss, all part of a routine inquiry, and no need to own up to our unscheduled chocolate break. So long as the Rottweiler with the clipboard doesn't

149

spot we went off plan. Here . . .' He broke off a line of squares and handed it to Sean.

'Do you think he was meeting a girl?'

'Probably, or a boy,' Gav said.

'Surely not!'

'Why not? Because Pakistani boys can't be gay? Let me tell you something. A few years ago, I was based in Leeds and I was driving with a colleague round one of the outlying estates. We came across a group of lads, fifteen or twenty of them. I thought, hey up, this is some sort of gang. I was braced for trouble.'

'What was it?'

'Lads who took the bus out to the edge of town, or got on their scooters or whatever, to meet up where nobody knew them, nobody to tell their families. Young gay lads. Asian lads.'

'All right. Point taken. He got a text from a lover, or a prospective lover. He was on a promise and he ended up dead. That doesn't get us much further.'

Back on Attlee Avenue they encountered shrugs, monosyllabic responses and a door shut in their face by a toddler, who they could hear screaming inside the house. Eventually the mother opened the door and said she was sorry about that, but the little girl was scared of the police since they kept taking her dad away and no, they hadn't seen anything. Finally, as Sean was giving up hope, an elderly man outside his house said he'd been sitting in his front garden on Tuesday night, watching the world go by. He'd come out to do the watering and decided to have a bit of a rest on his bench as it was such a nice evening. He showed them a low stone bench under his window, flanked by roses and giant daisies.

'It was very quiet. A young lad went by, smoking a cigarette. I remember that because I could smell it. I've packed them in myself, but now and again I get the smell of one and it brings back the cravings, you know what I mean?'

The boy he'd seen was wearing a hood, that's all he could remember, strolling casually, not in any rush. He didn't see his face. He got the feeling he stood about for a while, because the cigarette smell lingered. Sean sat on the bench and realised that the hedge was so high, you saw people only as they passed the gate. The rest of the estate disappeared once you were seated and you could be a hundred miles away from the Chasebridge estate. They thanked the old man and carried on to the last few houses. Sean looked back down the hill.

'If you were planning to visit Eagle Mount Two,' he said, 'it would be straightforward. You'd turn the corner of Winston Grove, come up the centre of the estate past the school and the community centre and then across the rec at some point. You'd never be out of sight of Mrs Armley's window. Unless you were trying to hide from someone. I suppose he could have cut between the community centre and the back of the primary school and come up Attlee Avenue, where nobody claims to have seen him.'

'There you go, boss.' Gav said, handing Sean a clipboard with the house numbers all ticked off. 'Put your squiggle there.'

'Gav, mate, I'm not your boss.' Sean picked up the pen.

DS Simkins wasn't in the car when they got back to it. Gav set off in the direction of the low-rises to catch up with his new partner and Sean carried on to the tower blocks. In the entrance hall of Eagle Mount Two, Lizzie Morrison was crouching down, running a UV light over the floor of the lift.

'Hi!' Sean said, trying to sound casual. 'You got more to do here?'

'Something's bothering me, so I thought I'd do another sweep. How about you?'

'On the way up to see Mrs Armley.'

'Do us a favour, Sean. While you're there, see if you can get her mop. There might be blood traces on it. This lift was definitely cleaned recently, but I'm picking up a faint pattern. Blood's almost impossible to shift completely, even with Mrs Armley's arsenal of household chemicals.'

'OK.' Sean turned towards the stairwell. He was trying to puzzle something out in his head, which didn't add up. He came back to where Lizzie was working.

'Why did she stop cleaning the footprints at the door to the stairwell, if she took the trouble to clean the lift? Surely you would clean the worst bits first.'

'Go on.' Lizzie straightened up.

'Well, she made out that she stopped when she saw the body, but that doesn't make sense. The cleaning ends on the landing, just inside the door. I'm beginning to think she never saw the body. She said "it", not "he".'

'But she must have seen it. She called it in.'

'I think she said there'd been a fight. We thought she meant it had just happened, but it was hours before. I wouldn't mind knowing exactly what she did say.' He selected a number from his contacts. 'Hi, Sandy . . . um, it's Sean. If you get this, can you call me back?'

'Friends in high places?' Lizzie said.

'Friend in the call room. Anyway, she's not picking up, maybe she's finished for the day.'

'Some people have social lives. Apparently.' Lizzie puffed a cloud of white powder over the lift's control buttons and gently brushed the excess off. 'Not our Mrs Armley, though. It looks like she's been very busy. Not much left to go on here, but we need to get this lift back in use. The natives are getting restless.'

Sean looked at his watch.

'Are you waiting for someone?' Lizzie asked, without looking up.

'That DS from the Sheffield squad. Simkins.'

'The grumpy-looking one? She was here five minutes ago. She completely ignored me, so . . .'

'Shit. Why didn't she wait for me?'

Sean took the stairs two at a time and arrived out of breath at Mrs Armley's door. Bernadette Armley undid what sounded like five different locks, before she opened the door on the chain. He held out his badge.

'Hello, it's the police.' He decided not to bother with the 'acting detective constable' bit. 'I was here yesterday.'

She slid the chain off and opened the door.

'Someone knocked before,' Mrs Armley said, 'but I didn't let her in. She said she was police, but it could have been a ruse, don't you think? Like that lot I had in last year who said they were the gas board and took my watch and my rings from by the bed.'

She stood back and he went in. Mrs Armley relocked the door and padded in fur-lined slippers to join him by the window, which overlooked the heart of the estate. Apart from the faint rush of her nylon housecoat, she moved without a sound. Neither of them spoke while Sean listened to the outside world, deadened by double-glazing. He hoped he wasn't in trouble, but he was sure it wasn't his mistake. DS Dawn Simkins had come without him on purpose.

He could see where the cordon had been reduced to a triangle of tape, the apex tied to the lamp post. A police crime incident van was parked on the access road and beyond it the playground was empty. Two boys were kicking a football back and forth on the patch of rough grass. A small dog ran out through the tattered hedgerow that hid the bins behind the community centre. It circled hysterically, barked at the boys and disappeared, summoned by someone out of sight.

Sean looked down at the low-rise blocks, which cupped one side of an oval along Darwin Road. He glanced across the rec, the community centre and the primary school, to Attlee Avenue, curving around the other side. The ground sloped down until the rooftops of The Groves filled the view and above them, in the distance, Sean could see the Frenchgate Shopping Centre and the tower of Doncaster Minster. The view would be even better higher up, but the interesting thing from this angle was that he could see the road and even the path up to the flats. Only the side door to the stairs was out of view.

'Tell me again, where did the young man run from?'

She pointed towards the school. 'He cut across there. And I said: "there's someone up to no good." That's what I said. "There's someone on the run." Lost sight of him after that.'

He couldn't have vanished, and yet nobody on Attlee

Avenue had noticed him. Someone casually sauntering past with a cigarette didn't tally with a young man being chased.

'And you're sure you didn't see anyone else?'

'Quite sure.'

'Did he stop? Or did he carry on running?'

She peered out and shook her head.

'Did you keep looking? Or did you look away for a few seconds? It's important.'

'Like I said, I lost sight of him.'

'Was anyone following him or chasing him?'

'I can't remember.' She turned away from the window and sat down on the settee. She was so tiny and frail looking. She patted the seat next to her. 'I'm forgetting my manners, son. Sit yourself down. Would you like a cup of tea?'

'No thanks, I'll get one later at my nan's.'

'Who's that then?'

'You probably don't know her.' He recalled DCI Khan's sharp look yesterday when he nearly gave away that he was local. 'You said you saw the boy running, but did you see anything else before that? Anything unusual?'

She shook her head. 'I was watching telly. Corrie and then that thing with the feller off *Bergerac*. I usually close the curtains early, even in the summer. I don't like the dark creeping up on me.'

'I see.'

'It'll be dark soon, I said, I'll close the curtains.'

'You saw the young man and closed the curtains?'

'Yes.'

He was trying to picture it, but it wasn't helping. He hoped it might make more sense to DCI Khan. He got up to go, pausing by the glass-fronted cabinet to look at the framed school photographs.

'Would you mind if I borrowed your mop?'

'My mop?'

'Just to get it checked over by forensics.'

'Well, I suppose so.' She went through into the kitchen and on to the small concrete balcony, where Sean could see the mop standing in a bucket. She squeezed the water out of it and gave it a shake.

'Try not to let it drip on you trousers, son, it's got a bit of bleach in the water.'

He said goodbye and carried the mop, at arm's length, down the stairs.

Lizzie was waiting for him in the foyer by the main front door.

'Let me see if I've got a big enough bag for that,' she said. 'Might have to be two.'

'Don't hold your breath, she's had it in a bucket of bleach.'

'Blood is thicker than bleach, Sean.'

He returned her smile and looked away fast; it wasn't fair that she could still look so good, when he didn't stand a chance.

'I'll see you around,' he said and headed for the door.

'Yeah, see you.' She was already focusing on her work again, her voice muted inside the lift.

CHAPTER TWENTY

Doncaster

Sean sat up in bed and scooped his clothes off the floor. His phone started to ring on his bedside cabinet at the very moment he was shoving his head into his T-shirt. He got one arm into a sleeve hole and grabbed blindly, but as his fingers brushed the screen, the phone clattered to the floor. The neck of this T-shirt had always been too tight and he was still trying to force his head through, upside down over the side of the bed, when he heard Khan's voice.

'Hello?'

'Hello! Sean Denton speaking.'

'Did I wake you?'

'No, I . . . No, sir, I'm awake.'

'You sound like you're having a fight in a shoebox.'

'Dropped the phone. Hang on . . . there, that's better.'

'Can you meet me at Doncaster Royal Infirmary as soon as possible? A stab victim came in late last night. At the moment the hospital doesn't have a name. All we know is that he was found behind the shops on Winston Grove, on the edge of the Chasebridge estate. The ward sister's just phoned to say he's woken up, and he's all ours.'

'Is the victim Asian or white?' Sean said, upright now and half-dressed.

'Sorry?'

'Asian or white, or black, even?'

'Asian, since you ask. And he's refusing to give his name.'

'OK. I just . . .'

'Denton?'

'Nothing, sir.'

He put Saleem's veiled threat to the back of his mind. 'They take one of ours; we'll have to take one of theirs.' Not this time. He made a mental note: don't jump to conclusions.

At the hospital they found their way to the ward and stopped at the nurses' station to ask where their patient was. A student nurse waved them towards a bay, but Khan turned back.

'Do you have any details from the ambulance crew that brought him in?'

'I've just come on shift. Look, sorry, I'll try and find out, but I've got to sort out a leaking catheter bag.'

DCI Khan was breathing hard through his nose.

'Are you all right, sir?'

'Fine, but hospitals don't agree with me.'

They walked along the corridor, glancing into the bays until they came to the one they were looking for. A thin figure was lying in a bed near the window. The other occupants of the bay were finishing their breakfast, but their target was lying on his side with his back turned. The toast was cold on his plate and his cup of tea untouched.

'Morning, son,' Khan said.

'I'm not your son.' He didn't turn his gaze from the window.

Khan gave Sean a nod and he walked round the other side of the bed and pulled up a chair.

'Hello, Saleem,' Sean said. 'Are you going to tell us what happened?'

The other patients had stopped talking and Sean suspected they'd stopped chewing too. Saleem Asaf turned on his back, wincing.

'I ain't talking to you lot.'

'We want to find out who did this to you. You're the victim of a crime. But you'll have to help us,' Sean said quietly.

The boy continued to stare above his head, trying not to blink. A muscle pulsed in his cheek.

'Do you have the clothes you were wearing when you came in?' Khan's voice was quiet too, but more insistent. 'We'll need to take them for forensic testing, to see if your attackers left any evidence. Are they in here?'

Khan opened the cupboard by the bed and the boy tried to turn towards him, but the pain forced him back.

'Fuck off! You can't touch my stuff.'

The man in the bed opposite paused with a spoonful of Rice Krispies suspended in mid-air.

'I can take what I want, especially if what I want will help us find out who hurt you.' The cold steel in Khan's voice made Sean's skin prickle. 'And I don't need a warrant, if that's what you're thinking, because this is a public place. Now, why don't you calm down and I'll see if the nurse can give you something for the pain.'

Sean looked at the tense face, eyes fixed on a light fitting above him. It was the first time he'd seen the boy so still. Khan went to find a nurse.

'Saleem,' Sean said, 'who was it?'

'I don't know. I didn't see them. They jumped me and that was it.'

Sean thought about the conversation they'd had at the college. Not just a wind-up merchant then. Someone really was out to get Saleem. Perhaps he could have stopped this from happening, but if Saleem was too stubborn, or too scared, to give them anything, there was a limit to what he or Khan could do. He got up and looked out of the window. There was a sepia haze hanging over the town; and out there someone was going about their business, someone who had attacked a teenage boy, perhaps the same someone who had murdered his cousin.

In the call room, Sandy Schofield, a middle-aged civilian whom Sean had known since his days as a PCSO, handed him the transcript of Mrs Armley's 999 call.

'It's odd that she doesn't describe the victim as a man or a woman,' she said, 'just as a body.'

'I know, it's been bothering me, too.'

'Do you want to hear the original?'

'It's OK, another time. I'd better get back up to DCI Khan. There's a briefing in five minutes.'

'No problem.' Sandy peered over her reading glasses at him. 'You all right? You look a bit worried.'

'I'm OK. But I need to keep on my toes around DCI Khan.'

'You'll be fine. You're a people person.'

'Er, thanks.'

'Any time, pet!'

He dragged his feet on the way back to the incident room. The grit in the treads of his trainers pulled against the concrete. It had been a relief when Khan told him to leave the suit at home.

'Can't have us both looking like loan sharks,' he'd said on the phone.

Sean had shuddered, inwardly. He wished Khan had never clapped eyes on his father.

The board in the incident room had Mohammad Asaf's picture in the centre, next to an aerial photograph of the estate, the dates and estimated time of the assault. To the right, Khan had written 'College' and three bullet points, one for 'teachers', one for 'other customers' and one which read: 'Saleem Asaf, first cousin of deceased. Non-fatal stab victim'. As the room filled up with officers, Sean hung back by the door. Khan saw him and gestured for him to take a seat at the front. As he worked his way through the tangle of chairs he heard someone quietly, but distinctly, say 'Paki lover' as he passed. He turned, but no one was looking in his direction. The colour rose up his neck and into his cheeks.

Khan called the room to order and talked through the events so far. He explained what had happened to Saleem.

'This lad,' Khan said, 'referred to his cousin by the nickname, "Mocat".'

The pen squeaked on the whiteboard as Khan began to write it up.

'He also made an overt threat against young white males on the Chasebridge estate,' he continued.

'Sean, did he say "Mocat"?' The voice came from behind him. Sean turned to face Lizzie Morrison.

'Hi Lizzie.' Casual. Or so he hoped.

'Hang on,' she said. 'I've got a picture on my phone which might be interesting. Oh, flip, how do I . . .'

'Shall we continue while Miss Morrison sorts out how to operate her mobile phone?' Khan's tone was icy. Any laughter that threatened to start up was quickly muffled.

Sean felt a hand squeeze his elbow and Lizzie's lips almost brushed his cheek, as she whispered: 'Here, look.'

Don't touch me. For God's sake. His cheek burnt and he could feel the pressure of her hand long after she'd taken it away.

'This was on the wall outside the Keepmoat Stadium,' she said. 'It's fresh.'

The screen showed an image of green and purple lettering sprayed onto a concrete wall. 'MOCAT RIP'.

'What's the point of media silence now?' Sean wondered out loud.

'Denton?'

'Graffiti, sir.' He passed the phone to Khan. 'Saleem knew about Mohammad's death, even before we told the family, didn't he? So maybe this is his work.'

He wondered what Lizzie was doing at the stadium, but then he remembered that her dad was on the board of the football club. She used to go out with the marketing manager there, before she went down south.

'Is your friend Guy still working at the Rovers?' He whispered back to her. She didn't reply.

Khan was asking if the house-to-house inquiries had

been fruitful, but the response was depressing. Nobody had seen or heard anything. Doors had been slammed in officers' faces, if they were ever opened at all. One of the constables observed that while nobody was interested in talking about Mohammad Asaf, they were downright hostile when asked about the cousin, Saleem. Rick Houghton, as Doncaster's drug squad lead, stood up to give a brief account of Mohammad's known connections.

'He was a small time supplier before his arrest last year. We're working on the theory that this particular supply line is controlled from Sheffield, but we haven't successfully traced it back to any group or individuals. Mohammad Asaf has kept his hands clean since he got out, which is very nice for Her Majesty's Prison Service and their resettlement targets, but bugger all use to us. We'd given up watching him because he was being such a good boy.'

Lizzie spoke next, presenting the forensic analysis of Saleem's possessions, taken from his bedside locker. She looked great, Sean thought, in slim black trousers and a cropped jacket. She was thinner than when he'd first known her, or maybe just more toned. He imagined her at the gym, wondering if she'd joined a local one since moving back. Wouldn't it be great if it were the same gym he went to? She caught his eye for a second and he snapped back to the moment and tried to look as if he'd been listening.

'It's Saleem's own blood on his clothes and no one else's. We're checking a fingerprint from his sleeve, which looks as if someone made a grab for him. The shoes are still waiting to go to the lab. I'm sorry but we're having trouble keeping up with the workload as it is, so I'll have to get back to you on this in a day or so.'

Lizzie sat down, catching Sean's eye with a strained smile, as she slipped back into the row behind him.

'Thank you,' Khan said. 'Saleem's injury wasn't life-threatening, and my guess is, that was quite deliberate. It's possible someone wants him to keep quiet, perhaps he's the missing link in the drug supply line.'

'It's possible,' Rick grunted.

After a few questions from the floor, Khan announced that Doncaster and Sheffield CID homicide and drug squad officers would remain active, but all uniformed officers were being pulled off the estate to let things settle. There was a commotion of voices questioning the decision.

'That's all for now, folks. I think we have to accept that we're not going to get anything out of these people by asking straightforward questions. We're going to have to try something different. Right, on your way, people.'

'Whose idea is this?' A male voice called from the middle of the room.

Sean thought he recognised it as the one who'd called him a Paki lover. He turned to try to match a face to the voice, but people were standing up, blocking his view. He felt a tap on his shoulder; it was Khan.

'Meet me in the CID office in ten minutes.'

'Yes, sir.'

'Oh and Denton?'

'Sir?'

'Get me an Americano from the canteen, small splash of milk.'

The long corridor which led from the ops room to the CID office was lined with rooms belonging to senior staff (opaque glass above the door, knock before entering) and larger offices which housed uniformed teams and civilians (clear glass, doors left open to air the overcrowded hot boxes). A wolf whistle came from the PCSO base as he passed. He suspected it was Carly. The door ahead of him at the end of the corridor had clear glass, over which someone had stuck a home-made poster:

Rules of the CID Office

1. Forgive your enemy but remember the bastard's name.
2. Many people are only alive because it's illegal to shoot them.
3. Alcohol never solved anything but then again, neither did tea.

Sean turned the loose metal handle and the glass rattled in its frame. The room was packed with furniture. Desks, pushed back-to-back, lined the wall under the window and a central table was laden with box files. Tucked behind the door another long table was piled with a nest of cables, one leading to a grubby computer monitor, others trailing off between mismatched chairs before snaking across the floor.

'Can I help you?' A head was appearing from under a desk in the far corner of the room. The head was partly covered by DI Rick Houghton's thinning hair. 'Sean, mate. Didn't recognise your feet in trainers.'

'Khan asked me to come in dressed down. Is he around?'

'He'll be back in a minute.' Rick stood up and dusted off his trousers. 'I was trying to reconnect my telephone line. We're sharing with the Sheffield crew.'

'What? They unplugged your phone? Cheeky buggers.'

'That's one word for them. That coffee going spare?'

'No.' Sean hoped he could remember which was his cappuccino and which was Khan's Americano. 'Although it is probably going cold.'

'Shame. I'm gasping.'

Sean nudged some box files aside on the central table to make space to put the cups. Rick picked one up and peeled back the lid. The froth had stuck to the plastic.

'What do you call this? Looks like a frigging milkshake.'

'Get your mitts off. That's mine.'

'What's the other one?'

'Americano, but that's for DCI Khan.'

'Are you his personal servant now?' Rick grinned at him. 'Scared you'll be back in uniform if you give him the wrong brew?'

'I don't have a clue what he thinks I am, to be honest.'

'Yeah? Well be careful around him. He's got a reputation.' Rick licked off the froth from the inside of the cappuccino's lid.

'So people keep saying.'

Sean heard a door close further along the corridor. He turned to see Khan heading towards the CID office.

'Ah, coffee, excellent and you got one for DI Houghton.

Good work, Sean. Right, we need to talk through a plan. Shut the door. I've had an idea, but this is strictly between the three of us.'

Rick picked up the cappuccino and licked his lips behind Khan's back, before taking a slurp of Sean's coffee.

'Right, Denton. As you know, I've pulled the house-to-house team off for now, but I want you to go back on the estate.'

'Sir?'

'I don't want you to do anything, just be there. Hang out, and relax,' Khan said. 'Spend some time at your dad's place.'

Sean nearly choked. 'I don't think he'll want me, especially if I'm on the job.'

'Not a big fan of the force is he?' Khan said.

'That's an understatement, sir.'

'Why's that then?'

'My dad was a miner,' Sean said, suddenly noticing a mark on the knee of his jeans. He licked his thumb to rub it off. When he looked up, Khan was waiting for more. 'Uh, well. This was before I was born. He got his hand broken on a picket line by a member of the South Yorkshire Force, as it happens. It never healed properly and he couldn't go back to work, and then there was no work to go back to. He's a drinker, has been for years. End of.'

'Did he try to stop you joining the force?'

'He didn't know for a long time. I haven't had much to do with him, to be honest.'

'I think you should stay with him for a few days. Would that be possible?'

Sean looked at Khan in horror. 'You're kidding? Shit. You're not kidding.'

'I want you to be right there, where you can overhear conversations in stairwells, or hang out in the pub, picking up gossip.'

'Not much chance of that, sir, the pub was burnt down last year and it's not going to be rebuilt.'

Khan took a sip of coffee. 'Tell him you've changed careers. Taken up money lending.'

Sean said nothing.

'Another thing, Denton.'

'Sir?'

'What have you done to upset DS Simkins? She says you didn't turn up at Mrs Armley's and she was somewhat inconvenienced yesterday.'

'She was early. The old lady wouldn't let her in. I don't know why she didn't wait for me.'

Khan sighed. 'I can hazard a guess. Don't take this the wrong way, son, but she's not over the moon that I seconded you for the investigation. She thinks you're too inexperienced. Don't worry. We can use this to our advantage. If anyone asks, you're off the case while I explore a complaint by another officer.'

'A complaint?'

Rick had just taken a mouthful of coffee and nearly spat it across the table. 'With respect, Sam, I don't think Sean . . .'

'Hang on, hang on, the pair of you! It's a game Simkins is playing. But we can play too, can't we?'

'I suppose so,' Sean said, although he hadn't got a clue what this was about.

'So?' Khan's eyes were fixed on him, unblinking pools of persuasion.

'OK. I'll stay at my dad's, if that's what you want me to do.'

'Excellent.'

Sean felt sick.

Twenty minutes later, he parked his moped by the recreation ground, where he could keep an eye on it, and set off on foot to see who was around on the Chasebridge estate. The whole place felt deserted. The day had turned out muggy and heavy with clouds.

He sat on one of the swings in the little playground and watched a taxi turn the corner, down Darwin Avenue and on to Winston Grove. He recognised the rear seat passenger. Jogging down the pavement to the corner, he was just in time to see a young woman helping someone out of the rear door. As the car pulled away Saleem Asaf shuffled slowly towards the shop, his hands over his abdomen and shoulders hunched against the pain, his sister's hand on his shoulder. Sean phoned Khan to let him know that Saleem was home, then walked back up to where he'd parked the moped. The blank windows of the Eagle Mount flats stared back at him. What was that phrase his nan used? Between a rock and a hard place.

He got on the moped and drove down the hill, turning below the school. There was a group of four men painting a wall. He pulled up and three of them stopped what they were doing and turned towards him, white paint dripping from their rollers. He could still make out the outline of a purple design on the wall, ghosting through the white. They were going to need a couple more coats to obliterate 'MOCAT RIP'. Sean flipped up the visor on his helmet.

'This a council thing? Anti-graffiti?'

'What's it to you?' A stocky, bald man with a thick neck spoke without looking up and carried on painting. Sean thought he recognised him from the CUC meeting.

Sean felt naked without his uniform. 'Just curious.'

'We're putting things right,' another man said. The bright blue eyes were smiling at him. 'All right, Sean?'

'Terry.'

'We don't want no Paki kids messing up our estate,' the thick-necked one was saying. 'Messing with our girls.'

'What do you know about them?' Sean said.

'Who?'

'The . . . Asian kids you think are responsible for that?' Sean pointed to the outline of 'MOCAT RIP'.

No one spoke.

'Not much, bro,' Terry said, 'except they're not wanted round here.' He spat neatly on the ground. As he tipped his head, Sean could see the tattoo on his neck: Made in England.

'What d'you care anyway?' The bald man stepped towards Sean, the roller like a weapon in front of him.

'Gary!' Terry growled.

'I heard there was a lad got hurt,' Sean ventured. 'An Asian lad?'

'You heard right,' Terry said. 'It's got to stop. These gentlemen are here to help this community get itself back in working order.' He held Sean's gaze and smiled again. 'See you later.'

Then he turned away and carried on painting the wall. The other two followed him. The one called Gary lowered his paint roller and watched Sean until he got back on the moped. He revved the engine and took off along Winston Grove. He needed to get his sleeping bag and a few things to take back to his dad's; he wasn't looking forward to explaining his plan to Maureen.

At a quarter past eight that evening, Jack opened the door to Sean.

'What d'you want?'

'Hi, Dad, I've had a bit of a fall out with Nan. Is it all right if I stop over?'

The fall out bit wasn't even a lie. Maureen said she might as well wash her hands of him if he was going to sleep at his dad's. He couldn't explain that it was on Khan's instructions. He'd put on his old clothes and told her he was going to help Jack decorate.

'Where's me hat?' Jack said.

'Sorry?'

'I said where's me hat?' Jack jabbed a finger at him. 'You had it when we went to that meeting. I'll need it if I'm to go on the march. I'll catch my death without a hat.'

'What march?'

'Reclaim Chasebridge. Torchlit parade. You know. They were on about it at the CUC meeting. It's tonight. You should come.'

Maybe that's what Terry Starkey meant when he said 'see you later'. Jack was still blocking his way into the flat.

'Can I come in and put my stuff down first?'

He was trying to remember where he'd put Jack's hat. And then it came to him. He couldn't get off the estate quickly enough after the Clean Up Chasebridge meeting. Gav had

171

picked him up at the garage on the dual carriageway and driven him back into town for a drink. He had the hat on when he got in the car and then he must have taken it off and left it there.

'Sorry, Dad. I'll get it back for you.'

Jack stood aside and Sean took his sleeping bag and holdall into the living room. From the window he could see a group of people gathering on the grass behind the community centre. The light was fading in the dusk. A flicker caught his eye. Then another. Soon there were half a dozen flames dancing at the end of sticks; hardly a parade, more like a small gathering.

'Looks like they're starting, but there's not many there.'

'What is?' Jack said, sitting heavily on the settee and digging his hand down the side of the cushions. 'Ah, there they are. I thought you had them.'

'Eh?'

'My fags. Here they are. I was looking for them.'

Sean watched Jack shakily take one out of the packet. He'd done a bit of research about liver disease. The medical websites were hard work, he had to look up a lot of words, but the bit about toxins building up in the blood and causing the brain to deteriorate was clear enough. It made sense of the vacant look that had come over Jack's face again.

'Do you not want to go out, Dad?'

'No, lad. Let's get the telly on.'

Sean flicked the curtain shut and switched on the TV.

'Do you want anything to eat?'

'No,' Jack dragged on his cigarette. 'I'm not hungry.'

They sat in silence watching a reality show, in which a

bunch of teenage kids got drunk in a holiday resort. Khan had made a mistake sending him back here. He wasn't going to learn anything except what an arse people made of themselves in front of the cameras. The show ended and another one began, only this time it was set in a supermarket and the cameras were following a team recruited from an old people's home, posing as mystery shoppers.

He thought Jack was asleep, but he lifted a thin arm and rested his hand on Sean's shoulder. It felt like he might be about to squeeze him, but then Sean's phone started to ring and the arm dropped back.

'Hello?' Sean said.

'It's all kicking off at the shops on Winston Grove. There's a right crowd, with flaming torches. People are throwing stuff.'

'Nan?' He moved away from his dad to the window. 'Are the police there? Have you rung 999?'

'I expect they've been told, there's alarms going off. Bloody hell!'

'Nan? Where are you?'

'Something's happening at the newsagent's. It's on fire.'

'Get out of there, Nan. Go home.'

CHAPTER TWENTY-ONE

York

The IT class is late starting.

'I understand you have staffing issues – don't we all,' Kath from the council says to Darren, 'but I'm only paid until nine, so we really need to get going.'

He shrugs and ambles over to plug one of the laptops in at the wall. Taheera hasn't been back into work and people are saying she's off sick. Chloe keeps her mouth shut. The class has dwindled to her and Emma. There are soaps on the telly and anyway, the others say they know all this stuff.

Chloe's heart is racing. She digs her hands deep into her pockets and clenches her jaw to keep her excitement from bubbling over. She has so many things to look up. Kath starts them on bus timetables, which suits Chloe fine, because she's learnt something new in the last few days and it's genius. She can have two windows open at once, one hidden and one showing.

'Windows,' she says to herself. 'Get me! I'm using all the lingo now.'

Emma's sitting opposite her tonight and shoots her a look. Chloe realises she's spoken her thoughts out loud. She's glad Emma can't see her screen. She hasn't dared put her old self into a search yet because there's always someone watching, and even now, there's one more thing she wants to look up before she lets herself take that risk and find out what's been said about her. She waits until Kath is leaning over to help Emma and launches her second window, rapidly typing in a name. There are more answers in the list than she's expecting, but as she scrolls down, a sharp stab of recognition causes her to catch her breath.

'Everything all right?' Kath says.

Back on the bus timetables, Chloe pretends to care about the Sunday service until Emma demands Kath's attention again. That's something she's noticed about Emma, she's never happier than when people are fussing around her. Chloe, on the other hand, is quite happy to be left to her own devices. She opens her search results and clicks. There it is. The report of a conviction for armed robbery. He'll have been away almost as long as her. No mention of his family. The picture is old, but she's sure it's him, looking straight down the lens of the mugshot camera, straight at Chloe, like he can see her soul.

Kath is talking about recipes. She reads out the name of a site where they can type in cooking ingredients and it will tell them how to cook them. Some chance, Chloe thinks. In Meredith House all the meals are cooked for them, not that she ever gets back in time to eat any of it. She decides to humour Kath, and chooses random vegetables and meat, as her stomach twists and gurgles. She invents stews and pies and even a pasta dish that she'll probably never make, but she still has more searches to do.

Chloe types in 'Chasebridge, Doncaster'. Her fingers hover, she daren't click 'enter', not yet. She wonders if she'll find herself at the top of the list or whether she'll be hidden further back. She dreads the words she saw in the paper, but she needs to know. Kath comes round to her side of the table and Chloe quickly goes back to the food site. Kath shows her how to add or remove ingredients from her list, tells her about the shopping list function, which links to an online delivery page. Emma catches Chloe eye and pulls a face. They're both in agreement that Kath is from another planet: Planet Polenta.

Finally, Kath moves away and Chloe reopens her hidden search for Chasebridge. At the top of the list is the *BBC Look North* site, updated eight minutes ago. She clicks. The picture is astonishing and there's a video too. She mutes the sound as her screen fills with flames.

CHAPTER TWENTY-TWO

Doncaster

Orange and red filled the evening sky, throwing everything else into shadow. People were rushing towards the source of the fire. Teenagers mostly, but Sean saw a man with a child holding his hand and another with a toddler on his shoulders. The small group he'd seen from his dad's window had swollen to a crowd. As he ran down the hill, he heard the high quiver of a burglar alarm reaching him in waves. There were people shouting and sirens getting closer. An enormous bang punctured the air and a thick column of black smoke rose ahead of him. Then he was on Winston Grove and saw Khan getting out of a car.

'Sir!'

Khan looked at him and took a moment to focus. Sean was out of breath and probably looked like shit. He had Jack's coat covering his T-shirt and his painting jeans underneath. He felt for his badge and was comforted to find it still in his trouser pocket.

'Nice outfit,' Khan said.

He wore beige cotton trousers and a buttoned-down shirt under a bomber jacket, all of which screamed plain-clothes policeman. He nodded to Sean. 'Come on, you can fill me in as we go.'

Ahead of them, a police van was already parked across the road and a young female officer was trying to wave people to safety behind it. Another officer was attaching incident tape to the side of the library building. Sean spotted Gavin and Carly positioned outside the old people's flats. He looked for his nan, but he couldn't see her. Opposite the shops, the fire engine crew was pumping water into the broken window of AK News, while beyond it a parked car was burning. Sean saw the outline of three men. Gary and the other two, who'd been painting over the graffiti, were pushing people back, allowing a second fire engine to get near the burning car. He couldn't see Terry Starkey.

'Let's get a bit closer,' Khan said.

They made their way through the crowd of onlookers. People stepped aside without Khan needing to show his badge. They reached the cordon and a female officer let them step inside. The windows of the newsagent's shop had shattered. Shards of glass were spread across the pavement, glinting with the reflection of flames. Sean could feel the heat from thirty metres away. Torrents of water were being pumped in by the firefighters and clouds of smoke and steam rolled into the street. The fire hadn't spread to the neighbouring buildings yet. Sean hoped they'd be able to save the library. Maureen would be lost without her Romance Readers' Book Group.

'Tell me about the burning property,' Khan said. 'Anything significant?'

'AK News. It's the Asafs' shop. Saleem's father and uncle own it. I assume the uncle is Mohammad's dad.'

'So someone's targeting the whole family now. Have they got any known enemies locally?'

'Not that I know of. But I understand there was a meeting, a community thing, and a torchlit march.' He heard his own words as if someone else had spoken them. He'd made out he wasn't actually there.

'What was the meeting for?'

'Something to do with a clean-up campaign, but I think it was just an excuse, sir, to stir up trouble. A bit extremist, if you know what I mean.'

'You knew about this and you didn't think to mention it?' Khan's tone was quiet but cold. 'The purpose of gathering intelligence, Denton, is to pass it on.'

The burglar alarm stopped and the sound of rushing water and steam filled the silence. Khan walked away from him without speaking and repositioned himself by the police van, surveying the scene. Sean stood for a moment, wondering what to do. He turned away from the crowd and followed the police tape down the side of the library, where it was knotted round a drainpipe. He ducked underneath and looked up the narrow track, along the wall of the library building, to the service road behind the parade. It was dark here, and much cooler away from the fire.

At first he didn't see the figure leaning against the wall, about twenty metres ahead of him, until it stood up straight and slipped away into the darkness. Sean quickened his pace and heard the footsteps ahead of him speed up too, until they were both running. Sean turned the corner but there was nobody on the service road. It was a dead end. Either the figure had entered the back of one of the other shops, or he'd scaled a six-foot wall, topped with the jagged lines of high-security razor wire.

Sean approached cautiously. The back doors of the library were covered with security shutters. The newsagent's was the same. If anyone was in the shop when the fire started, he prayed they'd got out. The bookies looked similarly shuttered, which only left the last building in the block, the Health Centre. He spotted an open hopper window above a frosted pane of glass. It must be a toilet. If anyone had got in there, they must have tiny, narrow hips. He watched the window and instinctively felt for his radio, but he didn't have one, only his phone.

He tried to concentrate on what was happening in front of him. He was sure the person who'd run away must have got into the back of the Health Centre. He kept it in his sights and backed down the alley, glancing over his shoulder to make sure he didn't back into the wall, or anyone else who might be skulking in the dark. When he got to the corner, he stopped. He had a feeling he was being watched. He called Khan's number. It rang and rang; the noise of the fire must have been drowning it out.

Khan finally picked up.

'Sir, I'm behind the shops. I've got a potential suspect who I think has got into the back of the Health Centre.'

'Description?'

'Male, about 5'5, 5'6, I think.'

'IC?'

'I wouldn't like to say, sir.'

180

'Don't worry. You won't offend me.'

'I'm not. Worried, I mean. But I didn't get much of a look. It's dark back here. I think he's young from the way he moved. Fifteen, sixteen?'

'Saleem?'

'Could be.'

He could hear footsteps in the side alley before he'd even put his phone back in his pocket. A female uniformed officer and DCI Khan were coming towards him. He ran ahead to make sure nothing had changed around the Health Centre window.

'Did you look inside?' Khan said as they reached him.

Sean shook his head. The female officer had her torch out and was shining it at the window frame.

'There's blood here,' she said, 'but the glass is intact.'

'Good work, Denton. Now, make yourself useful and see if you can find a number for a keyholder for this place. They're bound to have a security contract with someone.'

Sean scanned the back of the building for a sign or a plaque. There was a CCTV camera but it was too high up to read the writing.

'I'll have a look round the front. Back in a minute.'

He looked towards the dead end of the service road, but it was surrounded by the same brick walls, topped with razor wire. He'd have to go the long way round, past the burning shop front and the audience of onlookers.

On the street, the riot police had arrived. They were parked beyond the second fire engine, crouched inside their van like bees waiting to swarm and sting. They hadn't been stirred up to attack yet; their presence was a warning to a section of the crowd who looked like they might fancy a fight.

'All right, mate.'

Someone jostled Sean's arm. It was Terry Starkey. The moving crowd pushed them closer together until Terry put his arm round Sean's shoulder. Sean felt his grip and looked in vain towards the Health Centre. There were over a hundred people between him and the information he needed to get a keyholder. He could see that the front of the building was completely shuttered up, so the suspect must still be inside. Maybe Khan and the officer had given up waiting and kicked the window in by now.

'Here, look, it's the TV,' Terry shouted and swung round with Sean still in his grip, right into the path of a cameraman. 'This'll make you famous.'

At that moment, a woman in a red coat pushed a microphone in front of them.

When Sean got to his nan's house, a PCSO jacket was hanging over a chair in the kitchen. Carly was in the living room, a smut of soot still smeared across her cheek, sharing the settee with Maureen.

'All right, Nan,' Sean said. 'See you've made yourself at home, Carly.'

'Sorry, mate, have I pinched your spot?' She made no effort to move.

'No, but you've pinched one of my beers.'

'No fighting. They're my beers to hand out as I please and Carly was kind enough to see me home.' Maureen looked up from the television. 'There's one left in the fridge, love.'

'Be quick though, Sean,' Carly said, 'the news is coming on. You might see me in a starring role.'

Sean helped himself to a beer. He wouldn't mind skipping the news. He had a nagging feeling that he'd be the one in the starring role. They sat through a long piece about a slump in UK manufacturing.

'Nothing new there, it's been slumped round here since the Three-Day Week,' Maureen said. She settled the cat on her lap and lit up a cigarette.

When the local news came on, they could see the fire crew pouring water into the broken window of AK News. Sean spotted Carly's back on the far right of the screen, arms wide like a one-woman human cordon.

'A girl's got to do what a girl's got to do,' she said.

Sean didn't need *Look North*'s help in reliving the evening. By the time he'd got the number of the security firm, from a plaque above the front window of the Health Centre, Khan was on the phone to say they'd got a couple of lads from the riot van to batter in the back door. Inside a locked toilet they'd found a very miserable looking Saleem Asaf. Sean was told to stand down, but he was to report to Khan, back at the station, first thing in the morning.

The programme cut to Winston Grove. A familiar figure was standing next to the *Look North* woman, leaning towards the microphone as if he was about to burst into song. Terry Starkey. He had his arm round the shoulder of someone off-screen. Sean sipped his beer but he couldn't swallow it.

'It's people from outside, coming onto our estate,' Terry Starkey told the camera. 'Dealing drugs, bringing trouble in, that's what the police are telling us. They can have dozens of coppers down here for one dead Paki, but on an everyday basis? We don't see no one.'

Then the camera pulled back and there was Sean, smiling. Fucking smiling. What the hell had come over him?

'Who the . . . ?' Carly spluttered and sat bolt upright, sloshing beer onto Maureen's carpet.

'Is that you, love?' Maureen turned to look at him, taking in the same T-shirt, the same haircut, as if he could possibly have a double out there who'd stolen his clothes. By the time she looked back at the screen, the image had changed back to the burning shop. They sat silently, staring, but he didn't reappear. Carly took out a tissue and mopped at the beer on the carpet.

CHAPTER TWENTY-THREE

Doncaster

'Who was that man and what did you say to him?' Khan was clicking the end of his ballpoint pen.

'Terry Starkey. I saw him earlier in the day, painting over a slogan. I did speak to him, but I didn't . . . I don't know . . .'

'You don't know?'

'I didn't say anything about Mohammad Asaf.'

'So you never told this gentleman about, and I quote, "one dead Paki"?'

'No,' Sean's mouth was so dry his tongue was sticking to the inside of his cheeks. 'He doesn't know I'm a police officer and I never said "Paki", I mean, I would have used the word "Asian".'

'You mean you said, for the point of argument, "dead Asian" instead of "dead Paki" because that's better in some way, is it? And which part of "media silence" did you not understand? The press office has been bombarded with calls since last night.'

The ballpoint pen cracked in Khan's fist. Sean was glad there was a desk between them, and the door was on his side of it. *Always check your exit is clear if there's a risk of attack. Personal safety. Unit 1.*

'You're suspended, Denton. Hand your badge in. Speak to your union rep and get out.'

'Excuse me?' There was no air in his lungs. He felt his mouth open and close like a fish landed on a bank. 'But . . .'

'You heard.' Khan spun his chair away and fixed his stare out of the window.

Sean found Rick Houghton in the canteen.

'He'll have to follow formal procedure,' Rick said. 'You'll be suspended on full pay until it's sorted. I expect you'll have to have another meeting with the lovely Wendy Gore from Professional Standards.'

'But I haven't done anything!'

'Can you prove it?'

'Look, this guy, Starkey, he's stirring it up for some reason. Maybe he wants another bloody riot, I don't know.'

He'd said nothing to Rick about his dad or the CUC meeting. It wouldn't help his case, especially as he needed to convince them that Starkey was nothing to do with him.

'It's a shame you're suspended, Sean. I was hoping to show you some mugshots of the lads we've had in our sights for drug dealing on your manor.'

'Is it connected to our case? Sorry, Khan's case. Not mine any more. I don't have a fucking case and I'm not going to have a job soon, thanks to that bloody Nazi.'

'Calm down, man! Anyone hears you calling Khan a Nazi and you'll definitely never work again.'

Sean realised the canteen had gone quiet.

'I'm not talking about DCI Sam Nasir Khan.' He was speaking to Rick but he made sure everyone else could hear. If they were so keen to listen to his conversation, they might as well get the truth. 'I'm not the racist here. I'm talking about the guy on the telly. Terry Starkey. A man with a "Made in England" tattoo on his neck.'

'You want to know his story?' Rick lowered his voice. 'That shouldn't be difficult, especially with a tattoo like that. I didn't see the news myself. Sounds like I missed a treat though.'

'Check it out on iPlayer. But the tattoo's on the other side. He knew which way to turn from the camera.' Sean pushed his chair back and stood up. 'By all means look into it, Rick, as a mate. But beyond that, forget it. Don't do me any favours that are going to get you into trouble.'

'Wouldn't dream of it. But it might help the investigation, two investigations actually. Look, you get off home, enjoy your extra bit of paid holiday and call me if anything comes up.'

Sean had never had a dog of his own, but he'd seen plenty, and right now he felt like one who'd been kicked very hard and had its nose rubbed in its own shit. He walked out of the station and across town, eyes on the pavement in front of him, counting the fag butts and pressed circles of gum. He stopped at the edge of the market and watched the stallholders and shoppers, busy like ants. He wondered if Lizzie Morrison had found the other half of the ant corpse from the shoe prints. He'd probably never find out. The Red Lion on the corner had a pie and a pint special offer in its window and there was no reason not to go in.

'We're not serving food until eleven-thirty, love,' the woman behind the bar said.

He looked at his watch and realised it was only quarter past ten.

'I'll just have a pint then.'

After another two pints, he was ready for pie and chips, not to mention the peas and gravy that came with it. He found himself thinking he should bring his dad in here some time, get some decent food in him. It was cheap and the landlady was doing her best to make it cheerful. Then he remembered the AA meetings and the liver problem. Perhaps a pub wasn't the best idea.

It was warm and Sean was full of food. His eyes were closing, as if lead weights were pressing on his eyelids. He shuddered awake, checking to see if anyone had noticed, but the pub was the same as before. He rubbed his face but it was no good, his head nodded forward until his forehead rested on his arms on the table in front of him. He drifted into a dream of blood on concrete, soaking into his shoes, and Rick Houghton calling his name.

'Sean, mate?'

He jerked upright and realised Rick was standing on the other side of the table. He could only have been asleep for a few minutes. The beer was pressing on his bladder.

'Hang on,' he said, 'I'll be right back.'

It was cooler in the gents' toilet and he felt more awake. He had what must have been the longest piss in the world, washed his hands and splashed his face with water.

There were two cups of coffee on the table when he

got back and Rick was laying out photographs on top of a brown envelope.

'Stills from the CCTV at Winston Grove shops,' Rick said.

Sean peered at the grainy images, each of which included Terry Starkey.

'That's him, right?' Rick asked. 'What about the others, the ones you saw painting the wall?'

'This guy,' Sean pointed. 'He's called Gary. Right little fascist, he is.'

'We've got footage of him being quite the model citizen, helping the fire brigade and keeping the youth out of the way. He's not known on our patch, but I'll send his face around the other forces.'

'What about that face recognition thing they're using in the Met?'

'No budget for it up here, mate. And to be honest, it's not that great. You're sure he's not local?'

'Not as far as I know. Sounds Mancunian, or some place like that. Starkey gave the impression he'd got these guys in to help. Maybe he met them inside.'

'Well he had plenty of time to make friends at Her Majesty's pleasure. He served a long stretch for armed robbery, so your hunch was spot on. Put a ring round any of the others you think are part of Starkey's crew, then we can have their prints ready for comparison with anything at the scene.'

Sean found the other two faces easily.

'They'll have kept their hands clean,' he said, 'but you could get them on incitement to racial hatred.'

It was a mistake not to have told Khan he'd been at the meeting, but Sean wasn't sure how he was going to get away with suddenly remembering something he couldn't possibly have forgotten. Then it came to him. Maureen.

'Give my nan a ring. She might be able to tell you what was said at the Clean Up Chasebridge meeting.'

'Nice one.' Rick drained his coffee and put the photos back in the envelope.

'And, Rick, she might mention I was there too. I just sort of forgot to tell DCI Khan.'

Rick hesitated.

'You know the oath in court, Sean?'

Sean nodded.

'The reason it's "the truth, the whole truth and nothing but the truth" is because anything else will tie you in knots. A white lie here and there, and before you know it, you're up to your neck in shit. Why didn't you tell him?'

Sean shrugged. 'I don't know, I thought it would come out wrong. I went to the meeting with my dad, to bond with him or something stupid. I felt sort of dirty just hearing that stuff and you know what? I didn't want to offend Khan. That's pathetic, isn't it?'

'No. It's naïve.' Rick sighed and leant heavily against the back of the seat.

When they'd finished talking, and Rick had paid for another two coffees, they said goodbye and went in opposite directions. Sean left the moped parked in the yard at the police station – he didn't need to add a drink-driving conviction to his problems – and set off to the bus stop. As he passed the estate agents' shop, he paused for a moment, pushed the door open and went in.

The well-appointed studio apartment had already been let. He wasn't entirely surprised. But there was something else, if he was interested. He found himself agreeing to a viewing there and then. The estate agent drove him to a pretty Georgian square only five minutes' walk from the police station. At least the agent said it was Georgian. Sean just thought it looked old, seriously old but very smart. He was already shaking his head and trying to form the words 'out of my price range' but the agent kept on talking. Gavin Wentworth had told him about attending a burglary on this square and the money people had here was eye-watering. Never mind a studio, it would have to be a broom cupboard before he could afford it.

They stopped in front of a tall, brick building, maybe not as old as some of the others, but certainly dating back to the time when the Chasebridge estate was fields, covered in deer or bears or something. Sean was beginning to regret the three pints. In spite of the coffee, his mind was all over the place, and he was dying for another piss. The house had an imposing flight of stone steps up to the front door and at least ten doorbells to choose from.

'It's right at the top,' the agent said. 'Super views.'

As the agent was fumbling with the keys, the front door opened and there stood Lizzie Morrison. The agent said 'thank you' and walked in, but Sean stayed where he was, frozen to the top step.

'Hello,' she said.

They ended up round the corner in The Salutation, a

friendly pub with a good choice of beers, but Sean wasn't tempted. When he got back from the toilet, Lizzie had already ordered two double espressos. If this didn't sober him up, nothing would. The estate agent had left him with his card, unable to understand why Sean had changed his mind about the viewing. He wasn't sure himself, he just knew he couldn't live in the same block as Lizzie; it would drive him insane.

She listened as he told his story about the Clean Up Chasebridge meeting and how he wished he'd tipped someone off about the torchlit parade. He described the fire and the television crew and Khan's reaction.

'It'll be OK,' she said for the third or fourth time.

She sounded like she was on his side, but she had no advice to give him other than to wait and see.

'He'll calm down, I'm sure of it. He's got no proof that you leaked Asaf's death. I'm sure the whole estate knows who the victim was. Let's face it, the locals usually know more than we do.'

'It's a nice square,' Sean wanted to change the subject, talking about his job was making him feel miserable. He forced a smile. 'Have you lived in your flat for long?'

'Are you drunk?' Lizzie said. 'You sound a bit drunk.'

'Slightly, but as I don't have to work, it doesn't matter.'

'Fair enough.'

She studied the dregs at the bottom of her cup, as if she was playing for time. He didn't want to hear about it if the flat belonged to a boyfriend, the successor to Guy of the Rovers, or whoever she'd been seeing in London. He was beginning to wish he hadn't asked.

'I moved in when I got back from London. My dad

192

bought it,' she said finally, and looked at him as if he was going to criticise her.

'Nice. That was nice of him.' And he meant it. She lived there alone. Probably. That was nice, very nice.

'Were you really looking to rent a flat?' she said.

He was startled. 'Yes, why? Did you think I was stalking you?'

She laughed and shook her head. 'Of course not.'

'Lizzie?'

'Sean?'

'How am I going to get out of this mess?'

'I don't know. But I do know I've got to go to work. There's a burnt out shop needs checking over.'

'If you fancy a brew while you're up there . . .'

But he didn't finish. He wasn't sure she'd be welcome at his nan's. She'd been there once before, when they first knew each other, and it hadn't gone well. Different worlds. He suddenly thought about Jack, about the cleaning equipment he'd left there and the sleeping bag he'd taken up, before the whole estate went mad. He wouldn't be making Lizzie a cup of tea in that kitchen either, but he might be able to make his dad something to eat and have a go at cleaning up the bathroom. A caffeine-induced sense of purpose was stirring within him. Stuff DCI Khan; Sean had work to do.

When the bathroom floor was clean again, right to the edges, the knees of Sean's jeans were black and his throat was parched. He resisted the urge to sneak off to the shop for a beer. There was no AK News and Convenience Store now anyway, just a blackened frontage between the library and the bookies, where right now Lizzie was probably picking over the wreckage.

'Stop it,' he said to himself. 'Leave her alone, or she really will think you're a stalker.'

His dad had perked up.

'I'll make you something to eat, lad, if you don't mind that I can't cook.'

He'd been shovelling down all kinds of pills and he told Sean he had good days and bad days. This was a good day.

'There's a tin of mushroom soup,' Jack said, 'if you fancy it and I've got some sliced bread in that top cupboard. Toaster still works, more or less. More than can be said for its owner,' he wheezed, laughing at his own joke.

They didn't talk much that evening. Sean's arms and back ached. He'd never realised what hard physical work cleaning could be. They watched the television, with Jack's running commentary, until he limped off to bed and Sean unrolled his blue sleeping bag on the settee. He took his jeans off and hung them over the back of a chair, kept his socks on, and his shoes close by. The carpet was dark and stained with unidentifiable marks and he couldn't be sure there wasn't some broken glass among the discarded newspapers.

He slid inside the bag, pulled the hood round his head to keep his face away from the greasy fabric of the settee and let exhaustion wash over him. Tomorrow he'd go out and get more bin liners and some carpet spray. Cleaning this place up would keep his mind off Khan, and Starkey, and the mess he was making of his career.

CHAPTER TWENTY-FOUR

York

Everyone at the hostel is sick of Chloe using mugs from the kitchen to water the plants, but they'll shrivel up and die if they don't get a drink, and she's the only one who cares. Eventually, Darren brings a watering can from home and lets her use that. She carries it, heavy and sloshing, into the back garden and rations each pot, being careful not to splash the leaves. She asks Darren if he's got the sprinkler rose to put over the nozzle, but he says he lost it years ago. He's not much of a gardener. That's obvious from the amount of spiders and cobwebs in the bottom of the watering can.

No one says anything about Taheera's absence. Even when Emma asks Darren directly, he shrugs and says he's not sure when she'll be back. A new woman has started covering the night shift. Emma says she used to be a screw and none of the girls like her. Chloe hasn't formed an opinion either way, but the woman let her use the computer early this morning, so she's prepared to give her the benefit of the doubt. She found out that the fire in the newsagents' may have been started deliberately. Chloe would happily have started it herself, to burn up all those copies of *The Doncaster Free Press* with her picture on the front page.

It's Emma who calls out from the doorway to tell her she's got visitors. It's odd the way she says it, sort of snarky. Chloe hesitates. Who would visit her here? She pours the last bit of water onto the soil around the busy Lizzies. They might be the world's most boring bedding plants, but she's not going to let them die.

'Are you coming?'

Chloe lays down the watering can and turns round. She wipes her palms on the back of her jeans and follows Emma inside the building.

They're standing by the office door. Even as her eyes adjust to the gloom, it's easy to see what they are from their outline: two female police officers who just want a quiet word. Darren shows them into the office. Chloe wishes he would stay; she's afraid of what she might say, but he doesn't, probably not his remit or something.

'We've been asked to come and speak to you, to rule something out. Do you understand?'

Chloe nods, but she doesn't, not really. Now they haven't got the light behind them, she can see one of them is plain-clothes. Must be CID. The suit is an ugly dark grey. It's as if the woman wearing it would rather have the security of her old uniform, so she's got herself a suit cut in the same style.

'We want to know where you were on Tuesday night,

that's the night of Tuesday the seventh of June,' the detective says and glowers at her, square-jawed like a boxer.

Tuesday the seventh. Chloe's good with dates. Years and months and weeks of counting down the days have given her an excellent memory for these things. On Monday the sixth she had her first day at work then breached her licence by going to Doncaster. On Tuesday the seventh she went to work again, and early on the eighth Taheera got a phone call which made her cry. She begins to guess what this might be about.

'Here. Meredith House. I mean, I've been here since I left prison, except when I go to work, which is at Halsworth Grange, near Halsworth Main, South Yorkshire.' The truth is easy and clear, she hopes they can see that.

'Can anyone confirm that?'

Her memory blanks out for a moment, she almost panics, then it comes back.

'I was at the IT class that evening. There's a trainer. She's from the council. Kath. She's called Kath. I did the IT class, then I went to bed.'

'Thank you, we just needed to be sure.'

'Ask Darren, ask . . . well, the other girl's off sick, but she'd know. She was on duty that night.'

'And what's her name?'

'Taheera. Taheera Ahmed.'

Chloe chews her lip. She mustn't say any more. What she's told them is real, so far. If she adds to it, she may get it wrong. All she understands is that this visit has got something to do with Taheera and the boyfriend. Suddenly an image flashes into her mind of the young man on the tower of York Minster and Chloe is pushing him; he's flying through the air, turning and falling. But that's wrong. She didn't go up there. She stayed on the ground. There was a nest with bird skeletons. He wasn't the one falling in space. She gave the nest to a little boy. That was last week. She needs to focus on the truth. Tuesday evening. The class, her bed, Taheera crying on the phone. The bus. Work. That's it. It's all in place. She needs to keep it there.

CHAPTER TWENTY-FIVE

Doncaster

Sean woke up with his hip squashed under him and his arm tingling with pins and needles. The slope of the settee had prevented him from turning over in his sleep. He adjusted the hood of the sleeping bag where it had slipped down. He stretched out on his back, his feet up on the arm. He felt his spine click straight again. The morning light filtered through the dirty nets, picking out dust in the air. Yesterday he'd cleaned and swept and scrubbed until every muscle ached. The kitchen cupboards were spotless and he'd managed to replace the fuse in the water heater.

The sitting room was getting warmer and a rank smell was rising from the carpet. He thought about hiring one of those steam cleaners. They weren't pricey. His legs itched inside the sleeping bag and he longed for a shower, so he extricated himself carefully and put his feet in his shoes. The bathroom was looking better than when he'd started. The black mildew was gone from around each tile, but the bath itself was still scratched and stained. It looked like the inside of an old teapot. There was no shower as such, just a rubber attachment shoved on the taps. He didn't like the look of it so he ran water into the sink, filled his hands and drenched his face. He dried it on his T-shirt and decided he needed some air. His nan would be up by now, she was an early riser. A proper shower and a decent breakfast were calling.

The estate was quiet apart from a car changing gear, coming down the hill towards The Groves. He caught a glimpse of the driver, a woman in a green uniform tabard, an agency carer he supposed, or a cleaner, up and out early.

Particularly observant with an eye for detail was the final comment on his police training report. Not observant enough to keep his bloody mouth shut and stay away from Terry Starkey when a camera crew turned up, and now he was facing a disciplinary, and he wouldn't get off as lightly this time. He kicked a stone so hard it ricocheted off the base of a lamp post with a surprising clang.

He was so focused on wishing he could turn back the clock that his eyes and ears nearly let him down, and he would have missed it, if the sound of a car door hadn't caught his attention. In front of the shops, a woman had got out of a taxi. It was like an action replay of the scene he'd witnessed a couple of days ago. Only this time the young woman's hijab was askew and her face was grey with tiredness. She held out her hand to help someone struggling to get out of the car, beseeching them to hurry up so they could get inside, but the figure who emerged did so slowly, holding his waist with one hand and gripping the roof of the car to pull himself to standing.

As Saleem Asaf turned to slam the car door shut, he

looked up and his eyes locked on to Sean's. He was as thin as a whippet, apart for a thick band around his middle, pushing against a rusty brown mark on his tight T-shirt. Sean could make out the contours of a newly-applied dressing.

As Ghazala and Saleem approached the front of the shop, a police officer waved them away. They stood for a moment and Sean saw how lost they were, like two refugees in a scene from the ten o'clock news. He told himself not to be so soft. Saleem Asaf deserved to be in the nick, not constantly slipping through their fingers, but as Ghazala adjusted her hijab and straightened her drooping shoulders, he found himself approaching them.

'Anything I can do to help?'

'You can tell that bastard that we need to get into our flat,' Saleem began, but was cut short by Ghazala slapping him round the side of the head.

'Why don't you just shut up for once? Eh?'

Saleem looked at his feet.

'Yes, please,' Ghazala turned to Sean. 'You're police, right? We need to get upstairs to the flat. I need to find the insurance documents.'

Sean was going to tell her that he wasn't working, but at that moment the officer by the shop recognised him and beckoned him over.

'All right, mate? It's PC Denton, isn't it?'

'Aye, that's me,' Sean said.

He couldn't remember the other man's name. He worked the day shift in a different unit. There was nothing in his open smile that suggested he knew anything about Sean's suspension.

'Look, technically I'm off duty,' Sean said, 'but would it be OK if I accompanied the young lady into the flat? I think we can get around the back without disturbing the crime scene.'

'I don't see why not, if you're quick.'

Ghazala followed him and Saleem tagged along behind her.

'No, son,' Sean said, 'you stay right here, where my colleague can see you.'

'What you saying? I can't go in my own home? You saying you don't trust me?'

'That's right, Saleem, that's exactly what I'm saying.'

Saleem gave an exaggerated shrug, sucked his teeth at Sean and flounced off to sit on the low wall in front of the library. A flicker of annoyance passed across Ghazala's face but she shut it out. She and Sean walked quickly up the alley beside the library to the back of the shop. He was impressed by the way she was handling this situation; the more businesslike the better, as far as Sean was concerned. Any moment now, the officer at the front of the shop might catch on and call in to the station, then he'd find out that Sean had no right to be here.

Ghazala opened two padlocks on the security shutter and pulled it up. She unlocked the back door and Sean followed her. They were in a hallway with a flight of stairs ahead of them and an internal door to their right. The air smelt of burnt plastic and the paintwork was clouded with smoke stains. Ghazala pulled her scarf across her mouth and nose as she climbed the stairs to the inner door of the flat.

Inside the living room, the smell was overpowering.

'Please touch as little as possible,' Sean said. 'Just find the papers and then we need to leave.'

202

She stood still and looked around.

'Everything's ruined,' her voice cracked as she swallowed back tears. 'My dad doesn't know yet, he . . .'

Sean stood helplessly, wanting to comfort her, but knowing he shouldn't touch her.

'Saleem said your father was in Pakistan with your uncle.'

She nodded, her eyes coming to rest on a bookcase with an inbuilt sliding cupboard at eye level. She took a tissue out of her pocket and made sure she didn't touch the wood as she slid the cupboard open. The tissue was grey with soot as she let it fall to the carpet.

'Are they on their way back?' Sean said. 'I imagine your uncle, at least, would want to bury his son, and now this fire. It's not fair to leave you to deal with everything.'

He felt cruel, reminding her of Mohammad's death on top of the disaster of the fire, but it had been bothering him that there was still no sign of the two heads of this family. Ghazala didn't answer. She lifted an A4 box file out of the cupboard and opened it.

'Do you mind me asking, miss, what they're doing there? In Pakistan?'

She shrugged. 'Family business.'

'But what about their family here?'

'Are you interrogating me, officer?' Ghazala's eyes flashed as she spun round, almost dropping the box file. 'Because if you are, I want a solicitor. I know my rights. Do you think I'm just some young girl you can push around and hint at all kinds of things?'

Sean opened his mouth to speak but nothing came out.

'Well, I'm not stupid,' Ghazala continued. 'What are you

203

trying to say? That we're all criminals? Because Mo and Saleem have been stupid boys and mixed with the wrong people? Or because you assume all Pakistanis are drug dealers or terrorists? Is that it?'

Her voice was shrill now and Sean was afraid the officer outside would be able to hear them. He held up his hands in surrender.

'I'm not saying that.'

'My dad and my Uncle Hassan have taken my granddad home. He's old and sick. We haven't told him about the fire. It'll probably kill him, because this was his shop. You see? He opened it with his sons twenty-five years ago. Now all he wants is to see his village, one last time.'

Sean didn't know what to say. The acrid smell from the fire was biting into his throat. He swallowed and his saliva tasted bitter.

'My granddad was planning to stay over there for a few weeks, say goodbye to all his relatives, but he can't now, can he?' Ghazala continued, not looking at Sean. 'He has to come back and bury his grandson, as you said.' Her voice faltered and she turned towards the window where net curtains hung grey with soot. 'They're still trying to find a flight with spare seats, while my cousin's body lies in the mortuary because your people aren't even close to finding out who killed him.'

Sean cleared his throat. 'I'm sorry.'

'Are you?' Her voice was low, but anger pulsed through it. 'I saw you on the TV. You were right here, outside on the pavement with that mob. Hanging around with those thugs. I know who you are.'

'Miss Asaf, please, I'm not . . . Look it doesn't matter. We need to go. The smoke damage, I mean, the air we're breathing, it's not healthy. If you've got the papers you need, let's get out.'

She held the box file close to her chest and looked around the room. It was clear that it would take a lot of work to get everything back to normal.

'I hope the insurance covers all this,' Ghazala said quietly.

'I hope so too.' Sean gestured towards the door and she responded by walking slowly down the stairs, the fight gone out of her.

Outside, Saleem came to meet them.

'How are the stitches?' Sean tried to sound sympathetic.

'OK,' Saleem said. 'They had to redo a bit.'

'You want to take it easy, no more climbing into windows.'

'You can't resist having a go, can you?' Ghazala snapped at Sean. 'He's been in hospital half the night and for your information he's not been charged with anything, so leave him alone!'

'Really?' Sean said.

Saleem nodded. 'Just got told off. It's all right, Ghazala. He's OK, really.'

He looked like he might have something else to say, but his sister put her arm round his shoulders and hurried him away to the bus stop without a backwards glance.

When he got to his nan's, Sean found Maureen on her knees in front of the oven. The kitchen smelt of caustic soda. Only his nan would think it was normal to clean her oven this early in the morning.

'Hello, love.' She straightened up, out of breath. 'I

thought I'd get this done before the day gets too hot. I'm not going to complain about a decent summer for once, but they say we're due for another heatwave. I reckon it's that global warm-up.'

'Warming, Nan. Shall I put the kettle on?'

'Aye, why not. I'll be done in a minute, just need to rinse the gunk off.'

She didn't question why he was there or mention him staying at his dad's last night. When the tea was brewed and she'd finished what she was doing, she piled his plate with toast and he lathered each slice with a thick, melting slab of butter. He started to tell her about DCI Khan, about how it had all been going so well and how he had suddenly got it so badly wrong. He was careful not go into too much detail, especially about Mohammad Asaf, but he mentioned bumping into Terry Starkey. He told her he was simply in the wrong place at the wrong time when the TV crew turned up. He didn't tell her he'd been suspended. For some reason the words got stuck and when he tried to form them, his head rushed like it used to when he was a kid and he thought he was about to cry. He told himself it was the fumes from the flat still making his eyes sting. He sank his face into his tea mug and she nodded, reassuring him that she'd never for a moment thought he was in with Terry Starkey's crowd.

'You know him?'

'Of course, I thought I told you,' Maureen said. 'He's batty Bernadette's lad, different name because he was from the first husband, John Starkey. John used to work at Markham Main with your dad. Died in a scaffolding accident not long after the strike. Fell off drunk probably. Anyway, then she married Bob Armley.'

Sean tried to process what he was hearing.

'That poor woman,' she said. 'As if she hadn't had it hard enough after losing the younger one, that Terry went and got himself banged up for armed robbery.'

'Come again?'

'I thought you knew. The one that got pushed off the flats, that was her younger son. Terry tried to use it in court, in whatsit . . .'

'Mitigation?'

'That's right. But his was a nasty crime. Armed robbery's armed robbery, at the end of the day.'

He thought about the pictures in Bernadette Armley's flat – two young boys with red hair and freckles.

Maureen topped up his tea and sat back in her chair, lighting up a cigarette.

'First one of the day,' she sucked on it with her eyes closed.

'Nan, you shouldn't. It's not ladylike,' he joked.

'My days of worrying about being ladylike are long gone. Anyway, some fellers still think it's sexy,' she laughed a deep smoker's laugh.

He could sense a dangerous change of subject and sure enough, she was asking him about girls and whether there was anyone special in the picture. He decided to tell her he'd seen Lizzie Morrison, but regretted it as soon as the words were spoken.

'What's she doing back in Doncaster?' Maureen's eyes lit up. 'Is she still seeing that bloke from Donny Rovers?'

'I don't know Nan, I've not really thought about her.'

'Well you be careful with that one.'

It struck him as ironic that the people who cared about him were constantly warning him to be careful of the people he admired. He wondered if he was gullible, or maybe he trusted the wrong people. But were Lizzie Morrison and Sam Nasir Khan the wrong people? Or were they just people who were out of his league socially, professionally and in every way he could imagine?

'It's not right,' Nan said, 'the shop being attacked. They've gone too far with that Clean Up Chasebridge thing, let it get out of control. I told your friend Rick, I said to him, they're just jumping on the bandwagon most of them.'

'He rang you, then?'

'Yes, I told him you left the meeting early, reckoned you didn't want to be associated with that lot.'

'Thanks.'

'Don't mention it.'

Maureen refilled his cup, the tea darker than ever.

At that moment his phone pinged with an incoming text and interrupted their conversation. He wouldn't have recognised the number, but Lizzie Morrison had thoughtfully signed her text. She wanted to know if he was all right. That's all she said.

'Who's that then?' Maureen said.

'Lizzie.'

'Ah,' Maureen tapped the side of her nose.

'What's that supposed to mean?'

'You summoned her. You sent out a temporal vibe and she caught it.'

'What are you on about?' Sean said.

'There was a talk at the library. Some woman who'd written a book about telepathy. It was very interesting. There's a lot of things we put down to coincidence, which are no such thing.'

'OK,' he nodded. 'Maybe I'm getting temporal vibes from Terry Starkey then. He keeps turning up all over the place. Call it coincidence or whatever you like, but I can't shake him off. Have you still got the weekly paper? The one with the girl who killed Starkey's brother?'

'Outside in the recycling bin. You're just in time. It's collection day tomorrow. Now I need to go up and get ready, or I'll be late.'

He found the paper near the bottom of the box and glanced at the headline. There was the photo of a girl in school uniform, ears sticking out through her straight, dark hair. If only we knew how those terrible school portraits could come back to haunt us, he thought, we'd refuse to have them done.

Back at the kitchen table he read the article carefully, looking for any mention of Terry Starkey or Bernadette Armley, but there was no reference to the family, beyond saying that James Armley was a 'loving son and brother'. Sean underlined the girl's name and the year it happened, ten years ago. He circled the words 'cold-blooded' and 'innocent schoolboy'. James was sixteen at the time, which was stretching the definition of schoolboy a little. The same age Saleem was now. Sean went back to the beginning and read more carefully: *The victim had been lured to the top of the Eagle Mount flats by jealous Marilyn Nelson, a local girl with whom he'd had a secret love tryst.* He saw the word 'manslaughter', tucked in the final sentence. So, not a murder then; he wondered why not.

'I'm surprised Terry Starkey didn't try to make something of it at the CUC meeting,' he said, thinking out loud. 'Wouldn't hurt his profile to have the sympathy vote.'

His phoned pinged and he remembered he hadn't replied to Lizzie's text. He typed his response carefully. Three words. *Yes fine thanks.* Then he saved her number in his address book. He realised she must have kept his, two years on from their last job together.

Maureen came downstairs in a tracksuit top and leggings.

'I'm off to Bums and Tums. I don't like to miss it and I'm going to be late at this rate. See you later!'

She closed the back door and he sat for a while in the silent kitchen, trying to decide what to do next. Nothing. That's all he could think of. Nowhere to go and nothing to do. He stared at the kettle and wondered about making another pot of tea, but he didn't move. He looked at his watch and saw it was creeping towards nine o'clock. He didn't think Jack would be awake yet, but the supermarket on the ring road would be open.

Sean stood up and rinsed out the teapot, leaving it neatly on the drainer. He wished he could stay here, where everything worked and you didn't feel as if you would stick to every surface you touched, but he knew he had to go back to his dad's; it had something to do with finishing what he'd started.

He went through to the sitting room and looked around. It was spotless, as usual, with a scent of lemongrass coming from the aroma sticks Maureen had put in a glass vase on

210

the mantelpiece. She'd done away with the plug-in room fresheners when she decided they gave her asthma. He'd tried to suggest that giving up smoking might help with that, but she wouldn't be told. Maybe this new exercise regime would put her off, although knowing Maureen, she'd probably find time for a fag break at Bums and Tums. He sat heavily on the settee and his head fell back into the soft corduroy cushions. Tiredness crept through every limb, weighing him down. He closed his eyes and let himself drift.

He woke up with a crick in his neck and realised it was nearly midday. In the kitchen, he ran the cold tap and poured a glass of water. He downed the glass in one, rinsed it out and put it on the drainer. The newspaper was still on the table with his annotations in blue biro. He rolled it up, tucked it under his arm and pulled the back door shut behind him. As he turned down the side of Maureen's house and onto Clement Grove, his phone rang.

'Hiya! How are you doing?'

'Hi, Lizzie. I'm. . .'

'What?'

'Nothing. I'm doing nothing, there's nothing to do. The high point of my day will be scrubbing the rest of the mould off the bathroom tiles in my dad's flat.'

'So you are on the Chasebridge estate?'

'Near enough, just leaving home.'

'Really? Brill. Any chance you could get us that coffee you were offering? I'm at the paper shop.'

'Again?'

'Got turned away yesterday. It wasn't safe inside the shop.

211

Something to do with the electrics. Now I've got to wait until the fire investigators give it the all clear, and they're late.'

He was glad she hadn't been there earlier and seen him going upstairs with Ghazala.

'I'll see what I can do,' he said. Lizzie's stint down south had obviously raised her expectations. This wasn't coffee bar country, but he had an idea. 'I'll be there in a minute.'

She was sitting in her car outside the parade of shops, window down and one bare elbow resting on the door frame. He thought about creeping up to surprise her, but she was obviously checking her wing mirrors because she waved out of the window as he approached. He leant in and she smiled up at him. The radio was playing Mumford & Sons. It wasn't his kind of music but it suited her.

'You after a coffee?'

She nodded.

'Fresh from my nan's Thermos!' He produced the red tartan flask with a flourish.

She laughed. 'Wow, vintage!'

'I brought a spare cup, if you don't mind me joining you.' He wondered where it came from, his newfound confidence around Lizzie Morrison, but as long as it was just about drinking coffee together, he felt he was on safe ground.

'Let's sit in the sun and make the most of it,' she said. 'I feel like I'm missing the whole summer. I'm either in the office or sweating it out in a plastic suit.'

She got out of the car and clicked the locks on. Sean sat down on the low wall in front of the library and poured the milky instant coffee into two cups. They were both quiet for a while until Lizzie broke the silence.

'Sean?'

'Yes.'

'When I was in London, I missed all this.'

'Yeah?'

'Yeah. I actually missed Donny, and I missed crappy places like the Chasebridge estate. Funny, isn't it?'

Sean took a slow mouthful of coffee. Lizzie didn't notice his lack of response; she was looking at something behind him.

'What did Mohammad Asaf study at the college?'

'Media or something,' Sean said and turned to see what had caught her attention.

In the window of the library, a series of black and white photographs hung from thin steel wires. One was of a tower block taken from below, which made it appear to be toppling forwards away from a cloud-filled sky. In another, a beautiful young Asian woman was on a swing in the playground, her head thrown back and her hair trailing out behind her. Brick walls, concrete, more sky; they weren't pretty, but there was something moody and artistic about them. A small white sign with black lettering said: *Mohammad Asaf, first prize, Chasebridge Community Photographic Competition.* Dr Angus Balement might not appreciate Mohammad Asaf's talents, but someone did.

'How sad,' Lizzie said. 'He made it look beautiful. He didn't know he was going to die in that very building.'

Sean peered closely, about to correct her that it wasn't the

213

same block. Asaf had died in Block Two, whereas this was clearly Block Four, but he stopped himself. It would have sounded a bit callous to be that picky and anyway, Eagle Mount Four had its own ghosts. It was the block where the boy had been pushed off ten years ago. He shivered, despite the warmth of the day.

A red fire investigation van drew up and Lizzie put her cup down and walked towards her own car to get her kit.

'Thanks for the coffee,' she said, turning back for a moment. 'Don't forget your paper.'

She nodded to Maureen's copy of *The Doncaster Free Press*, lying on top of the wall. He picked up the newspaper, glancing at the circles and underlinings he'd done earlier. There was something about Mrs Armley that he needed to get clear in his head. If Terry Starkey was her son, where was he living? *And I said, there's someone up to no good.* Mrs Armley hadn't mentioned anyone else, and they'd assumed she meant she was talking to herself, but what if she'd said it out loud, to someone standing by the window with her?

Lizzie was talking to the fire officer, who stood with his arms folded to maximise the bulging muscles crammed into his short-sleeved shirt. She was getting animated. As he got closer, Sean picked up something about procedure and priorities. The fire officer was expressionless, waiting for Lizzie to finish.

'I can't let you in there, darling, until we've isolated the electrics and I'll need our specialist guy to come down for that.'

'Meanwhile the evidence is deteriorating.' She looked

214

round as Sean approached. The other man glanced at him, trying to decide who, or what, he was.

'Some people don't understand protocol,' he said to Sean, smiling through bleached white teeth.

Lizzie went back to sit on the wall and Sean followed her with a backward glance at the fire officer, who winked at him. If it was meant to be a sign of blokey solidarity, he'd got the wrong man.

'What a complete tosser,' Lizzie said. 'I understand they have their own teams and their own way of doing things, but he's actually obstructing us now and I've got a good mind to report him.'

'So what are you looking for?' Sean said.

'How much do you know?' She shot him a sideways glance.

'Almost nothing. Except when the fire was raging I followed a suspect who disappeared into the back of the Health Centre. That same suspect and his sister were here this morning. She got some documents from the flat, but the boy stayed clear.'

'Has he been charged with anything?'

'Not as far as I know. Just another ticking off. He collects them.'

'And you just happened to be here when they turned up?'

'I was passing. On the way home from my dad's, as it goes.'

He hoped he hadn't given himself away. Rick was right about little white lies tying you in knots.

'The flat's not part of the crime scene, as far as we're concerned,' Lizzie said.

Sean stifled a sigh of relief.

'Does the CCTV tell us who started the fire?' he said.

'Sadly not. There's a camera on the Health Centre and one on the library, so although you can see people coming and going, there's a gap in the middle of the parade.'

'What about mobile phone footage?'

'Rick Houghton's on to that. He's got half his team scouring the Internet. By the time the shop went up in flames, there were over a hundred people here, so there's bound to be something.'

Sean was wondering what Saleem was up to.

'Someone should check the appointments at the Health Centre for the day of the fire,' he said.

'You've lost me.'

'Saleem might have been running because he saw me, or he might have been running because he had a plan. What if he had an appointment at the Health Centre during the day, to check his stitches or whatever, went to the toilet while he was there and left the window open, ready to squeeze himself in later?'

'What was he after?'

'The usual. Prescription drugs to sell on. Anything he could get in his pockets. Living near such an easy source must be quite tempting.'

'And the fire enabled him to cover his tracks?'

'Or a happy coincidence,' Sean said. 'Perhaps he took the opportunity when he thought nobody would be watching.'

'You should talk to DCI Khan.'

'No chance. I'm suspended, remember? You tell him, if you like.'

The fire officer was coming back towards them. Lizzie adjusted her equipment bag on her shoulder and was about to say something, but Sean cut her off.

'And while you're at it, tell him someone needs to ask Terry Starkey where he was on the night of Mohammad Asaf's murder.'

CHAPTER TWENTY-SIX

Halsworth Grange

Chloe is praying for rain. She rakes the gravel on the path into straight furrows and at every pass wishes she'd had a shower this morning. She lingered too long in bed after her alarm went off, and when she got up there were people moving around. The broken lock on the bathroom door makes it too risky. Now the Icy Mist has worn off and she hates her body's vinegary odour. If her mother could smell her now, she'd be horrified. She was a woman who moved around in a cloud of perfume, who sprayed the air if it didn't smell gorgeous enough. Air freshener, beer and fag smoke all mingled together in the pub, but at home it was like a spring meadow, all year long. Well, Chloe smiles to herself, not a real one, not like the meadow here at Halsworth Grange, which prickles the back of your throat with the dry smell of hay and the sweetness of clover. But sometimes she catches the scent her mum wore, on the bus or the train, and she misses her. She looks at the patterns she's been making with the rake. They've gone a bit wobbly. She needs to concentrate. She straightens them up and keeps her distance from the visitors.

After her break, Bill tells her there's more mowing to do. He jokes about the dodgy haircuts she gave the long grass under the apple trees and she's relieved he's not annoyed about her poor mowing in the orchard. He points out a grassy slope next to the car park. It's like a small field, fenced in from a wild patch of shrubs and trees below. Above it, a dry, brownish lawn is currently laid out with wooden picnic tables.

'We'll move the tables down there tomorrow. Give the other patch a rest. Let's get it as short as we can while it's clear of visitors and all their rubbish. OK?'

Under her ear defenders the buzz of the ride-on mower seems to be coming from miles away. The vibration through her spine is like the hum of bees. She's the hive and the bees are inside her. She keeps a straight line, eyes fixed on a fence post at the foot of the field. As she gets close to the edge, she eases off the accelerator and prepares to turn, looping round to make the upward cut. The smell of newly mown grass and engine oil fills her nostrils. At the top of the field, in the existing picnic area, families cluster round tables covered in rubbish. Some of them will make the effort to transfer it to the bins. Some of them won't. She drops her gaze, focusing on the line she's following, and turns again.

At the bottom edge of the field another smell drifts across the perfume of grass and oil, but she can't place it. Once she's made the turn it fades away behind her. From somewhere in her memory she thinks of a fox's scent, dark and musty. Maybe it's something Jay taught her about. There were foxes on the allotment. He taught her so many things about nature.

219

Her Jay, with his flapping coat and wild red hair, smoking a joint or just hanging out in the shed when it rained. He was almost happy there.

Ahead of her a group of teenage girls jump up from their picnic table screaming. They flap pointlessly at a wasp, but Chloe doesn't care. The rhythm of mowing lulls her into drowsiness. Their screaming barely reaches her through the ear defenders as she steers around another loop and faces back down the slope. Beyond the wooden post-and-rail fencing, rhododendrons as tall as trees have escaped from the formal gardens and run wild. Their season is over and their spent flower heads are browning and sodden. For a moment she wonders if it's the rotting flowers causing the smell, which is getting stronger and more metallic.

She steers away, back up the field. She's mown about half the area Bill asked her to cover. It's satisfying to see the effect of before and after. The thick stripes are neat and orderly, but the lush green of the unmown section, where bumblebees settle on clover heads, is open and free. The picnickers ignore her, even though they have to pause their conversations at the noisy approach of mower. To them she's just a gardener in a uniform Halsworth Grange hat, part of the furniture, like the ticket sellers or the room guides in the big house. She turns again, coming down the field with the house behind her, and wonders what it must have been like to live here, before the tourists took over. It would have been a laugh to be lady of the manor. She imagines having a butler to wave the wasps off the wicker picnic basket, bottles of champagne and jellies in the shape of rabbits. She sees herself and Jay, in old-fashioned clothes, sitting on deckchairs that don't fall apart.

Jay cried more after the night they played at being Mr and Mrs Clutterbuck at the allotments. There were new scars on his hands and sometimes bruises on his neck. She never asked any questions, until one day she did and Jay got angry with her, slapped her across the face. It still makes her skin sting to remember it, even though it was years ago. He was sorry he'd slapped her, so sorry that he decided to tell her the truth. After that, their friendship changed forever.

Something causes her to put the brakes on before the next turn: a change of colour in the rhododendron leaves, a darker green in the low-spreading skirts of the shrubs, marking a space, as if a large animal has crashed clumsily into the undergrowth. Chloe stands up on the footrests, immediately cutting off the power to the engine. The silence is sudden and total. In that moment, the light catches an object glittering in the long grass beyond the fence. On the ground, among the thistles, lies a pink sequined sandal.

She looks at it for a long time before she notices her legs are shaking. She sits back on the seat of the mower and takes the ear defenders off. The sandal is out of her line of sight now, but she can't wipe it from her memory. Inside the sandal was a slim brown foot with painted toes and an ankle leading to a bare leg, but the rest was hidden in a dark green tent of rhododendron.

Someone is screaming and she thinks they must have seen it too, but when she turns round it's just the girls at the picnic table, laughing and running round, flapping stupidly at the wasps. Under the bushes, flies are buzzing, rising into the light like fighter pilots, before bombing back in for their next raid. She sits on the mower, wanting it to be a fox, wishing she hadn't seen a sandal and a leg, but unable to change any of it, any more than she is able to move a single muscle in her body. She is still sitting there when Bill comes striding over the field calling her name.

'Chloe, pet, you OK? Has it run out of juice?'

She knows he can smell it now because he coughs, chokes on the foulness and swears. He comes to a halt by the mower and looks over the fence. He steps forward, his hand over his mouth and nose, tentatively peering into the bushes and then he stops still.

'Christ. Christ almighty,' he whispers. 'It's that lass. Christ, Chloe, it's the one who came to see you. What have you done to her?'

CHAPTER TWENTY-SEVEN

Doncaster

No sooner had Lizzie got started on a fingertip search of AK News, than her phone buzzed in her pocket. Fully covered in protective gear, she decided it could wait. She was mapping the trajectory of petrol traces and collecting up sooty glass fragments: clear, green and brown. Window and bottle glass, she guessed, but a quick look under the microscope when she got back to the lab would confirm that. The shelves of alcohol behind the counter had been badly damaged but the newspaper section had come off worst, spirits accelerating the fire had caught the dry paper. Next to the till the lottery stand had melted and bent over, like a Dali clock. A few minutes later her phone buzzed again. She stepped out into the street and peeled off a glove. The fire officer was watching her as she unzipped her white suit. She turned her back on him and pulled the phone out of her trouser pocket.

The voicemail said to drop what she was doing and get to Halsworth Grange, where someone had kindly provided them with a fresh body. Dr Alf Huggins, the pathologist, had a dry sense of humour, but there was an element of honesty in his delight: it was usually easier to gather evidence from a recent death than a crowd attack on a property.

She put in a call to Donald Chaplin to ask him to come and finish off here. He was a gentle, avuncular soul, who might bore the fire officer to death with the chemical properties of the reagents he was using, but he'd do a thorough job while he was at it. She slipped out of her over-suit and shoe covers, bagged them up and left them for Donald to dispose of, in case she caused cross-contamination with the next site. She started the car and cruised past the parade of shops. The name, 'AK News', was just visible, but 'and Convenience Store' had blistered and peeled into a blackened mess. The broken window was covered with a temporary screen. Most of these shops had heavy toughened glass and it would take more than a bottle to smash through a window like that.

'Of course,' she said and put her foot on the brake. She dialled Donald's number.

'Sorry to bother you, Don,' she spoke to his voicemail, 'but when you get to the scene, can you have a look to see if there's something in there that shouldn't be? A mark made by a pole or something else that you'd use to break strong glass?'

Lizzie set her satnav and let the voice of Elvis Presley guide her to Halsworth Grange. The satnav had been a Christmas present from her ex-boyfriend, who'd loaded the programme of celebrity voices and preselected the King. She kept expecting it to say, *Elvis has now left the motorway*, but it never did. She remembered the framed Elvis print at Sean Denton's grandmother's house, that night, a couple of years back, the night she'd realised he fancied her. He'd changed a lot since then, grown up, she thought. She hoped he'd got a nice girlfriend now; he deserved one.

Lizzie didn't think she would ever be nice girlfriend material. She'd tried to keep things going with Guy, the Doncaster Rovers marketing manager, when she moved to London, but she saw less and less of him and began to see more and more of someone else. The overlap was messy and she wasn't proud of herself, but life was changing so quickly. She was seconded to a unit in Scotland Yard and briefly believed that this was the beginning of a new life, until she discovered the new boyfriend had a serious coke habit, which could have jeopardised her career. Breaking up with him felt like a physical injury. She couldn't eat, she couldn't sleep and she couldn't think straight. She was signed off sick and came home to her parents, who fussed and faffed and said: *I told you so*. Then her dad put the keys of the flat in Regent Square in her hand, put a good word in with his friend, Commander Laine, and suddenly she was a crime scene manager again. As Elvis guided her out through the villages she'd known all her life, an idea began to take shape. She could speak to Laine about Sean's suspension. He'd listen to her, she was sure, and he could be made to see that it would be madness to lose such a promising young officer. She pulled into the car park of a pub and dialled his number.

The road to Halsworth Grange took her back to a family outing, years ago. Her mother thought it dingy and couldn't understand why they didn't do it up, but that was the point. The inside of the house had been left exactly as it was when the last Lady Halsworth died. The cracks in the walls and ceilings were testament to how the family made their money from the coal seam underneath. Her dad told her and her brother, for the hundredth time, that their great-grandfather had mined that very seam and if it hadn't been for the grammar school they'd be down there still, digging for coal in the darkness.

'Except the pit's shut now,' her brother had pointed out.

'And I'm a girl,' Lizzie added, 'and girls haven't gone down the mines since Lord Shaftesbury banned it.' And then they took their overeducated, smug little selves to play outside on the play equipment. God, she marvelled at how snooty they were.

At the bottom of the Halsworth Grange drive, she waved her ID at the constable manning the gate and drove up to the car park, where another constable flagged her down and showed her where to leave her car. The car park itself was cordoned off. As she passed it, she noticed a group of angry people remonstrating with a woman at the ticket office about when they could get their vehicles out.

'When I'm good and ready,' Lizzie said to herself.

It amazed her that people could be so lacking in public spirit. You would think it was in their interest to solve a crime, but they behaved like it was a deliberate attempt to personally inconvenience them. At the foot of a half-mown slope of grass, a small white tent had already been erected. The whole field was taped off in a wide strip from the car park to the edge of a wooden fence and there were groups of police and CSIs nervously clustered on either side.

A tall, thickset man was in conversation with one of the uniforms. He occasionally nodded or shook his head. Every now and then he stole a glance at a woman cowering in the back seat of one of the police cars. Lizzie's new deputy was coming towards her. Janet Wheeler, ex-hockey player for the Scottish national team, held out her hand and shook Lizzie's with gusto.

'Great. Good,' Janet said. 'Glad you got here so quickly. The pathologist is down there now. He wants us there *tout de suite* so we can get what we can before CID get their feet all over the scene.'

It was warm in the protective suit and once she was inside the tent, she realised they were going to have to work quickly. The smell told her that the body was fresh, but decomposing fast and they were competing with flies. She wished she hadn't been so stubborn about waiting to check her phone in the shop. Janet was an excellent deputy, and everything was how it should be, but she should have been here sooner herself.

The photographer was covering every angle of the young woman, but Lizzie needed to stand back and make her own mental picture before they moved her. What she saw was almost a mirror image of the boy in the stairwell: a foetal position, the body left where it fell, except this victim's wound was to her neck, a deep cut to her throat, which ended below her left ear. When they turned her, they'd be able to see where it started. Blood had soaked into the ground, spreading across grass and compacted leaf mould. The blood had sprayed out and spattered the victim's top.

'Left-handed killer,' Lizzie said out loud.

'Go on,' said Dr Huggins, who was testing the body temperature with an ear thermometer.

'That looks like the end of the wound, because the skin's wide open as the blade exits,' she said. 'It's commensurate with the perpetrator being behind her, so he's slit her throat from right to left. Odd though, a messy exit as he's pulled the knife away. Like it's snagged and he's had to yank the wound wide open.'

'Any reason you're using the masculine?'

'Sir?'

'It's just that the prime suspect is female.'

'That woman they've got sitting in the car? You're joking.'

'I wouldn't joke about a thing like that,' Dr Huggins said. 'We need to be very clear about what's in front of us, Lizzie. If you have the slightest shred of doubt that this is the work of a five-foot, six-inch female, who looks like she weighs in at less than eight stone, than you'll need to be cast iron with the facts. Otherwise CID will throw the book at her and she doesn't look like she's got the strength to dodge it.'

'Did she find the body?'

'We don't know. She's not speaking. The big fellow called 999. Mr Coldacre. The young woman was mowing the grass and had come to a standstill. But Coldacre says she knew the victim, so it would be useful if she did decide to talk. There's no ID on the body, no handbag, no wallet and no cars unaccounted for in the car park, but I'm sure the detective will fill you in.'

Lizzie squatted down by the victim's feet. The pink sandals were marked with fresh grass stains and had picked up the crushed head of a clover flower. She bagged the flower and handed it to Janet.

'OK, let's start a fingertip of the field. Look for footsteps in the long grass. And get someone to go through the cuttings from that lawnmower.'

'Here,' Huggins was pointing to a mark on the girl's arm. 'Someone gripped her hard. That mark is recent, discolouration is what I'd expect from the estimated time of death.'

'Good, we'll be able to get something off it, prints hopefully or maybe sweat. But first, my little beauties,' Lizzie opened her kit box and took out a piece of sticky paper. She peeled off the backing and drew the paper carefully through the air where a couple of flies were trying their luck over the pool of coagulating blood. 'Come to mama. Gotcha!'

'Delightful,' Huggins said dryly. 'I'm pretty much done until we get her on the slab.'

'Time of death?'

'About five hours ago.'

'We'll see if the flies agree. Meanwhile, I'm OK for CID to come in now. Just need to swab this bruise.'

She brushed gently over the darkened skin and allowed herself, for a moment, to feel a wave of sorrow for this young woman who had either walked, or run, to her sudden and violent death in the undergrowth. She felt the ghost of a breeze as Huggins left the tent and heard the sound of low, male voices.

'Miss Morrison,' Khan nodded formally as he ducked into the tent, his eyes large and dark over a paper mask. She tried to set her face and her feelings to neutral. The way he'd treated Sean had lost Khan most of his remaining allies on the Doncaster team, but she had a job to do, so she tried to push that from her mind.

'DCI Khan, you're just in time to help me turn her over.'

'Were you hoping for someone else? Another detective?'

She clearly hadn't done the neutral face as well as she thought.

'Not necessarily,' she lied.

'DI Houghton and DS Simkins are both on the Chasebridge estate today, following up the Asaf murder.'

'Really?' She was genuinely surprised. 'I thought that was your case?'

'I've been informed I am too emotionally involved,' he said, with a completely level voice, not meeting her eye. 'Apparently that's not seen as a problem when attending the untimely death of this young woman.'

He stretched out a gloved hand and lifted a gold chain that hung loosely over the girl's breastbone. On his fingertip lay a tiny gold pendant, spelling out a trio of Arabic letters. His lips moved silently.

'Shall we?' She indicated it was time to turn the body.

As she slid her latex-gloved hands beneath the girl's back, she felt the bone of the shoulder blade under her fingers. It was just like the scapula of a living person, the part you feel when you throw your arm round a friend's shoulder.

'Clothes appear intact, no obvious sexual assault?' His clipped tone indicated he was back on the job, the moment of sympathy had passed.

'As far as we can see,' Lizzie said.

The young woman lay on her back, but the rigor in her limbs kept her knees bent. If there wasn't a huge gaping wound in her neck, you might think it was someone lying on the grass to watch the clouds go by. The skin beneath her eyes was smudged where her mascara and eyeliner had run. Lizzie took a sample pot and swabbed the victim's tear ducts and the skin beneath her lower lids.

'It's going to have a high sodium content,' she said. 'She'd been crying.'

She carefully picked a crushed purple rhododendron flower off the young woman's thigh and lifted the thin cotton of her patterned smock to reveal that her calf-length trousers were done up, clean and undisturbed. 'Huggins will do a proper check when we get her back. But you're right. Her clothes show no sign of sexual assault. Nothing's torn. Here, look, this stain's too dark for grass. Algae maybe? On the lower inside of her trousers.'

'What if she climbed over the wooden fence? Not dragged, at least I don't think so, that would have made more mess.'

'She definitely died here,' Lizzie said. 'Aside from the obvious fact she bled out where she fell, look at her knees.' The fabric was slightly stained, not green, but yellowy brown and on one knee the body of a spider was pressed into the cotton. '*Pisaura mirabilis*. It's their favourite kind of habitat. The rhododendron roots, not the cotton, I mean.'

'Are you saying that someone persuaded her to climb over the fence into this dank undergrowth and got her to kneel down, before slitting her throat like a butcher?' Khan said.

'It looks like it.'

'So someone who knew her? Who she went with willingly?'

'That's not a forensic question, Detective Chief Inspector. Unless the body tells us there wasn't a struggle.'

'And unless we already have a suspect for you to forensically examine.'

'The girl in the car? What's the connection?'

'Her name is Chloe Toms. She's on probation. Bill Coldacre, the tall chap you'll have passed in the car park, doesn't know the details, but says she handed over a disclosure letter, which he passed on to his boss without reading. He also said the victim visited Chloe and gave her a lift home last Monday. Chloe left in the victim's car, a little cream Fiat. Coldacre was quite precise about that. The remake, he said, of the Cinquecento, and in his opinion, an improvement.' Khan's eyes creased in a momentary smile. 'Coldacre hasn't seen this young woman since, not until he found her lying here, dead.'

'Does she have a name?' Lizzie said.

'Chloe isn't speaking and Coldacre says he can't remember if he was told, but he thinks it was a foreign name.'

'Handy,' Lizzie shook her head.

She looked again at the mark on the victim's arm and held her own hand above it, trying to match the bruising with the spaces between her own fingers. 'Let's see if Chloe Toms has got bigger hands than me.'

The tent opened and Janet stuck her head in.

'Sorry to bother you,' Janet said, 'but Dr Huggins is keen to get her bagged up, says the heat's going to make his job harder when he gets her on the slab. And Lizzie, we've found two pink sequins in the grass mowings.'

'Damn.'

Khan looked up, frowning.

'Well, it means she walked across that bit before it was mown,' Lizzie said, 'making footprints or any other DNA much harder to find. Janet, bag up all the grass cuttings, just in case.'

'A handy way to cover one's traces,' Khan said. 'Use an industrial lawnmower to obliterate your footprints.'

Khan stood up, as much as the low tent would allow, and offered her a hand. She pretended not to notice and sprung up from her squat with a quick abdominal contraction.

'She's all yours, detective.'

The air outside was warm and dry, but degrees cooler than the tent. She felt her blouse unstick from her back as she stretched. On a branch of the rhododendron, which had been pushed aside to fit the tent over the body, something caught her eye: a long black hair, hooked to the broken stem of a leaf. She reached up for it and held it for a moment, before tucking it away in an evidence bag.

Chloe Toms was sitting in the back seat of the police car. Lizzie needed the young woman's clothes, but there was nowhere obvious for her to change. Lizzie spotted a low brick shed.

'What's in there?' she asked a female officer.

'Potting shed, ma'am. Where the gardening team has its base.'

'Can you ask the girl to come with me?'

The officer opened the car door. She reached to her belt for her handcuffs, but Lizzie stopped her.

'It's not my decision, of course, but do you think that's really necessary? She's not under arrest yet, as far as I know.'

The girl didn't look like she had the strength to run. She got out of the car and stood still, waiting to be told what to do. Her face was pale and drawn, her limp, blonde hair pulled back in a ponytail. A patch of sweat had made a map of Africa through her olive green vest. Her limbs were spindly, shoulders pressing through the skin, but Lizzie could see she had strong, tight muscles roping up and down her arms. She clutched a baseball cap in her hands and as they started to walk towards the potting shed, she put it on, tugging the brim low.

In the cool, earthy stillness of the shed it took Lizzie a moment to become accustomed to the lack of light. The girl stared at the floor.

'I'm a forensic specialist, Chloe. I'm not a police officer; I'm a scientist. I need to check your clothes for evidence, to see who's been near the victim.'

The bony shoulders gave a barely perceptible shrug.

'I need you to get undressed and put this plastic suit on. We'll need your shoes too.'

She wished she didn't have to put this young woman through the indignity of taking off her bra, but she'd learnt that the cleavage was a surprisingly useful place for catching particles. The girl didn't care, she pulled off her vest top and held it out for Lizzie to catch in an evidence bag, unsnapped her bra and did likewise. Then she kicked off her shoes, peeled off her socks and let Lizzie pick them up while she dropped her trousers and offered them up for bagging. She stood naked except for her knickers. Lizzie was reminded of the pictures of liberated concentration camp victims. This girl might be muscular, but she didn't look like she'd had a proper meal for weeks.

'I'm sorry, but I need your knickers too.'

The female officer was watching and not watching at the

234

same time, struggling to show Chloe Toms some dignity. She need not have bothered. Lizzie thought about what Khan had said. If she'd already served a sentence, she must have undressed in front of people in uniform many times over.

Lizzie handed her the forensic suit.

'I'm going to swab your mouth and your fingers. And then the skin around your neck and chest.'

Lizzie couldn't see any blood on Chloe's clothes or skin. If she'd killed the victim as soon as she arrived at Halsworth Grange that morning, she would have needed access to a shower and a full change of clothes. Close up, Lizzie could smell she hadn't been near a shower for a while.

When she was done, she sent Chloe Toms back to the car with the police officer. She hesitated in the cool quiet of the potting shed. Coldacre kept the place very neat and tidy. Brooms and rakes hung from wooden racks in the ceiling. A drawer in an old dresser revealed pairs of stiffened gardening gloves in large, medium and small sizes. Lizzie bagged them up. A cupboard was labelled 'Hand Tools'. She pulled open the double doors and was confronted with an Aladdin's Cave of axes, secateurs, trowels and saws, all dangling from leather loops on their handles from rows of horizontal pegs driven into the back of the cupboard. Her eyes scanned the gently swinging objects until they came to rest on a wooden-handled blade, which scooped round and ended in a sharp point.

'That could do it,' she said aloud in the silent, dusty shed and reached for it, barely noticing as the metal sliced across the fingertip of her latex glove.

CHAPTER TWENTY-EIGHT

Doncaster

Sean wandered slowly up towards the Eagle Mount flats. His dad would surely be awake by now, and, if he'd remembered anything at all about Sean staying there, he might be wondering where he was. Sean couldn't face the stinking lift and took the stairs instead, his footsteps echoing off the concrete. He reached the first floor and heard the clunk of the lift arriving at the same level. He opened the door to the landing slowly, waiting to see who would step out of the lift. The metal doors jerked apart, but whoever was in there was moving with an equal degree of caution. Sean stayed on the stairs, letting the door close on the tip of his shoe, and levelled his eye up to the open crack as the slight figure of Saleem Asaf stepped out. The boy stood for a moment, listening, then approached Jack Denton's door. He put his ear to the door and listened again. Saleem obviously didn't like what he heard and pulled back.

Sean opened the door from the staircase and they looked at each other, frozen. Sean was about to say something when

Saleem put his finger to his lips. Sean shrugged and held the door wide open for the boy, who slipped through and took off up the stairs, his footsteps so light he made no sound. Sean followed him.

They kept going up and up, until Saleem pointed to the roof and Sean felt an old chill of fear. *Don't go up on the roof, some kid got shoved off.* But that was another time and another tower, and anyway, the killer had served her sentence. He put his hand on his back pocket to feel for the folded-up newspaper he'd been carrying that morning, but it wasn't there. He must have dropped it on the way up.

The metal door to the service ladder had a broken lock and they were up and through the hatch in moments.

'So?' Sean said, taking in the view, breathless from climbing up ten floors. 'What's so important that we have to meet up here? Were you looking for me or do you often pay my dad a visit?'

'Didn't even know you had a dad, till someone told me.'

'Who told you?'

Saleem shook his head. 'I said to that other copper at the police station that I wanted to speak to you, that I would only speak to you. He just ignored me.'

'Saleem, I'm not . . .'

'On the case . . . yeah, he said that. But you're safe, man. You're the only one that is.'

'You got into the back of the Health Centre right under my nose. Were you trying to get caught?'

Saleem grinned at him. 'That's what I mean: you're the only one with any brains.'

Sean sighed. He wished he had Saleem's faith in his

abilities because none of this was making any sense at all. He walked across the roof and sat on a low wall that surrounded a large air extraction unit.

'Can't talk there,' Saleem jerked his thumb at the white, slatted construction. 'All the kitchen fans come out here. They might hear us.' He walked towards the opposite corner of the tower, which looked across the ring road to the woods and the quarry beyond. 'I heard about you. You're the one that cracked that caravan case. You were famous, man. I wanted to be a copper for time after that, you know?'

'You still could.'

Saleem barked out a laugh that had no humour in it. 'Nah, I'm never going be like you. You're the real thing, CID, plain clothes now and all that.'

'Thank for your high opinion of me, Saleem, but I was only seconded, a temporary thing, and right now I don't know what's going to happen. I may be done with the police anyway; I've been suspended.'

'Seriously?'

Sean nodded, wondering why he was telling him all his secrets.

'Whose voice did you hear, Saleem? Downstairs?'

'If I tell you stuff, you never heard any of it from me, OK? I don't want anything to do with it. I get stuck in the middle and this happens.'

He lifted his sweatshirt and showed Sean the large gauze bandage over his stomach wound.

'So why do you trust me?'

'I want you to make sure Ghazala is looked after.'

'What makes you think I can help?'

238

'You know people: housing, social and that.' Saleem shrugged like it was obvious. 'Sooner or later, my luck's going to run out, man. I'll end up dead or inside.'

'I won't be able to stop that from happening. You need to make changes in your own life, Saleem.'

'Whatever. Look, what I'm trying to say is, I'm worried about Ghazala. The shop's gone, everything in the flat is ruined; she can't live there. But if I'm not there, she's got no one. People will push her around.'

'What about your auntie?'

'It's complicated.'

'Your dad?'

'Worse, don't ask.'

'Saleem, how old is Ghazala? She must be able to make up her own mind.'

'She's twenty-two. My dad wanted her to go with him to Pakistan, to help look after my granddad, but she was scared to go. She didn't want to come back with an old man for a husband, or not come back at all.' Saleem seemed suddenly older than his years; his fidgety, streetwise energy had all but fizzled out. 'She had some trouble with a boy, years ago. It messed up her marriage chances. Like I said, it's complicated, but trust me, I don't want her to be on her own.'

'I'll do what I can to help your sister,' Sean stood up, moving closer to the boy, uneasy now he was standing so near the edge. The rail was only waist-height and flimsy. 'But in return, I want you to tell me what you know about Terry Starkey.'

Saleem froze, the muscle in his cheek pulsing.

'Why don't you ask him yourself? He's sitting in your dad's flat.'

239

'That's whose voice you heard?'

Saleem nodded. 'That's him. He mustn't know I'm here and he can't see me talking to you.'

'Does he know I'm a police officer?'

The boy shrugged. 'Don't know. I ain't said anything. Does it matter?'

'God knows what my dad's told him, but I think Starkey might have got the idea I've been in jail.'

Saleem's laugh sounded more natural now and he was smiling when he turned round. 'Who's going to believe that?'

'Where were you when your cousin Mohammad was killed?'

Saleem's face dropped. 'I just got told the game was on, some sort of shakedown. I was hanging around the rec and some white guys I knew said I could earn a bit of cash, if I wanted to help. They sent me down Attlee Avenue. I had to keep a lookout and make sure no one got out down there. I didn't even know who they were chasing. I walked down to the bottom corner, then I walked back up, didn't see nothing.'

'Who were they?'

'Just some lads. There was some money in it. Seemed like easy money.'

'Who stabbed him?'

'Don't know. I stopped to roll a ciggy. Honest, I didn't even know who the target was until . . .' His voice caught in his throat and he turned back to the view of the ring road, hiding his face from Sean. 'I wouldn't have done anything to hurt Mo. He was my cousin. He stuck up for Ghazala.' Saleem sucked his teeth and spat over the wall of the block. 'They must be laughing at me now, those boys.

Same ones who came to burn down the shop, I reckon.'

'Why would they do that?'

'Because they're racists, of course. You want a name? There's an older guy called Gary MacDonald, fat and bald. You can see videos of him on the internet doing all the Nazi salutes at a football match.'

'So that's what this is about, is it? Far-right extremists? What about the drugs?'

'What about them?'

'Terry Starkey reckons drugs are coming in to the estate from the Asian community.'

'Of course he'd say that. Come on, you're supposed to be the clever one. You work it out. I've got to go. We're staying at my auntie's and I'm supposed to be tucked up on the settee, letting my stitches heal. My sister will kill me if she knows I've been here.'

Despite his wound, Saleem moved quickly and reached the exit door in three strides. He swung himself round onto the ladder, wincing only slightly from the injury. Sean thought how in another world, the boy could have been a gymnast.

'Wait! You can call me if you think of anything else,' Sean said. But Saleem had gone and the metal door clanged shut at the foot of the ladder.

Sean made his way back down the stairs. When he reached the first floor, it was as if the boy had never been there. He pushed open the door to the landing and stopped dead. Terry Starkey was standing by the lift with Sean's copy of *The Doncaster Free Press* in his hand.

'Did you drop this?' Terry said.

Sean nodded. 'Must have done.' He tried to think quickly,

thoughts scrambling round his brain. 'Look, um, I'm sorry for your loss. Must be hard to know she's out. The one who did it.'

Starkey's face was expressionless, the bright blue eyes fixed on Sean's. 'Yeah, thanks, it is. I was looking for you as it goes. The old man didn't know when you would be back.'

'Just got in. Been for a wander round.' He watched for a reaction but got nothing back. 'What can I do for you?'

'I thought we should get to know each other a bit, we've got a lot in common.'

'Really?'

'More than you'd imagine,' Starkey's laugh hit the metal door of the lift and bounced back off the concrete wall behind them. 'Jack said you might be able to help me.'

Sean's mouth was so dry he thought his tongue would stick to the roof.

'I've got myself one of these new smartphones,' Terry continued. 'Your dad was trying to help me set something up, but he hadn't got a clue. No offence, mate. Me mam's the same, out of the bloody ark, technophobic. We're two of a kind, aren't we?'

Sean forced a smile; it felt like a snake slithering across his face where his mouth used to be.

'I can have a go,' he said.

'It's that Twitter I want to get on to, for the CUC campaign.'

'Oh. There's always the library.'

'No, don't fancy that, too public. See what you can do with this. No idea how to do half the stuff on it beyond phoning and texting.'

He held out a phone. Sean took it. It was a very recent model. He turned it over in his hand and noticed a set of tiny lines scored into the gloss black. Not brand new, then.

'Nice phone. Shall we go back in? We might as will sit down while we're sorting it out.' Sean knocked and his father opened the door immediately, as if he'd been listening.

He had an idea that he might be able do something clever with Starkey's phone while he was installing Twitter, but he didn't really know what he should be looking for. The recent calls list might give him some names or numbers, but probably nothing that would mean anything. Added to which, Starkey was watching him with those blue eyes, hungry to learn how the phone worked.

'You miss a lot inside, don't you?' Terry Starkey said. 'There's always something new.'

Sean nodded and looked up to see his father winking at him. He'd like to know how long he was supposed to have been away for and what the charges were. Jack's mad grin suggested he'd been embellishing a story while Starkey had been in the flat.

'It's loading now. Do you want a beer or something while we're waiting?'

Starkey's eyes lit up. 'Sweet, mate.'

'Nowt in the place, lad. I told you,' Jack said. 'I'm on the Twelve Steps.'

'You don't mind if Terry gets a couple in for me and him?' He risked the first name. They were mates now, weren't they? He pulled a twenty-pound note out of his wallet. 'Have you got wheels? I'd go but I'd have to walk, and it's a fair hike to Tesco, now the shop's out of action.'

There was a moment in the stifling, musty air of Jack Denton's flat when Sean thought Terry Starkey had rumbled him. His blue eyes flickered and settled on the phone.

'OK,' he said finally. 'But don't put anything out on that Twitter until I get back. The first message from the CUC is coming from my mouth.'

'Of course. I'll have it all set up. No worries.'

Sean saw him out and positioned himself by the kitchen window. A few moments later, Terry came out of the flats and turned into the entry road which ran down the side of Eagle Mount One. If he'd been parked at the front Sean would have missed him, but now he had a full view of Starkey's vehicle. He pulled out his own phone, held it up to the window and snapped. The dark blue BMW started moving. He snapped again, hoping it wouldn't be a blur, as the car turned onto the ring road and out of sight.

The toilet flushed and his father came into the kitchen.

'You and him are getting on all right, son.'

Sean wondered which version of the truth his father could handle and decided to keep the white lies to a minimum.

'I didn't realise that was his brother, the one who got pushed off.'

'Oh, aye, terrible business. And they've let her out already.'

'Looks like it.'

Jack shuffled into the living room. Sean followed him and leant against the door frame, Starkey's smartphone in his hand. He checked that the Twitter app was loading and wondered what information he should be looking for on the phone. Somewhere, in the back of his mind, he knew

244

the answer was none. He was a suspended constable with absolutely no powers to go nosing around a citizen's phone.

He weighed the phone in his hand and the faint scratch lines caught his eye. He crossed to the living room window and pulled back the curtain to let the light in. The scratches were faintly tinged with fuchsia pink, like nail varnish. He slid the cover off his own phone. There were similar scratch marks, only on his phone they were white. Same as his cover. It looked like the scratches on Starkey's phone could have been caused by a pink plastic cover sliding on and off. He didn't think it was infringing anyone's human rights if he noticed something that was in plain view and it was plain to see that pink wasn't Terry Starkey's colour. It wasn't rocket science to assume it was stolen.

Sean looked up to see that his dad had fallen asleep, his jaw slack and a line of dribble running into the stubble on his chin. With nobody watching, Sean clicked 'Contacts', but it was empty. There were no missed or recently received calls either. It obviously had a clean SIM card.

Sean realised he needed to hurry up. He checked and saw the app had loaded, then started to set up the account. It was requesting an email address. He'd have to wait for Starkey to get that. He went into messages and sent a text to his own number labelled 'test'. He could say he needed to know Starkey's number as part of the account set-up, which turned out to be true. He went back to the home screen. Behind the date and time there was a photo. He didn't think it had the quality of a standard issue screensaver, more like a photo someone had taken. A tree full of pink blossom curved round the screen in a garden somewhere, and to the left of the picture he could make out the side of a house, a brick wall and white window frames.

He went back to the kitchen where there was no chance of his father opening his eyes and asking what he was up to. Then he put Starkey's phone on the drainer and used his own phone to photograph the cover image. He turned it over. He wasn't sure he'd be able to pick up the scratches, but maybe Lizzie would know if there was some way of enhancing the image. She popped into his head and lingered there for a moment, like the hologram of Princess Leia in *Star Wars*, but he shut her out; he didn't have time. If Starkey found out what he was doing, he'd probably beat him to a pulp.

He wasn't sure what all the icons meant, so he touched various things, but nothing made sense. Suddenly, like an open sesame, a swipe across the screen opened up the settings menu. He scrolled all the way down and there, nestled at the bottom, was an icon labelled 'About Phone'. He clicked it and scrolled slowly through a mess of words and numbers, trying to understand what they meant.

When the knock came on the door, he almost jumped out of his skin. He fumbled with Starkey's phone, to get it back to where he'd started, and squeezed his own phone into his pocket. As he opened the door, he hoped the lack of light in the dingy hallway would cover the heat in his face.

CHAPTER TWENTY-NINE

Halsworth Grange

Lizzie carried the evidence bags back to the police vehicles. The doors to the CSI van were open and Janet was loading several more bags into its temperature controlled interior.

Janet wrinkled her nose in the direction of the bag she was holding. 'I'm not sure this lot's going to tell us very much, but at least we've done our civic duty and left the place cleaner than we found it.'

'Have we finished with the cars?'

'The last one's being processed. The uniforms have collected all the personal details of the drivers, so once Khan gives the OK, we can let them go.'

'Good. I wonder if he's had a chance to talk to the woman at the ticket office.'

'Why don't you ask him?' Janet nodded to where Khan was sitting at one of the picnic tables. He pushed the hood of the white suit back and ran a hand over his hair, down his cheek and across his beard. He was staring across the field to the white tent.

'What's on your mind?' Lizzie said, laying the gardening implement she'd found in the potting shed down in front of him. This time she was careful the blade didn't tear the clear plastic bag she'd put it in. She'd narrowly missed slicing her finger.

'North Yorkshire police just called back.' His voice was deadpan, his eyes resting on the curve of the blade. 'Chloe Toms is better known as Marilyn Nelson. She's registered at a bail hostel in York. Our victim also has a name: Taheera Ahmed. She was a staff member at the hostel and Marilyn's link worker, supporting her resettlement. As it happens, DS Simkins went to have a chat with Marilyn, or Chloe as she's now known, about Mohammad Asaf. A local Doncaster woman thought she'd spotted Nelson on the Chasebridge estate the day before Asaf died.'

'She's the Chasebridge Killer? Jesus.' Lizzie sat down on the end of the bench. She stared out towards the slope of lawn and the bank of rhododendron bushes, where the white tent stood.

'Where's Bill Coldacre?'

Khan paused. 'Gone home.'

'Where's home?'

'He lives in a tied cottage on the estate. Why?'

'Did someone swab him before he went?'

'He has no motive.'

'And she does?' Lizzie snapped.

'She's certainly a suspect.'

'Have you spoken to the woman at the ticket booth?'

'Do you want to swab her too?'

Lizzie turned round to face him. She could have slapped the superior expression off his face.

'I don't mean to overstep any lines of command here, DCI Khan, but I do need to get forensic evidence from anyone who may have been on-site at the time of death. So yes, I'd like her DNA, please, and if it's not too late, I'd like the DNA of every single car owner before they leave.'

'Good luck with that.' He turned away and looked across the field again. 'I'm not a complete fool, Lizzie. I know you're pissed off with me about Sean Denton. On my way here I had a call from Commander Laine himself.'

Lizzie tried to keep a poker face. There was an old boy network in every walk of life, and even if she wasn't part of it, her father was, and those old boys hadn't wasted any time.

'All right,' he said. 'I accept I may have been hasty. I assure you, I will do the right thing and withdraw the disciplinary proceedings against Sean Denton. Are you happy now?'

It was difficult to know how to respond, so she said nothing.

'Look,' he said, 'taking up the time of all my constables to get swabs and fingerprints of twenty-two irate day trippers isn't going to improve relations now, is it? We have a prime suspect with a motive. What more do you want?'

'You are unbelievable!' She stood up. 'What happened to innocent until proven guilty? There's no physical evidence that Chloe, or Marilyn, or whatever we're calling her, killed Taheera Ahmed. In fact all the evidence I'm looking at suggests she didn't. You know what I think?'

'What?'

'I think it's some ritual thing, I don't know, like an honour

249

killing. She let her attacker march her across the lawn and over the fence. She didn't fight back.'

She held her breath, expecting a reaction, but he continued to focus on the white tent at the other end of the field.

'Did you know her?' she said.

'What?' He snapped round. 'You think I know every Pakistani girl in South Yorkshire?'

'No, of course not. That's ridiculous. But when you first saw her, it seemed personal. I'm sorry. It's none of my business. I'm prying.'

He sighed and looked back at the tent. 'It's our job to pry. I don't blame you.'

Lizzie replayed in her mind the order in which Chloe had unzipped her jeans, handed her the clothes and done up the white suit.

'Do you even know, detective, if your suspect is left-handed or right-handed?'

A wasp flew close to her ear and she waved it away.

'A bit of a coincidence, isn't it?' he finally said. 'A released killer and a murder in the same place? I don't believe in coincidences, Lizzie.'

'Neither do I, DCI Khan. I believe in empirical evidence and I'm not seeing any. What if the murderer is still in that group, biding his time until we let him drive out of here?'

'Call me Sam.'

'Excuse me?'

'Call me Sam. It's my name.' There was a softness in his voice and a weariness too.

She sat down again, opposite him this time.

'What's with the blade?' he said, as if he'd only just noticed the wooden-handled knife in the bag.

'It's not the murder weapon,' Lizzie said. 'It's too big. But it's very sharp and it's got me thinking. I want to ask Bill Coldacre where he gets his knives. He's got a whole selection in there that we don't usually see in town.'

Khan shook his head. 'He's not our man. If he wanted to kill someone he'd snap their neck in one squeeze. Have you seen the size of his hands? No, this is much more precise, more personal. You're right in that sense. She was crying. Not fighting.'

Lizzie thought about the imprint on Taheera's arm. The hands were bigger than hers, but were they as big as Coldacre's?

'I'd like to check him over all the same.'

A uniformed officer was approaching the table. 'Sir, Mrs Coldacre wants to get home to see if her husband's all right. Someone's told her she'll need to give a statement. She says she's ready, so if you could . . . sorry, her words, not mine . . . get a move on.'

'Mrs Coldacre?' Lizzie looked up. 'Happy families?'

'His wife. She was on duty in the ticket office this morning,' Khan said. 'I'm sure when you meet her you'll agree she's not the type either.'

A woman as broad as the gardener, but a foot shorter, was making her way over the grass towards them. Her wavy grey hair was short and neat and she wore a spotless white blouse over a navy skirt. Her Halsworth Grange badge read – 'Brenda, Ticket Office, Happy to Help'.

'Are you the detective?' she spoke directly to Lizzie.

'Er, no. This is Detective Chief Inspector Khan. I'm Lizzie Morrison, Crime Scene Manager. I'm sorry if those members of the public were giving you a hard time. It's my fault we've had to keep their cars here.'

All the time, she was looking at Brenda Coldacre's hands, trying to judge the size of her grip.

'Don't worry, pet. Water off a duck's back to me. You get all sorts in my job. Now, Detective. I'll give you five minutes then I need to get back to my Bill. He's had a terrible shock and his heart's not what it used to be.'

Lizzie tested the hypothesis in her mind that Brenda Coldacre was capable of marching a young woman across a field, over a fence, forcing her down onto her knees and slitting her throat. It had a certain efficiency that suited the older woman, but beyond that it was unlikely.

'Do you mind if I take some DNA from you,' she said, 'while we're here?'

'Be my guest. Do you take it from my mouth like they do on the telly?'

Lizzie nodded and got a sample pot from her case, while Brenda opened her mouth like a willing dental patient.

'That tickled!' Brenda Coldacre laughed for a moment, then caught herself. She reset her mouth to a grim, tight line.

'Now. This is what I wanted to tell you. I got to work at eight-thirty this morning, as usual. That gives me an hour to tidy up the hut, process the numbers from yesterday and get everything ready to open at nine-thirty. Bill went up to the big house for a meeting with Giles, the land manager. The girl, Chloe, she came in shortly after nine-thirty. She's allowed to start late because she comes all the way from

York. She has a long journey, but she's very committed.'

There was a challenge in Brenda's voice that made Lizzie warm to her.

'Did anyone else arrive before Chloe?' Khan said.

'Well this is what I wanted to tell you about. At around nine, a car came in. Now normally I wouldn't have had the barrier up, but Bill said should he do it on his way past to save me the bother later? I've had this problem with my shoulder, you see, so I said yes.'

She paused for breath and Khan waited. Lizzie hoped Brenda would get to the point before his patience ran out.

'It was a little car, white or off-white, with a dark red roof.'

'The make?'

'I'm not very good at car names. But you see them around. They look sort of old-fashioned, but I bet they cost a bomb.'

'Did you see who was in it?'

'Just a driver. I didn't get a good look but I think female and she had dark hair. I was going to go and tell her she was too early, but I figured she'd work it out. She didn't come by on foot, so I thought she must be waiting in her car. Anyway, at about twenty-past nine, I went to put the sign out. You see where it is?' she pointed to the corner beyond the picnic area, 'another car came in then. Well, that's not so unusual, to be ten minutes early, so I didn't take much notice.'

'Can you remember anything about it, Brenda?'

'Dark, blue or black, quite a posh make. A feller driving and someone in the passenger seat.'

'And did they come to buy a ticket?'

'Well, it all got very busy after that. There were three

253

minibuses full of cub scouts. So I was sorting out their group ticket, then it turned out there was a fourth minibus on its way, and they wanted to wait, because the scout leader was in the last bus and he had all the money. Anyway, you can imagine, they were all milling around and then the families started arriving and there was a disgruntled pensioner and his wife, who'd driven from Spalding and didn't expect to have to wait around with nowhere to sit. They could have been the people from the dark coloured car, couldn't they? I mean there are some very generous pensions nowadays. But no, they wouldn't be, because they came in after the cub scouts arrived.'

Khan waited while she caught her breath again. Another wasp buzzed over the table and he ignored it.

'Try to picture the driver of the first car, Mrs Coldacre. Was there anything about her, apart from the fact she was female?'

'I didn't take a proper look, I'm sorry.'

'Did any woman come in on her own to buy a ticket? A young woman of Pakistani heritage, perhaps?'

Brenda shook her head. 'I'm not saying we don't get Asian visitors, because we do, Mr Khan, and we offer everyone here at Halsworth Grange the same welcome and the same treatment, but to be honest, I would have noticed, because at this time of year it's usually families.'

'And as far as you can tell, the driver of the little cream coloured car never appeared at the ticket office?'

'I don't believe she did. No.'

'And Chloe Toms walked up the drive after both the cream car and the dark coloured car, but before the cub scouts?'

'Definitely after the two cars, because I'd already put the sign out.'

He rubbed his beard in circles and smoothed it down again. Lizzie was distracted for a moment by trying to guess whether it would feel soft or bristly. She pulled her attention back to Brenda Coldacre.

'Are the older couple or the cub scouts still here?'

The older woman shook her head. 'The cubs were doing us in the morning and the farm park this afternoon, so they left at about noon, but I can give you a contact name and number, because someone lost their camera and I said I'd ring if we found it. I can't help you with the miserable pensioners though. Oops, I'm sorry, I shouldn't say that. I'll be one myself before long. It's just what we call them when no one's listening.'

A half-smile twitched across Khan's face for a moment. Lizzie had come across people like Brenda before. The shock of a horrific crime made them burble and make jokes they would later regret.

'Thank you, Mrs Coldacre,' he stood up and shook her hand solemnly. 'You've been very helpful. I'll walk down to the ticket office with you and get that phone number, if that's all right. Then you should go and see to your husband.'

'Mrs Coldacre, do you mind if I pop in and see Mr Coldacre in about half an hour? I need to get a DNA sample to rule him out,' Lizzie caught Khan's eye as she spoke and he nodded. She hoped he was right about Bill, almost as much as she hoped she was right about Chloe. Ruling people out was the only way to start ruling people in.

CHAPTER THIRTY

Doncaster

Under the harsh lights of the pathology unit, Lizzie watched Alf Huggins explore Taheera Ahmed's body with the delicacy of a surgeon who still has a life to save.

'Good skin, healthy nails and hair.' He lifted the fleshy tissue of her upper lip and looked at her teeth. 'Money's been spent on some top quality orthodontic work.'

'Was she sexually active?'

'Hymen intact.'

'Not bad for a twenty-three-year old.'

'Now if I'd made that remark, you'd tell me off,' Dr Huggins said. 'It may seem old-fashioned to you, but a crime of passion doesn't have to involve sexual intercourse.'

'Could it involve, for the sake of argument, a staff member and a vulnerable client? Both young women?'

'Not my department, I'm afraid.' Alf Huggins stood back and looked at Lizzie. 'Khan says the family wants the body to be released as soon as possible, on religious grounds. Any particular requests about what organs you'd like me to keep, as we're pushed for time?'

'The wound itself is our main clue. Without a murder weapon, that's all we've got. One of the girls in the lab is getting something oil-based from the neck swabs,' Lizzie said. 'It would be good to know what we're looking for. Running a test for every lipid could take weeks.'

'I don't think they'll be very happy if I send her back without a neck. Hard to detach it from her head, you see.'

The slit in Taheera's throat looked like a second mouth, flat lips of skin pushed opened in a grimace.

Dr Huggins leant in for a closer look. 'It's almost surgical, a very clean cut, but then the exit is so messy. Makes me think of a cheese knife, except they're never sharp enough for a decent piece of cheddar.'

'Are you into gardening, sir?' Lizzie saw the surprise shoot across his bushy eyebrows.

'More my wife's department. She's into the good life, grows all our veg, flowers for the table, that sort of thing.'

'What sort of tools does she use? I mean, is there a particular brand of gardening knife she favours?'

He straightened up and shifted the weight off his hip. 'Let me think, yes, there was something I got her for Christmas, professional sort of knife. Swedish name, I think. Bloody sharp.'

'Like a pathologist's scalpel?'

'Almost. But a little thicker.' He smiled and pinched the two sides of the wound together through his latex gloves. 'Yes, yes. Sharp but wider than a scalpel, maybe one, one and a half millimetres at most. Crikey, don't tell me you think my wife Anne's responsible.'

'Don't worry,' Lizzie smiled. 'But thanks, that's very useful. How long have I got before we have to hand her over?'

'Well, it's pretty clear what killed her; I just want to check for anything that tells us who. I won't rush it. Three hours? Four at the most?'

'Perfect. Let me see if I can find something to fit that wound.'

She turned to go and then remembered something else. 'I'll send the crime scene photographer across, if he won't be in your way. I'd like a light source treatment on her arm and her face. Hopefully someone left some prints.'

Lizzie went back to her office and picked up her car keys. She nearly collided with Donald Chaplin as she rushed out of the door.

'Got a minute?' he said.

'Thirty seconds. I've got to catch the garden centre before it closes.'

'Here.'

Lizzie looked at the sheets of paper Donald was holding in front of her and tried to understand what she was seeing. He pointed with the tip of his biro at a smudge the shape of the Isle of Wight. Around the edge, it was just possible to see the frilly lines of a partial fingerprint.

'It's bottle glass and it was wedged under the bottom of the fridge at AK News, protected from the heat. I've picked up concentrated petrol residue and a few tiny drops of human sweat. Here are the fingers that held the bottle that started the fire.'

'Nice one.'

'We can have a go at matching the print,' Donald said, 'but it's a bit of a long shot as it's only partial. Any chance we can get a DNA test on the sweat?'

'Yeah, go on. Leave it with the paperwork on my desk.' There was already a neat stack of samples waiting to go off to the lab; Lizzie tried not to think of the budget implications.

Donald chewed on his pen. 'The fire officers didn't find any petrol on the pavement, right? Even after everything's been soaked in water, you'd still expect to find traces of droplets falling away from the angle of an object being thrown. And here's another thing, the window glass had mainly blown outwards, most of the glass inside the shop is from the stock, and from the front of a chiller cabinet. You said it yourself, how do you break a window that thick with one little bottle? You don't. The back of the shop is shuttered up. The internal doors to the stockroom at the back and the flat upstairs are all closed. The smoke spreads but not the fire. Don't you think that's a bit too neat?'

'Maybe,' Lizzie said.

'We know the crowd was getting out of control. Several people were carrying these torches – well, they're more like a big candle wrapped in brown paper – and if one or two of these are thrown at the shop door, no harm done, but the incendiary device was meant to do real damage. The fact that there are no casualties inside the shop is bothering me.'

'I'd say that's a good thing, wouldn't you?' she said. 'Otherwise we'd have another murder inquiry to deal with.'

'Perhaps they were tipped off.'

'Who by?'

'Someone they knew.'

Lizzie looked at the whorls on the partial fingerprint, like the edges of geological contours. 'That could be anyone on the Chasebridge estate, Donald. It's the local shop.'

Within half an hour, Lizzie was standing in the tools' section of Fulton's Garden Centre. She found the Scandinavian brand of tools that Huggins had mentioned. It was definitely the upper end of the sharp knife market, with the same leather loops she'd seen in Bill Coldacre's potting shed. There was a long blade, like the one that had cut into her glove, then a stand of folding knives, ranging from tiny finger-length knives to heavier items that looked like they could slice the branches off a small tree.

'Can I help you?' A man wearing thick spectacles and a green apron was watching her. 'Are you looking for something in particular?'

'Yes, I am.' She looked back at the display and willed him to go away, but he was still there.

'These are excellent tools. A very popular range. What sort of task did you have in mind?'

She could hardly say throat-slitting, although she'd like to see the look on his face if she did. 'Do you have something that's shaped like a cheese knife? But not for cheese, obviously.'

'A cheese knife,' he looked at her as if she was simple, his eyes behind the spectacles almost as large as the glass lenses that covered them. 'Do you mean like a pruning knife?'

He reached over her head and took something from the shelf with a wooden handle and smart leather sheath. He was about to take its cover off but she held her hand up to stop him.

'That's OK. Don't open it. Is this how it comes from the manufacturer?'

'Yes,' the assistant sounded puzzled.

'Thanks. I'll take it.'

Lizzie walked over to the till and got in the queue.

'Darling!'

It was her mother's voice, loud enough to carry across Yorkshire, as her dad always said. Lizzie looked to see where it was coming from and spotted her mother in the company of two other ladies she recognised as neighbours from the village. They were sitting at a table in the garden centre café, separated from the main part of the shop by a stretch of ornamental trellis.

'Come and join us!'

Lizzie waved the pruning knife hopelessly and nodded towards the till, where she was third in line. The neighbour women were grinning at her and she half expected one of them to blurt out some platitude about how much she'd grown. The queue moved forwards and Lizzie heard her mother's voice, only partially lowered.

'She works very hard,' and then in answer to something one of the others must have asked, she added in a stage whisper, 'oh, yes, much better off without him. We were terribly worried.'

Lizzie could feel the skin on her neck reddening. She needed to be back at the lab, measuring the width of a knife blade, phoning the manufacturer and finding out what oil was used to treat the metal before they were packaged for sale. The man with thick glasses was stacking some boxes next to the till and she called to him.

'Excuse me, but what should I use to keep it sharp?'

He straightened up and came over. 'Honing oil. Shall I find you some?'

'Yes, please.'

'Right you are, Elizabeth.'

She was startled that he'd used her name, but as she looked at him more closely she realised how she knew her. He was the son of one of the women at her mother's table, thirty going on fifty, and still living at home. She snatched a glance across to the café and shuddered. She wasn't meant to come back here, slip into a life she'd grown out of, where everyone knew her business and felt no shame in discussing it while she was in the same room.

She paid and clutched her plastic bag in front of her like a shield, walking slowly over to the table, where her mother and her two friends were finishing off a pot of tea. They'd each had cake. The remains of cream, jam and chocolate were still smeared on the china.

'The evidence suggests Black Forest gateau. Was it good?' She smiled at her mum, conscious how proud she would be of this pathetic party trick.

'Oh, Mary, isn't she clever?' One of neighbour women gushed.

'It's my job,' Lizzie shrugged.

If only it were as simple as that. Part of her would have loved to accept the offer to sit down and play the guessing game of who ate what for afternoon tea. She could let the village gossip wash over her, the everyday stories of planning objections and divorces. The mother of the man with thick glasses had tried to push them together once, years ago when she was about seventeen. Lizzie was praying he wouldn't be called over to join them. The other woman was chattering away about her own son and his life abroad, an American wife, a child on the way. Tremendously happy. How lovely. How lucky.

'I'm sorry, I've got to go. I'm in the middle of a job.'

'Darling, surely you can stay for five minutes, there's still some tea in the pot.'

'I really do need to get back. See you later, Mum. I'm not sure when I'll be over, maybe next weekend?'

Lizzie turned away and her mother's voice followed her out of the garden centre.

'Why don't you come back home for supper when you finish, darling, and stay the night? What about a nice piece of chicken and some couscous? She doesn't eat properly you know, living on her own in that flat . . .'

Her mother's voice was silenced by the closing glass doors. You don't choose your family, she thought. Outside she blinked in the bright sunshine and decided she needed to focus on the job. Taheera Ahmed was lying on a slab in the morgue, lost to her family forever.

CHAPTER THIRTY-ONE

Doncaster

A dog was barking. Barking then silent. Barking. Silent. Barking. Sean tried to turn over but his head was pinned to the hard ground. His tongue was thick, stuck to the roof of his mouth. He opened his eyes and a bright light burnt into his retina. He closed them again and the light lingered, an orange glow the other side of his eyelids. The barking had stopped but there was another sound, like an animal choking, gasping for air and exhaling in a shuddering grunt. It came again, choke, gasp, grunt. Sean tried to reach out around him to feel what was there but he couldn't move his arms, they were trapped inside some kind of bag, a bag that rustled and slipped. This is my sleeping bag, he thought, and this is morning.

He turned his head slowly, weighed down by a dull pain, and forced one eye open. An army of beer cans stretched in front of him across the carpet, some still upright, others fallen in battle. Beyond the troops lay the enemy, snoring on the settee. Last night they had got very, very drunk. Sean was still drunk but he guessed Terry Starkey was in a worse state. He remembered trying to pace himself, keeping each can going longer until he was downing one for every two of Starkey's. He focused on the empty cans and tried to do the maths, but the pain intensified between his eyes and he let them close again. Snatches of their conversation jerked back into play. Starkey talking about his brother's death, how it had messed him up. Something about how that girl had to pay the price for what she'd done to his family; he knew where to find her now. He remembered Terry grabbing the front of his T-shirt and twisting it up under his chin.

'I like you,' he'd said. 'You're Jack's lad and I'm going to trust you. But you fuck me over, Sean Denton, and I will kill you.'

Sean remembered his dad appearing in the doorway and mumbling something about the noise and how he was trying to get to sleep and Starkey letting go and laughing that loud, hard laugh, like it was all a game and they were mates, weren't they? It was getting late when Terry Starkey asked the question Sean had been dreading.

'So what were you inside for?'

'Drink-driving. Caused a bit of criminal damage.' It might have been true. He knew plenty who did it and got away with it.

'Your old man thinks you did time for drug dealing!' Starkey laughed and Sean brushed it aside, mumbling something about how his dad got mixed up on account of his liver disease.

'Old bugger says the first thing that comes into his head!'

'You must never drink and drive.'

Now Sean was remembering when Terry said that, and how he'd been wondering whether he should make something up about his prison life, but he didn't need to because Terry started on some story about his car, the BMW, which wasn't his at all. Sean tried to recollect what he'd said. It was something about being nobody's chauffeur, so he reckoned the car was his now. Sean couldn't follow why he thought this.

'Could get a fucking house off him if I wanted it.' Terry had grovelled in his pockets and pulled out a pouch of tobacco and some papers. 'Got any blow, mate? I could kill for a bit of blow.'

Sean shook his head.

'Good job I know his number!' he tapped his head with the phone. 'I can memorise numbers, me!'

He prodded the screen and put the phone to his ear. 'Yo, man! It's me. Yeah, me . . . No, you never said . . . Don't fucking put the phone down on me . . . Shit.' He dialled again and listened for a moment. 'OK, have it your own way, I'll leave a message. This is my message. I want some gear, can you sort that? Some nice bud, you can get it off my boy, Gary. Get a fucking taxi to the snooker hall and pick it up and bring it to me at number 9, Eagle Mount One, Chasebridge, you got that? You better have got that, because I fucking own you man. I own you . . . What the . . . ? Fucking ran out of time, fucking thing's beeping at me. Still, I think he got it.'

Now it was morning and Sean realised the delivery had never arrived. Which was just as well. He remembered going to the toilet and gulping handfuls of water from the tap.

When he came back, Starkey had slumped on the settee, fast asleep. He took the cigarette out of Starkey's hand and took off his shoes, tucking his feet up on to the settee gently, so as not to wake him.

With the light drilling directly into his brain, Sean tried to focus on what else had happened, what else had been said, and whether he'd remembered the gist of the evening. He'd had an idea. Had he followed it through? Yes, it was coming back to him; he'd used one of Terry's trips to the toilet to find the recording function on his own phone and he'd recorded some of what Terry had been saying. He lay back and covered his eyes with his arm. That was better, darker. The snoring from the settee was steady and rhythmic. Soon Sean's own breathing fell into the same pattern and he let sleep overtake him again.

The next time he woke it was because someone was speaking. It sounded like they were saying 'worry folk' but then it became clearer and Sean recognised his dad's voice and he was saying 'what the fuck.' Then his dad kicked his leg through the sleeping bag.

''Ere you little bastard, what the fuck have you done to my living room?'

He didn't feel drunk any more. He sat up and looked into the angry face of Jack Denton, spittle gathering between the gaps in his teeth and his hands balled into fists. He felt the old fear from his childhood and the urge to run. He was on his feet before he knew it. Something slid down inside the sleeping bag and hit the floor with a muffled clunk through the padding. He knew it was his phone and that it was important. As he bent down to retrieve it, he took his eye off his dad and missed the foot that was heading for a sharp kick to his kidneys. Sean staggered, tripped on the sleeping bag and fell, scattering the beer cans and their remaining contents across the carpet. He landed with his face next to the settee. Looking up, he saw it was empty. Terry Starkey had gone.

The room stank of beer and something sharper, which he hadn't noticed last night. As he sat up, more carefully this time, he saw it in his father's hand: a small bottle of Bell's whisky, half empty, lid off. His father put it to his lips, his eyes shining, and swallowed a mouthful.

'Good lad, that Terry, knows how to show his gratitude for my hospitality, not like you, you little shite. I thought you'd come to help me out. What you up to? Police work is it? Not in my fucking flat. He warned me you were up to summat. Taking pictures. I saw you. Where is it?'

'Where's what?'

'Your phone, what you've been taking pictures on. He wants it. He'll pay me good for it too.'

Sean sat still. He needed to grab his jeans and T-shirt, find his shoes, and get past his dad. Jack took another swig from the bottle. Sean spotted one shoe behind the door and the other under the settee. The smell of whisky was the smell of his childhood and it made him want to retch. He reached for the shoe and Jack stiffened at the movement.

'You're not going anywhere until you give us that phone.'

'It's round here somewhere. You're welcome to it. There's nothing on it.'

Jack grinned at him. 'You lied to me, didn't you? Saying you'd come to tidy up. You're just a frigging snitch.' He gulped from the bottle again. There was only a couple of inches left in the bottom now. 'We sort things out our own way round here.'

'You shouldn't be drinking, Dad. What happened to the Twelve Steps?'

'They made me blind,' he shouted, thumping the door frame with his fist. 'See this?'

Jack Denton held his hand up in front of his face. 'See this hand? This arm? Twisted out of shape, broken by a dirty pig.'

Sean knew the story off by heart. The strike, the picket line, the police, the dogs. The broken wrist and fingers that wouldn't heal. The stiffening, the tingling and the numbness and the way the hand closed into a permanent fist. The way the alcohol took away the pain so it didn't matter when the fist hit out at brick or glass or plaster, or flesh and bone. The last drop of whisky disappeared into Jack Denton's mouth and the bottle hung by his side, empty. He blinked as its contents hit the back of his throat. Sean drew his knees up and tucked his feet under him. He pushed himself to standing and gathered the sleeping bag in front of him. The bottle in his father's left hand swung up and back towards the door frame, where it shattered against the splintering wood.

Sean ran forwards, roaring words that he'd stored inside for years. Names filled his mouth and spilt out.

'You fucking tosser! You bastard! You filthy fucking bastard!'

He slammed into his father, pushed him over, shocked at how light he was. It was like felling a feather pillow. Jack landed, gasping, on the pile of dirty clothes on the hall floor. Sean glanced back into the living room where his own clothes and shoes were strewn between the beer cans, but Jack was already getting back on his feet, the broken bottle still firmly in his hand. Sean ran, in underpants and socks, to the front door, clutching the sleeping bag. He threw himself out onto the landing and the bottle arced up and flew past him, shattering in front of the lift. He yanked open the door to the staircase and headed down to the exit.

At the bottom of the stairs he stopped. There was a pain in the heel of his left foot. When he looked back, he saw he'd left a trail of smeary blood marks. He must have stood on a piece of glass. Balancing on one leg, his back against the outer door, he peeled back his sock. There was a neat cut on the heel. He pressed it carefully to check there was no glass still in it, but it felt clean. Covering it again, he pressed it hard to staunch the bleeding. He couldn't believe the irony. Assault on a disabled man in Eagle Mount One, forensic trail leads to suspended police constable. Maybe he should call it in himself. At least he'd get a ride back into town.

He stood there, naked except for his socks and pants, with only a sleeping bag for cover. His wallet and keys were in his jeans. All he had was his phone, his precious phone, loaded with evidence against Terry Starkey, safely at the bottom of the sleeping bag. He let his head fall back against the cool metal door. Evidence of what though? He couldn't remember Terry telling him anything that made any sense. Maybe he should just wipe it all and go back up to his dad, talk him round, at least get his clothes back. As he slid his hand into the bottom of the sleeping bag and fished out the phone, he heard the mechanism of the lift, ascending from the ground floor. Prising open the door to the street, he glanced out. There was a man standing, hands on hips, on the edge of the pavement, with his back to the building. Jeans, bomber jacket and a thick neck under a bald head. Gary MacDonald. A passing car had covered the sound of the door opening and Gary hadn't turned round, but there was no chance of Sean getting past him.

He let the door close. The lift had stopped. It had only gone up one floor. He couldn't go out on the street, so he'd have to go up and he'd be trapped if he couldn't get past the first floor landing. He held his phone tight in one hand and grabbed the banister to launch himself back up the stairs, trying to keep the weight off his bleeding heel.

At the first floor he could hear voices. It sounded like Terry Starkey and Jack. He thanked God that the access door had no window and took the stairs two at a time. He passed the second floor, pausing to catch his breath at the third. He listened again. Nothing. He risked another floor and almost didn't make it. A door was opening onto the stairwell beneath him and he had a fraction of a second to duck into the doorway of the fourth floor landing, bracing himself as flat as he could manage.

'Here, Terry! Look at this!' He heard Gary's voice and heavy feet on the concrete. 'He's dropped his sleeping bag.'

'I told you to stay out there, he could have got past you when you came inside.'

'He won't have gone far.'

Sean gambled on the fact that Terry would be looking down, not up, and hooked his hand behind his back to grab the handle of the door. It was fire safety standard, with stiff sprung hinges. Silently and slowly, Sean prised it open.

'He's bleeding, look! The old bugger's cut him up.'

The sound of their mirthless laugh covered any sound Sean made as he slipped through and closed the door softly behind him. He reorientated himself on the fourth floor. Same layout, same smell. He had to keep off the stairs now so he pressed the lift button and felt a surge of relief as it rattled up towards him. He stood to one side, ready to run, as the metal doors slid apart, but it was empty. Once inside he selected the top floor. He didn't know what he was going to do when he got there, but he couldn't keep running, leaving a trail of blood for them to follow.

He was passing the fifth floor, straining to hear any sounds outside the lift. A door banged, but he couldn't tell if it was above or below him. The sixth floor went by and he realised he had to do something to stop the bleeding. He stood on one leg, leaning against the cool steel wall of the lift and held his foot in his hand. There was nowhere to put his phone, and he needed both hands, so he placed it carefully on the floor. He pressed hard on his heel, hoping the pressure would help. At the seventh floor his phone lit up, the dog-bark ringtone resonating inside the metal box. Of course, it wasn't a dog he'd heard in his sleep, it had been ringing when he woke up and he hadn't answered it. He'd been mucking around with his ringtones last night, half cut on cheap beer and trying to bond with Terry Starkey.

The caller ID on his phone read Gav. He picked it up and answered.

'Mate!' Sean said. 'Am I glad to hear you!'

'Where are you? I tried earlier . . .'

'I need some help, urgently,' Sean's voice was low. 'I'm at my dad's, I was . . . shit man, I'm in a lot of trouble, where are you?'

'Doing house-to-house on the bloody Chasebridge estate. That's why I called, to see if you fancied picking up your badge and doing some work for a change. You're off the hook, by the way. Khan's pulled his complaint.'

'That's great.' He was passing the ninth floor. 'Can you do me a favour? Probably a life-saving favour as it happens. Can you get to Eagle Mount One with a car? Now? I need you to get me out of here. Can you? Oh, Christ . . . Gav, Gavin, can you hear me? Oh fuck, fuck, fuck . . .'

The lift juddered towards the tenth floor, but the phone was dead, the battery empty. The lift stopped but the number ten didn't light up and the doors remained closed. He was stuck between floors.

CHAPTER THIRTY-TWO

Doncaster

DCI Khan had turned his chair round and was sitting with his elbows leaning on the seat-back, his head resting in the cup of his hands as if his neck was too tired to support it. Another briefing was due to start in ten minutes and Lizzie wanted to make sure the AV equipment was working so she could share last night's discoveries from the lab. Khan's eyes were closed, so she crept past him, assuming he was as tired as she was. They'd both left late last night and somehow ended up wandering into the Taj Mahal restaurant. He hadn't talked about the case or asked her very much about herself, but he'd opened up a bit about his own life, and she'd ended up feeling guilty about how she'd behaved towards him at the crime scene.

'Oh, it's you.' His voice startled her.

'Yes, it's me. Who were you expecting?'

'I have very low expectations, Lizzie, and they're getting lower by the day.'

'I'll take that as an insult, I think.'

She turned on the laptop, but nothing happened to the projector, which was attached to the ceiling.

'Do it in a different order. Try turning the projector on first.'

'You're wasted as a detective, Sam,' she smiled. 'You'd be better off in technical support.'

But he didn't return her smile. He looked beyond her to the two boards where mirror images of Mohammad Asaf and Taheera Ahmed faced each other.

'Yesterday, I went to see another parent who'd lost their child,' he said, standing up stiffly and walking over to the picture of Taheera. 'I watched the light go out in her father's eyes. I've thought about your theory that it's a family thing, a so-called honour killing, but when I saw him, I saw that whoever took her life, took his too.'

She waited, but he didn't say any more. The silence between them was broken by the electronic whir of the projector lens opening up. She started the laptop again and eventually an image formed on the screen. The girl's arm and the finger-shaped bruises filled the frame. She clicked forward to an enhanced image of the prints, clicked again and added an electronic Post-it note that said 'pigskin'.

'Gloves?' Khan said.

'Standard gardening gloves. No fingerprints.'

'Like the ones in the potting shed that Chloe Toms had access to?'

'Yes. But clean. The pattern's the same, but the ones I took from the potting shed left traces of soil behind, which were easy to see under the microscope. This glove had never been used for gardening.'

She clicked on to another image. It could have been the wavy edge of a conch shell. When she zoomed out it became a section of the fatal wound across Taheera's throat.

'That's some sort of oil, you see? It's been picked up in the light source treatment. It may take a couple of days to run all the tests, but yesterday I discovered that the manufacturers use a specialist petroleum-based oil to finish new knives, whereas your average gardener buys an off-the-shelf, vegetable-based honing oil. There's no dirt or rust in the wound, which also suggests it was a brand-new knife. Like this one.'

Lizzie put the open pruning knife, in its clean plastic bag, on the table in front of Khan. He shuddered slightly.

'A new knife and new gloves?'

'Exactly,' she said.

'I'll get someone to phone Halsworth Grange to find out whether Bill Coldacre has been to the garden centre recently. He might have provided the girl with new equipment, she's only just started after all.'

'You still think she did it?'

Khan shrugged. 'She didn't deny it.'

'So she's spoken?'

He shook his head. 'Either she's mad, or clever, I can't decide. I was in there for four hours with her yesterday and she didn't utter a word. She wouldn't answer any questions, but she did draw this.'

He took a piece of paper out of his pocket and unfolded it.

'Who is it?' Lizzie said.

'I don't know. It's not a great work of art. I've got one of the constables putting it through EvoFIT to see if it throws up a name.'

'Do you think she saw this person?'

'Hard to say. But she drew it with her right hand.'

'So you believe me?'

'Possibly.' He rubbed his beard and she could see how tired he was. 'Yesterday, I was being harassed by the duty solicitor and her probation officer to either charge her or let her go. The probation officer said we could have her recalled to prison if we think she's breached her licence. The sighting of her on the Chasebridge estate would give us enough to get her locked up.'

'She seems very vulnerable.'

'More vulnerable than Taheera Ahmed, who's dead?' he said. 'More vulnerable than her grieving family?'

Lizzie flicked through her slide show and avoided eye contact with Khan. She couldn't get Chloe Toms' numb expression and bony ribs out of her mind.

'I'm not an ogre, Lizzie,' he sighed. 'You're right. We haven't got enough to hold her. When I came back from the restaurant last night, I arranged her transport and she went back to York.'

'To the hostel?'

'Yes. At least we know where she is. I've asked the North Yorkshire force to keep an eye on her and let us know if she does anything unusual. Thanks, by the way, for dinner, I appreciated it,' he was rubbing his beard again. 'Once she's over the shock, we'll try again. I'm sure she knows something.'

Lizzie was relieved, but she didn't have time to dwell on

it. She still had to put the notes from Donald's work into the next slide show. This promised to be a long briefing, with three cases to cover. Two homicides and an arson attack had sent Doncaster's crime statistics into orbit and Commander Laine wasn't happy.

CHAPTER THIRTY-THREE

Doncaster

Sean pressed the alarm but nothing happened. He put his ear up to the mesh of the speaker but there was no sound; he doubted whether it was connected to a control room. It was cool in the lift. The hairs on his arms and legs were bristling. The floor was damp and stank of piss. He looked up at the ceiling and tried to work out which section was the escape hatch. If he was in a James Bond movie, he would push it open and climb out. He shivered. It couldn't be a coincidence that the lift had stopped between floors. It must be something to do with Terry Starkey. They'd worked out where he'd gone and decided to trap him. He didn't think thick-necked Gary's hips would fit through the hatch, but Starkey's might.

He listened to the building. A door banged quite close, somewhere above him, and he heard the sound of a young child, giggling.

'Bye bye, dada,' said the voice.

'Come on cheeky!' A woman spoke, only feet away.

The lift had stopped just below the tenth floor. He could hear the wheels of a buggy squeaking and then coming to a stop. There was a pause.

'Bloody thing,' the woman said.

Sean wondered if he should call out.

'It better not be stuck again.' The wheels of the buggy squeaked and someone was banging on a door. 'Lift's broken. Here, Dave, give us a hand down the stairs, I can't manage her and the buggy.'

There was a man's voice, indistinct from behind the door of a flat, then the sound of the door opening. Sean didn't want them to go down the stairs, he didn't want them to leave him, trapped where Starkey could find him.

'Hello! Can you hear me?' he called.

'Hello, hello!' The toddler's voice sang out in reply.

It sounded as if the adults weren't there. Perhaps the man needed to get dressed, perhaps he was arguing about having to help. The toddler kept repeating 'hello' and it seemed like an age before he heard anyone else.

'I'm going to go down that housing office and I'm going tell them,' the woman was saying.

Sean took a deep breath and shouted. 'Hey! I'm stuck in the lift. Any chance you could call the emergency number for me? I've got no signal and the intercom's not working.'

But before she could answer, the lift mechanism whined into life, as if his words had undone a spell. It shook and lurched upwards. The doors slid open and Sean stood, in pants and socks, in front of a young woman, her little girl and a man in a Doncaster Rovers T-shirt. All three stared at Sean. Nobody spoke. Suddenly the door to the staircase was flung back. There was nowhere for him to hide.

'Come on!' Saleem said, breathless in the open doorway. 'Let's get up on the roof. We'll be safe there. I came back to talk to you and I saw Terry Starkey's lot running round in circles. They've been up and down the stairs and now they've gone back outside. They're looking for you, aren't they?'

Sean nodded, his muscles flooding with relief. He followed Saleem to the stairs and gave the young family one last look but they'd already turned away. The woman was pushing the buggy into the lift and the man gave her a peck on the cheek, as if this was the beginning of any normal day.

Twenty minutes later Sean was being driven away from the Chasebridge estate. It might have been PC Gavin Wentworth's driving, or it might have been relief, but Sean was feeling very sick. He opened the window and gulped the morning air.

'Steady on, mate,' Gav said, laughing. 'You'll catch a cold dressed like that.'

Gav had been laughing, on and off, ever since he'd set eyes on Sean crouching on the roof next to the air vents in nothing but socks and boxer shorts. Alerted by Saleem's shout of: 'Oi, copper, up 'ere', Gav had taken the lift and by the time he'd arrived, the boy had disappeared, but not before showing Sean the control panel, in its not-so-locked cabinet on the roof, in case he ever needed to stop the lift again. On the way down they'd hammered on Jack's door but there had been no answer. He'd either gone out or passed out.

'Can we go via my nan's? I need to pick up some clothes.'

'Well, make sure it's your uniform. You're back with me, son, as soon as the briefing's over.'

'Great news,' Sean said. 'I should have stayed on the roof.'

'Feeling's mutual!' Gavin laughed and pressed his foot down on the accelerator.

The briefing had started when they arrived. As he sat down, something caught Sean's eye. Stuck to the corner of the whiteboard was an A4 piece of paper with a childish drawing of a face. The cheeks and lips were out of proportion but the eyes were unmistakable. Terry Starkey was staring straight at him.

He couldn't follow what was being said. In his two days off the job the world had gone mad. A girl was dead. The picture of her body surrounded by leaves and flowers was like something artistically staged. He'd need to be very sure, but her eyes, the set of her nose, even in death, were familiar. Then it struck him. She was the girl in the picture in the library window, in the black and white photo of the playground.

He forced himself to listen. Each whiteboard had its separate family tree, its lines and patterns linking people and places, the fire at AK News, prints on a fragment of glass. DCI Khan was saying that the motive was unclear, but he drew a line in red pen to a photograph of Saleem, who was also being linked to low-level drug dealing on the estate.

Khan was talking about the Asaf brothers, the fathers who were both away in Pakistan. One had lost a son and both had lost their business, so why hadn't they come back? Sean's head was swimming and his mouth was dry, then DI Rick Houghton had his hand up, he was saying Sean's name.

'PC Denton might have some useful information, DCI Khan, can we invite him to address the briefing?'

Khan nodded and Sean made his way to the front. As he went past, Rick whispered:

'Tell them about the CUC and Starkey.'

His colleagues were egging him on with grins and even a thumbs up from Carly at the back. Even DS Simkins offered him a nod and half a smile. Sean felt a little light-headed.

'Excuse me. I think we need to consider that Mohammad Asaf's murder was racially motivated. I . . . um . . . I was at a meeting, by mistake, which turned out to be organised by a right-wing group. A key player in that group is a man called Terry Starkey and, look, sorry this isn't what I was going to say at all, but that drawing, on the other board, looks very like him.'

If he was expecting everyone to stand up and applaud him, he was disappointed. There was a brief silence, broken by Rick clearing his throat.

'Um,' Sean tried to get the ideas in his head into some sort of order. 'I think Terry Starkey is in the middle of this. It was something Saleem Asaf said. He knew the lads who'd been paid to chase his cousin, presumably to his death. Sorry if that's not much use, but if Saleem can identify those involved in killing Asaf, maybe we should talk to him again.'

'And he trusts you?' It was Khan. The question seemed straightforward enough, no hint of sarcasm. Maybe Sean had been forgiven.

'Yes. I think he does. He may have just saved my life.'

There was a ripple of laughter across the incident room and Sean realised that news of his escape in his underwear to the roof of Eagle Mount One was now common knowledge. He sat down again, his face and ears burning, but Khan was watching him, stroking his beard and nodding slightly, as if something had clicked in his mind. Sean needed this briefing to be over so he could fill Khan in on some of the other things he'd worked out, but first he needed get to the toilet. A cold sweat gripped him and his stomach was churning.

People were standing up and a hubbub of conversation broke out around him. Images from the briefing merged in his mind: bodies and fingerprints, Lizzie had been waving a sharp weapon and some gardening gloves, and all Sean could do was breathe in and out of his nose, deep, slow breaths to keep the nausea still. He got to his feet and pushed his way out.

He was only just in time. With one hand on the edge of the cistern he emptied his stomach and then some. He left the cubicle and washed his face, rinsed his mouth and stared at the hollow-eyed fool in the mirror. The more he stared, the more he could see his father's features starting to creep up on his own. He turned to go and let the door of the gents' toilet swing shut behind him. Along the corridor the door to the incident room was open and the rows of chairs were empty. He could hear two female voices raised in an argument. He looked in. Lizzie Morrison and DS Simkins broke off when they saw him.

'Sorry, am I interrupting?'

'You OK?' Lizzie said. 'You look pale.'

'Rough night.'

'Lucky you!' she said.

'Not really.'

DS Dawn Simkins was smiling at him. It pushed her cheeks into an unfamiliar pattern, as if the muscles weren't used to it.

'Good to have you back, Denton. If you've got a minute, there's something I'd like to discuss with you. In private.'

Lizzie was busy removing a memory stick from the back of the laptop. Sean didn't want her to go, but Simkins was pointedly waiting for her to finish and leave them alone.

'Catch you later, Sean,' Lizzie said.

'Yeah, where can I find you . . . ?' He faltered. 'If there's something I want to . . . I need to catch up a bit first, but . . .'

'Extension 205, any time.'

Then she was gone and the square jaw of DS Simkins was back to normal.

'Let's get down to business.'

Sean looked at the boards and the drawing of Starkey. He wasn't sure what it was he was searching for and then he saw it. Someone had written a list of vehicles under a heading which said: *Halsworth Grange. Small white Fiat. Scout minibus. Dark posh car.*

'Could "Dark posh car" be a blue BMW?'

He reached for his phone to find the photo, but the battery was still as dead as before. Someone here must have the right sort of charger. He'd have to go on a hunt.

'Never mind that, I want you to look at this,' Dawn Simkins was tapping the end of a pen on a document printed on green paper. 'Have a seat.'

Sean sat down.

'What is it?'

'Whistle-blowing Policy. Can't you read?'

Fuck off.

'Of course I can. I mean, why?'

If he'd been expecting to have the word 'whistle-blowing' put under his nose, he'd have seen it straight away, but he was still trying to break it down, match it to something on the incident board, but it didn't fit.

'Wendy Gore suggested we have a word. Professional Standards?' she said, moving closer, the soft muscle of her upper arm pressing against his. 'Now, I'm here to support you if you want to file a complaint against DCI Khan.'

'Dawn, can I call you Dawn?' Sean said, moving away. 'I don't need this right now, what I need is a phone charger, so I can get on with some police work. So you can stick your whistle-blowing policy up your arse, and unless you've got a phone charger up there too, I'll see you later.'

He almost skipped out of the room. He might be off his head on lack of sleep and lack of food, but he was buzzing. In the corridor he found Rick Houghton.

'What are you smiling at?'

'Nothing,' Sean said. 'Have you got a spare phone charger that fits this? I've got a load of stuff. I don't know what to make of half of it. God knows if it's even admissible evidence, but we need to look at it. Khan needs to see it too. Our very own DCI Sam Nasir Khan. Let's keep him here, shall we, where he's wanted? And send that old trout back to Sheffield.'

'Sean?' Rick said. 'Are you still drunk?'

'Probably.'

CHAPTER THIRTY-FOUR

York

The smell of burning wakes Chloe a few seconds before the high-pitched wail of the fire alarm kicks in. She lies still, letting the siren pound in and out of her ears. It'll stop in a minute. If she jumps up and heads out to the garden, she'll only be sent back when they work out it's just someone smoking in the toilet. She turns on her side and puts her pillow over her head to block out the sound. On the other hand, it could be a real fire and if it is, the smoke will suffocate her before she burns to death and she won't know anything about it. She shuts her eyes and wonders what colour the smoke will be that kills her. She opens them again to check it isn't really coming under her door. Next to her bed she notices a plate. She remembers Emma bringing it in late last night. There was a peanut butter sandwich on it. Emma didn't ask her where she'd been or what happened, she just gave her the sandwich and went away again.

Then it all comes back, everything that happened

yesterday. There is a moment when you wake up in the morning and it's not there. The thing that's happened, the grief. The waves are far out to sea and you don't even see them. When Jay died, they would come crashing in within seconds. She would be drowning in sorrow for the rest of the day. Only the first snap of light on waking was clear, then the rest was muddy and thick and impossible to breathe in. When she found out she would never see her mum again, she was already in prison. Three things to realise every day. Jay's dead. Bang. I'm inside. Bang. I'll never see my mum. Bang. Then they wrapped her up in medication, like a cotton wool nest that kept her up and away from the grief. The waves still rolled in, but she was safe from them, as if they were breaking somewhere far below her.

She knows how it goes now. This feeling before the big wave, the storm wave. She watches it, watches herself, wondering why she's so calm. She pulls herself up to sitting and looks at the plate, the fire alarm bashing her skull with sound. It's empty, so she must have eaten the sandwich. Emma will be awake now, lining up outside on the terrace for the fire drill. Chloe should get dressed and go out to join the others, or someone will come banging on the door, shouting at her. She loved Taheera and then she was so angry with her that she thought she hated her. Now it's too late.

She gets out of bed and takes a pair of jeans from the wardrobe. The screwed-up, white forensic suit is on the floor. They kept her work clothes and her boots at the police station in Doncaster. She wonders if she'll ever see them again. She pulls on her clothes and follows another couple of girls down the stairs, but nobody's hurrying. The new night officer, who used to be a screw, has a clipboard and is ticking off names.

'Come on, ladies. You need to get moving as soon as the alarm goes. No good waiting, could be fatal.'

There are some mumbled responses. Nobody believes it's real. Chloe crosses the terrace to where Emma's standing, rolling herself a cigarette. She feels seventeen pairs of eyes watching her.

'Eh! Someone came home late. On a date were you? Nice fancy dress costume you had on.' A voice cuts loud through the sound of the fire alarm, followed by a brittle, false laugh.

Chloe doesn't turn to see who's speaking. More than one curtain twitched at the front of Meredith House when she stepped out of the police car in her luminous white suit, long after curfew.

'You OK?' Emma says. 'Want a ciggy?'

Chloe shakes her head.

'Police were here yesterday, asking questions. She let them in your room,' Emma says quietly, flicking ash in the direction of Clipboard Woman.

The other women are watching Chloe. She wonders what they know.

'Don't worry,' says Emma. 'I told 'em nowt. Said you were dead quiet, no bother. Didn't even have to lie.'

'Thank you.'

Chloe startles herself with the sound of her own voice, even though it comes out as a whisper. It's the first thing she's said out loud since she climbed onto the lawnmower yesterday, and behind those first two words a whole surge is waiting. She bites down hard, clamping her jaw shut, jamming her knuckles against her mouth, her lips against her teeth. She stares at the green, open leaves of a geranium in a pot at the edge of the terrace, concentrating on its white flower head. Inside she taught herself not to show her feelings, to grow a thick skin and become an expert in keeping her thoughts to herself. Now she needs to think of something, anything, that will keep the tears back, so she thinks of the plant names Bill was teaching her. It's not really a geranium, he said, but a *pelargonium*. She starts listing all the Latin names of the varieties in her head. When she gets to *pelargonium formentosa*, the siren stops.

'That's it ladies, false alarm. Who's been smoking indoors?'

Talking and laughter break the stillness as the women shuffle back inside. Emma is standing in front of her. She's pinching the end of her cigarette and putting the stub in her pocket.

'Talk to me, babe. What happened to you?'

Her arms open and her hands come to rest on Chloe's shoulders. She squeezes gently, drawing a sharp needle of pain up through Chloe's chest, until she can't fight it any longer and falls forwards into Emma's waiting arms, sobbing against her shoulder. Her knees give way and Emma falls to the ground with her, until they're both kneeling and Chloe can't stop the torrent of tears that heave up and through her body, soaking her face and Emma's hair. They stay like that for a long time, until there's nothing left. When they disentangle their arms, she sees that Emma's been crying too.

'Look what you've done,' her friend says, gently, 'started me off now.'

They're both sitting on the ground looking at each other, unsure of what to do next. Emma gets up first and brushes a bit of dirt off her trousers before reaching out a hand. Chloe takes it and steadies herself, standing shakily, feeling so much lighter than she did before.

'Let's get out of here,' Emma says, 'go for a walk and then, if you want to, you can tell me what's been going on. And if you don't, well that's all right, I'll fill you in on last night's *Coronation Street*. Deal?'

Chloe tries to smile. She takes Emma's waiting hand and they walk in through the back door, past the TV room. They go past the front desk and Emma waves to Clipboard Woman. They go out of the front door and onto the street.

'Which way?' Emma asks and Chloe turns right towards the main road and the city centre.

They link arms and walk together. Chloe tries not to think about Taheera. She can't help her now. They walk in silence until they come to a familiar row of shops. Chloe stops outside the charity shop.

'When I've got some money, I'm going to buy that cup,' she points to the white china set with the blue irises round the rim. 'Then the plate and then the bowl, then I'll come back and get the saucer. I don't really need it, but it would be a shame to leave it. I'd like the full set.'

Emma starts to laugh but then she stops. She can see Chloe's not joking.

'I bet you could have the cup,' she says, 'if you gave them fifty pence.'

Chloe turns away.

'Here, I'll get you the cup. I'll get you the whole set. You can pay me back.'

Emma pulls something out of her pocket. It's a thick, folded wad of notes. She peels off a tenner. Chloe stares at the money.

CHAPTER THIRTY-FIVE

Doncaster

While Sean's phone was charging, he went to get a couple of coffees and a bacon sandwich from the canteen. He stuffed the food down as soon as he'd paid for it. Nothing had ever tasted so good. He looked out for Khan in the canteen and all along the corridor to the CID office, but he didn't see him. He wondered if his boss knew DS Simkins was trying to stab him in the back. Probably. But who was behind her, holding the arm that was holding the knife? She didn't have the drive to have thought of it herself.

When he got back to the CID office, Rick was on the phone.

'When was this? . . . And is that a regular order? . . . They have an account. Right. Do you have a record of who signed for them when they were picked up? Mm. Thanks . . .'

Sean put Rick's coffee down. 'Flat white, no froth,' he said.

'Speak for yourself,' Rick said.

'Funny. What was that about?'

'Fulton's Garden Centre, the only South Yorkshire stockists of the Scandinavian pruning knife, which Lizzie thinks sliced Taheera Ahmed's throat open. They took an order from Halsworth Grange about two months ago. A range of items, including a pruning knife, something called a bushcraft knife, an 8cm locking knife and several pairs of pigskin gardening gloves. They haven't sold anything to Halsworth since, except a pair of size five work boots that Coldacre picked up himself, first thing Monday morning.'

'Is that unusual?'

'Not particularly. But we need to have a word with Bill Coldacre and see if he's missing anything.'

'I'll ring him, if you like.'

Sean looked at his mobile, but it had only charged ten per cent. He picked up one of the phones on the desk and checked it had a dial tone.

'Nothing better to do until I can find Khan. Gav's on a break, so I may as well make myself useful.'

Sean got through to Halsworth Grange and asked for the gardens' extension. He listened to it ringing and ringing, and was about to give up, when it was answered by an out of breath Bill Coldacre.

'Sorry, couldn't find the bloody thing. It was easier when the phone was stuck to the wall.'

Sean explained why he was ringing.

'Why are you asking me?' he said, 'I thought you'd arrested the girl?'

'We think the murder weapon might have come from Fulton's. They don't sell many pruning knives in the

294

summer and they keep meticulous accounts for their regular customers. So I need to know if you're missing one, brand new, straight out of the packet.'

'I'll have a look.'

Sean could hear him moving about, the click of a door opening and the rattle of metal and wood.

'Thanks,' Sean said. 'And while you're at it, can you tell me the names of anyone else you've had working there in the last two months?'

Coldacre gave a hollow laugh. 'That's not hard. Until the girl started, I've been on my own for a month. We had to let the last trainee go.'

'Did he or she come via the Probation Service too?'

'Aye. Lazy bugger. Terry Starkey his name was.'

'Thanks. Thanks very much.'

Sean scribbled something on a piece of paper and showed it to Rick who frowned initially, trying to decipher Sean's writing, then let out an expletive.

'That policewoman that was here,' Bill Coldacre was saying, 'the one in the white suit?'

'Miss Morrison, yes, the scene of crime manager.'

'She was asking about knives. I keep them in size order, you see, so it's easy to find what you want. I've had three new ones this season. Hang on. There's a pruning knife missing, sharp little beggar.'

'Yes,' Sean said.

'It's not here. It's gone. Never even used the bloody thing.'

'Anything else?'

'Aye, there should be a little pocket knife, good for cutting twine.'

'Would that be what they call a "locking knife", 8cm blade?'

'Aye, that's the one.'

'Thank you, Mr Coldacre. You've been very helpful.'

As Sean put the phone down, Khan swept into the room, flicking his car keys back and forth like worry beads.

'Denton? Need a word. Not here. My car. Now.'

'But . . .'

'Now!' Khan was already heading back down the corridor.

'Here, take your mobile,' Rick said. 'Tell him what you've found out about Starkey.'

'Two knives, Rick, he's missing two,' Sean managed to say over his shoulder as he followed Khan.

The black Range Rover was parked at the back of the police yard, slantways across two spaces. Khan clicked the locks off and they got in.

'Where are we going, sir?'

'We're going to have a chat. Pigs have big ears, so we're going to have a little chat in private.'

'Right.'

'What are you playing at, Denton?'

'I'm not sure . . .'

'What did you call DS Simkins?'

'I don't think I called her anything. I asked if she might have a phone charger up her . . . OK, there's no way I can make this sound what it isn't. I was rude to her. But did she tell you why?'

'Go on.'

'She was asking me to make a formal complaint about your conduct.'

'Oh.' Khan stared straight ahead at the concrete wall in front of them. 'I see. And so it begins again.'

'Sir?'

'Do you know why they sent me here, Denton?'

'No.' He remembered Simkins sharing her theory with him, but he'd thought at the time it was bollocks.

'Because I brought a complaint against a senior officer for racism and it stuck. He was disciplined and ever since then I've been playing cat and mouse with one ridiculous accusation after another.'

'What a cow.'

'Steady on, son. She's just following orders and, at the end of the day, she's not a bad officer.'

'But she was sent to spy on you. To get something on you being sexist, I think she said.'

'Sexist? Oh my, they really are scraping the barrel this time; they'll be trying to stick me with being a communist sympathiser next. Sexist? Please.' He thumped the steering wheel. 'Ah, but I gave her almost as good, didn't I? I gave her bullying a junior, white working-class member of the force.'

'With a diagnosed specific learning difficulty. Serious shit, that,' Sean smiled. 'Mind you, she took the piss out of my reading, so maybe I could counter-attack with a complaint against her for that. Joking, of course.'

'Look, I appreciate your support, Sean. And I'm sorry you've been dragged into this. But it's my fight.'

Neither of them spoke for a moment, then Khan gathered himself.

'What was Rick saying about your phone?'

'It's about Terry Starkey,' Sean said, 'the guy in the drawing. His brother was killed, pushed off the top of the Eagle Mount flats . . .'

'. . . by Chloe Toms or Marilyn Nelson, as she used to be known.'

'Exactly. And Bill Coldacre's just told me that Starkey was also placed by probation on an apprenticeship at Halsworth Grange. He was there two months ago, when the last lot of tools and gloves were purchased. There are two knives missing. Damn, I forgot to ask about the gloves.'

'Don't worry,' Khan said. 'I'll put someone on to that.'

There was a silence in which it felt to Sean as if Khan was waiting for him to say more, like being in school when they all got told off for something nobody would own up to and he felt like putting his hand up, to make it end.

'There's something else, sir,' Sean licked his dry top lip. 'He turned up at my dad's place last night. You could say your scheme paid off.'

'My scheme?'

'Sending me back, as it were.'

'Really?'

'Well, I got him talking and I managed to record some of it. Listen.'

The Range Rover had a docking station for his phone, so they had the glory of Terry Starkey in four-speaker, high-quality stereo. Sean winced at the sound of his own voice.

'I sound so thick.'

'Let's just say you were in role.'

'Thanks.'

Sean hoped the click of the ring pull and the hiss of another beer can being opened wasn't too obvious.

'What did he mean by that? "Now I know where to find her" . . . ?'

'The drawing she did. If Chloe saw him at Halsworth Grange, then chances are he saw her. Look, I've got a picture of the car he was driving last night. Here.' Sean took the phone off the dock and flicked to his photos. 'Could that be the dark car Mrs Coldacre saw? I've uploaded it to Rick's computer; he's running some checks on it now. Terry said something about a guy owing him; the car was payment for something. That's coming up . . .'

Terry Starkey's voice slurred out of the speaker.

'He can't help showing off, can he?' Khan said.

'There's another thing; Mohammad Asaf took a photo of the second victim, the girl. It's on display at Chasebridge library. Here, I took a couple of pictures.'

'Sean, I wish you'd use a notebook like everyone else.'

'Fair point, guv, it's just I haven't really had time to sit down with a pen and paper. It's all happening a bit fast. You see? It's her. They knew each other.'

'I think we need to go back inside and get some of this stuff on the boards. Cassius and Brutus will have to wait. If we're going to be making an arrest, we need to be very clear what the charges are.'

'Who are Cassius and Brutus?'

'In this case, DS Dawn Simkins and the Chief Super back in Sheffield. You really should read *Julius Caesar*, Denton, you'd like it.'

'Yeah, right.'

They got out of the car and walked slowly across the car park.

'How was it with your dad?' Khan said. 'He looked like he needed a bit of help.'

'It started well, then turned nasty. Same old story. I don't know why I expected anything else,' Sean said. 'I'm going to have to go back. I left all my stuff there, including my keys and my wallet.'

Khan's phone rang at that moment. He answered and listened to the caller.

'OK, thanks, we're on our way. Come on, Denton. Looks like you'll have a chance to pay your dad a visit sooner rather than later.'

'Sir? I think I'm supposed to be on patrol with PC Wentworth.'

'Leave that with me.' He turned and headed back to the car. 'Come on or we'll miss the fun. You wanted to know where Terry Starkey was on the night of Asaf's murder? Well, I think we're about to find out. We've got a raiding party ready to do a full search on his mother's flat. I'm not in the habit of scaring old ladies, but I think it might be justifiable in this case.'

Khan started the car and turned out of the police station, onto the road behind the law courts. His phone rang again and Rick's voice burst out of the speakerphone.

'Message from the IT department, and I think you're going to like it. Mohammad Asaf's Blackberry records are in. Last received text from a SIM card registered to a Taheera Ahmed, 3 The Old Orchard, South Barnsall.'

'I see,' Khan kept his eyes fixed on the road as he swerved round a cyclist.

300

'So she wasn't a random subject for his photo project,' Sean said.

'Also, something else interesting,' Rick was saying. 'The car in PC Denton's photograph, the one Starkey was driving? I've got the results on the licence plate. It's registered to the same address as the girl's phone contract, to a Mr Kamran D. Ahmed. Thing is, the DVLA has him down as disqualified for a year.'

'That's not the father's name, he calls himself Raymond,' Khan said. 'Find out who this Kamran is and pay him a visit. Tread sensitively, they've just lost their daughter.'

'Sir?' Sean had a feeling of things sliding into place, not quite connecting, but getting closer. 'I took a picture of the screensaver on Starkey's phone. I had a hunch it was nicked. There was a garden, trees covered in flowers, like an orchard. Could be The Old Orchard – where her family lives? The phone had these scratches, like where a cover had been pulled off. Pink. Look, I think he had the girl's phone. Perhaps he sent the text to Mohammad?'

The lights ahead of them turned amber. The car in front went through.

'Or he took it off her body,' Khan said.

'Wouldn't he have thrown it away?'

Khan pulled up dead on the stop line. 'Rick? You still there?'

'Yes, I'm here,' Rick said.

'When you get to the Ahmed house, bring this Kamran in. He may have something for us on Starkey.'

'And if he won't come voluntarily?'

'Arrest him on conspiracy to pervert the course of justice.'

'Will you be back to conduct the interview?'

'I'll be there. Tell the custody sergeant to keep it nice and slow and make sure the solicitor doesn't get there before me.'

The lights were going green as Rick rang off.

CHAPTER THIRTY-SIX

York

Chloe looks at the roll of money in Emma's hand and looks away. She has to pretend she hasn't seen it, hasn't got a whole load of questions queuing up in her head about how Emma got it and what for.

'No. I don't know if I'd be able to pay you back.'

She looks at the china set again and Emma puts her money away. Something flickers in the glass, the reflection of a car behind them, slowing right down, close up against the kerb. She stands still, not wanting to turn round, her instincts telling her to keep her face to the window. The car stops and the driver's door opens.

'Let's at least go in and ask,' Emma offers.

'Yes.' Chloe moves quickly, almost pushing Emma through the door and into the shop. She elbows the door shut behind her and grabs a dress off the nearest rail. 'Can I try this on?'

A middle-aged woman behind the till waves them towards a changing cubicle at the back of the shop, barely looking up from her knitting. 'Help yourself.'

'Chlo? What you doing?' Emma has followed her. 'That's never going to fit you. It's massive.'

'Sh.'

She grabs Emma and pulls her into the cubicle as the door of the shop opens and a bell tingles.

'What?' Emma whispers but Chloe shakes her head.

'How may I help you?' This time it sounds like the woman has looked up.

'I'm looking for my girlfriend. I think she came in here.'

'Oh, really?' The lady is helpful, chirpy almost. 'Just a minute, I'll have a look.' She's walking towards the back of the shop, they can hear her humming under her breath. She turns and hums her way back. 'No, I'm sorry, there's nobody here. Perhaps she went next door? Cats Protection have more clothes in stock for young people at the moment.'

There's a pause and the door slams shut with a jangle of the old-fashioned bell.

'Some people have no manners,' the woman says, loud enough for it to be meant for them to hear.

Chloe lets go of the breath she was holding.

'Now what?' Emma says.

'Are you girls all right?' the woman calls to them.

They step out of the changing cubicle. Beyond the rails of musty clothes, the shop is empty and the road outside is clear. Chloe gives the woman back the dress.

'Have you got a back door?' Chloe says.

'Is that man troubling you?' The woman sounds like a social worker type. 'It's none of my business, of course. But we do have a closed-circuit television camera. You need to tell the police if someone's harassing you.'

'Who is he?' Emma asks. She looks first out of the window and then round the shop, as if she needs to double-check they're alone.

'I think you know,' says Chloe.

'What d'you mean?' Emma shoves her hands in her pockets and turns away.

'Like I said,' the woman says, 'I can save the tape. Do you want me to call the police?'

'They won't do anything,' Chloe walks towards the door.

It sticks for a moment as she pulls it and the bell jangles above her head. Outside, the car has gone. Emma follows her out to the hot pavement. He was here, and sooner or later he'll show himself again. Chloe thinks back and realises that she's been seeing that car, seeing him, everywhere. Like a ghost, she thought she was imagining him. From the first night at Meredith House, that was the car on the kerb and he was the waiting driver. He can't have known, then, how close he'd got to her, so when did he realise? After she went to the Chasebridge estate? Did he follow Taheera's car all the way back to York? On the dusty road by the cooling towers she thought she saw the tail end of a car following the skip lorry, and after that? Did he get to Meredith House and find Emma before she and Taheera got back or had they already met? Whatever has gone before, she understands that he's never going to let her disappear. Very well. Let him find her. Let him finish it.

'See you, Emma.'

'Chloe . . .'

'Leave it. Just ask her if she'll keep the set of china for me.'

'Where are you going?'

'I've decided to go to work today. I'm going to Halsworth Grange.'

'Chloe!' Emma called out to her, her voice thin like a child's. 'He said he's from a national newspaper. I was going to share the money with you. I did it for both of us.'

Chloe sets off running towards the city centre. She keeps to the edge of the pavement, dropping off the kerb every now and again to pass slower pedestrians. As the streets fill up with tourists, she slows to a walk. The tower of York Minster is watching her, but she looks away, keeps her eyes on the pavement. She presses on, head down, until she's on Lendal Bridge. Glancing at the red pleasure boats, she wishes she could hire one, take it as far down the river as she can go and out to sea, drift until she's found, a bone-picked skeleton rocking on the waves. She snaps back to the gritty pavement in front of her. Not a boat. Not starving or drowning. Not a church tower or a skip lorry in a narrow lane. No chance of anyone else trying to save her, only to make it worse. Because that's what they all do in the end, the do-gooders and the false friends. It's time to do it properly.

She thought she could trust them, Emma and Taheera. She even dreamt of a time when she'd have that place of her own, and she'd invite them in to say 'thank you' for everything they'd done, in to her little flat with the blue iris china and a cake she'd have baked. But that's someone else's dream. They've never done anything except make things worse, but she knows what to do now and she doesn't want to be distracted. She looks over her shoulder as she crosses the road near the city walls and thinks she sees the same dark blue car, tucked in behind a van. She quickens her pace and passes under the arch where the traffic is one-way, coming towards her. If it's him, and he's seen her, he won't be able to get to her without passing two sets of lights. She speeds up and runs out into the road as the pedestrian light flashes green. She sprints all the way to the station.

'Come on, Terry,' she whispers, 'let's see how clever you are.'

She finds her regular platform and the local stopping train. She takes a seat near the toilet, where she can watch for the guard. She has an old ticket in her purse and a story about throwing the wrong one away, but the train pulls out and there's no sign of anyone in uniform. She sits for a while, catching her breath, the sweat drying on her skin. In the police cell she sat like this, waiting. Unable to do anything except see what would happen next. There was no point in using any energy to shout or fight or argue. Taheera was dead. She got herself killed in that beautiful garden and they thought it was Chloe's fault. Maybe it was in a way. Maybe Taheera was tainted by being near her. Or perhaps it was to do with that boy. The one who died. Chloe can't understand it. Why would someone so smart and beautiful spend her time with criminals? Maybe she liked getting her hands dirty. Chloe sighs but there are no tears now.

She is startled by a man coming into her carriage. He's wearing a denim jacket and his hair is short. She sits up straight, staring ahead, willing him to catch her eye. He turns and she sees he has a goatee beard and glasses. He's carrying a guitar case. It's not him. She's not sure if it's relief or disappointment but she slumps down into the seat and lets her forehead fall against the hard, cool glass of the window.

When the train reaches the station near Halsworth Grange, her stomach contracts, a muscle memory that she should get off, but she stays where she is, holding her breath until the doors slide shut and the train jerks forward. Next stop, Doncaster.

The exit leads her into the Frenchgate Shopping Centre and she's confused for a moment, losing her bearings. This side of the Centre is new. A group of teenagers rush by, laughing, clutching cans of energy drinks in their hands. A fat boy pulls a face at her and shrieks like a parrot and they all laugh some more. One of them points at her and calls out: 'Freak!'

She looks around for the entrance to the old bus station. There's a sign for 'Transport Interchange' and she follows it to a staircase, which finally leads her to a line of bus stops. She thinks the numbers might have changed too, so she looks on the alphabetical list on the wall, but there it is: the number seventy-six still goes to Chasebridge.

CHAPTER THIRTY-SEVEN

Doncaster

The circus was back in town, squad cars ringing Eagle Mount Two. Bernadette Armley wasn't going to be happy about several pairs of regulation police boots messing up her carpet on the hunt for her eldest son, but the force wanted to know where he was the night she stood at her window, watching a young man run towards his killer. The same son who'd asked her to clean up after him, but spared her from seeing the body. They also wanted to question her about her refusal to let a female detective into her home, giving a suspect time to slip away before a second officer arrived.

DCI Khan had given the instructions, before returning to Eagle Mount One with Sean, in order to pay Jack Denton a visit. A knock on the door got no response. Sean opened the letter box.

'Dad, open up. Come on. I've come for my stuff. Come on, Dad, you owe me!'

Khan moved away and made himself busy, checking out the view from the far side of the landing, beyond the lift.

'Dad! I know you're in there. I'll start with my wallet and my keys but then you owe me, big time. You told Starkey I was police, didn't you? Fuck you, dad!'

He kicked the door so hard the wound in his heel throbbed. Bending down he pressed his ear to the open letter box. There was a sound of someone moving, a muffled groan.

'Come on, Dad. I'll give you ten seconds, then I'm going to kick the door in.'

Sean watched through the letter box as a clenched and twisted hand appeared at the partially opened bedroom door. Jack Denton steadied himself, squinted to focus and stumbled forward into his hallway, hair on end and wearing a filthy jumper, covered in something that looked like sick. Like father, like son, Sean thought. But at least he'd made it to the toilet in time, unlike Jack.

'Dad,' his voice softer now, 'come on, open the door. I need to get my stuff. Then I'll be off. We can pretend none of this ever happened.'

He straightened up and stood back as his father unlocked the door. The whisky breath was unmistakable.

'What d'you want?' he slurred. 'Who the fuck's this?'

Sean hadn't notice Khan moving in close behind him.

'Detective Chief Inspector Sam Nasir Khan. An honour to meet you again, Mr Denton. You son is a credit to you.'

Jack had nothing to say. He blinked his rheumy eyes and shook his head. Sean thought it was a nice speech, nicely wasted: his nan was the one who deserved the credit, but Khan's words had the desired effect on Jack, who stepped back, leaning crookedly against the wall.

'Go on then,' Jack said to Sean. 'Get your stuff and fuck off.'

Khan waited just inside the entrance to the flat. Sean headed towards the lounge and looked back to see the two men eyeballing one another, except Jack was still having problems focusing, rubbing his eyes as if he was seeing things, only to find the apparition of the detective still filling his hallway.

In the lounge the empty beer cans were where Sean had left them, but his shoes, jeans and T-shirt had been placed in a neat pile on the settee. He felt the pocket of his jeans and was relieved to find the familiar shape of his wallet in one pocket and the weight of his keys in the other. The tidiness was confusing though.

'Has he been back? Terry Starkey?'

'Aye.'

Sean came back into the hall, palming his wallet out of the jeans pocket and flicking it open. It was empty. Cards and cash both gone.

'He's robbed me, the bastard.'

'He needed some cash for petrol. He'll pay us back.'

'You mean he'll pay you back, I can't see him doing me any favours. But my cards, Dad, you let him take my cards.'

'He said it's a gas guzzler, that car. It'll be fifty quid for him to get to York and back. He said he's found that lass, the one who killed his brother.'

'York? Shit. When was he here, Dad? How long ago?'

'Hours ago. I don't know. I've been asleep.'

Khan ducked out onto the landing and spoke quickly into the radio.

'Funny,' Jack said, wheezing a laugh through his broken

teeth. 'I'd have liked to have seen that, you two having a happy family reunion.'

Khan hit the lift call button and called back.

'Come on, Sean. We've got to get to York before Starkey gets to the girl.'

'What d'you mean, "happy families"?' Sean said quietly, 'I'm not related to him.'

'Aren't you?' Jack was close enough for Sean to smell vomit through the whisky stench. 'She was a looker once,' Jack said quietly, a strange smile creasing his loose skin.

'Hang on a minute, sir.'

Whatever Jack was about to say, he would have to say it in private. Sean pushed his father towards the kitchen.

'Saint Bernadette, we called her,' Jack said. 'She used to do the soup kitchens during the strike. When I came out of the hospital, I helped her out and she helped me. He was on the picket line, old man Starkey, or down the pub. I walked her home a few times, and the rest.'

'You're full of shit.'

'Am I?' He said, whistling something tuneless through his teeth. 'She was kinder to me than your mam ever was. Mind you, that wouldn't be hard. They all showed me more respect than that bitch ever did.'

Sean fought the urge to grab him and slam him against the wall. He heard Khan's phone ring out on the landing.

'Yes?' Khan said. 'Mrs Coldacre, of course I remember. Did he? When was this? Thanks.' He called through the doorway of the flat: 'Sean? Are you coming? He was at Halsworth Grange half an hour ago; he must be heading north.'

Jack Denton was shrinking from his son, his back pressed against the cooker, but Sean wasn't looking at his father. Out of the kitchen window he saw a familiar car slow down and stop.

'Sir! He's here.'

Khan came into the kitchen and they watched as Terry got out of the car. He leant back for a moment against the bonnet, then pulled himself up as if he'd seen something, like a cat who's spotted a sparrow. And then he ran.

'Who's he after?' Sean said.

'Come on!'

Khan led the way out of the flat, radio in hand, as they took the stairs two at a time.

'Dawn? Can you see the front of the blocks? OK. IC1 male, cropped hair, denim jacket, could be following someone.'

The fire door clattered shut behind them.

'Shit. OK, get an ambulance for her and wait for instructions.'

Outside, the police cars were still. The estate seemed frozen, not even the swings moving on their chains.

'Mrs Armley spotted someone,' Khan said to Sean, 'while Dawn and the boys were searching her home. A slim young woman, apparently, running over the playground. But she wasn't running away, she was running towards the Eagle Mount flats.' He stood back, looking at each blank-faced tower block in turn. 'The old woman's so shocked, she's collapsed.'

'Chloe Toms?'

'Must be.'

Sean looked around them. 'Where did Starkey go?'

Still nothing moved.

'Which block did she push the brother off?' Khan tipped his head back and scanned the rooflines.

'Eagle Mount Four.'

Khan was already heading towards it.

CHAPTER THIRTY-EIGHT

Doncaster

Chloe's been running since she got off the bus. The grass of the rec is a relief, softer under her feet. She thinks she saw the car as she crossed the road by the shops, but she's still ahead. There are police cars at Eagle Mount Two. Jay's block. Where his brother watched from the window and saw him wave. Not now. She doesn't want to think about that now. She must push it down, keep it back. That was then and this is now. She crosses the top road and throws open the front door of Eagle Mount Four.

In the sun-filled lobby, ten years vanish. The smells and the colours, the sounds – distant voices, doors closing, resonating along concrete floors and metal pipes – are all exactly as they were. She's back. Marilyn Nelson, Linnie, her Jay calls her. They're back here together and this time she's going to get it right.

The lift is out of order. By the time she's half-walked, half-run to the top, her legs are shaking. She pulls herself up through the service hatch. On the roof her footsteps sound unnaturally loud, slapping down on the asphalt where it's bubbled and blistered. She stops at the edge, watching over the town. She remembers how her fingers brushed his sleeve and the brittle edges of her chewed nails caught the wool of his old army trench coat. She wished she'd worn something warmer. She slipped her hand into the crook of his arm and stood close, so that his body sheltered hers. Traffic and children's voices floated up to meet them.

She wanted to know if he was afraid, but his hair whipped round his face and she couldn't see his eyes. At the corner of the railing a crow perched, watching them, feathers ruffled by the wind. She want to say a prayer, but she didn't know any, just fragments remembered from primary school and nothing about being ready to die. She squeezed his elbow and they stepped up onto the wall. He raised his arm and waved to someone below. Then her hand was empty, reaching into nothing. He was meant to hold her hand, but he let go. The crow took off, hovered for a moment in the updraught; staring back at her with hard, shining eyes.

'Linnie.'

His voice is behind her. She turns and sees he's cut his hair short. He's put on weight. There are spots behind her eyes again, the image blurs and her mouth fills with saliva.

'Fuck you. You little bitch. I've got you now.' Blue eyes, red-rimmed, he's crossing the roof towards her. 'And I'm going to make you suffer.'

That was then. This is now. It's not Jay.

'Hello, Terry.'

She leans back against the railing. Above her the sky is blue and cloudless.

'You can't catch me, Terry,' she lets her weight take her, feels her chest open and throws her arms wide. 'And who's going to believe you didn't push me over?'

'Don't you fucking dare!'

'You killed him, Terry, with what you did to him. Made him hate himself enough to want to die.'

'Oi!' Another voice and footsteps across the roof, boots slapping down on the asphalt, but it's all too slow, she's falling back.

'I've got him,' a voice she knows, dark eyes and a black beard. 'Sean! Catch her!'

A scuff of sound, muffled, and the hard bar of the railing against her shoulder blades. Her head snaps back and it's all sky.

CHAPTER THIRTY-NINE

Doncaster

Sean dived for her legs, his fingers closing round the bones of her ankles as he fell face down on the sandpaper surface of the roof. He thought he'd lost her, the weight of her upper body carrying her over the rusting, broken rail, but at the last moment she tipped forward and slumped down next to him. She looked unconscious.

From a few feet away he could hear Khan giving Terry Starkey the standard warning, like a chant at a church service.

'Anything you do say may be used in evidence . . .'

Sean was breathing heavily, his fingers feeling for a pulse in her neck.

'Look at me, Chloe,' Sean said. 'Chloe? Marilyn? Open your eyes and look at me.'

Her eyes flickered.

'Hello, Terry. I knew you'd come.'

'What's that?' Sean leant in closer. 'Terry's not going to hurt you now.'

'Jay made me promise,' she said. 'He made me promise not to tell anyone what you were doing to him. What you'd been doing to him for years, from before he even knew the words for it.'

Her voice was so quiet, Sean had to strain to listen, as the words tumbled out.

'Until he couldn't live with himself. Until he wanted to fly away and I promised I'd fly away with him, but he let go, Terry, he left me, and I couldn't do it on my own. You want me dead. Go on, let me go.'

'Terry's not going to hurt you now. You're safe.' His hand was still on her neck, the pulse pushing softly against his fingertips. 'My name's Police Constable Denton, but you can call me Sean.'

Khan was cuffing Starkey, face down on the ground. Sean couldn't believe the girl had mistaken him for Terry Starkey; she was delirious and wasn't focusing. It didn't mean a thing. When Starkey turned his head, Sean searched his features for any evidence that he and Terry could be related and that his dad wasn't making stuff up. Terry definitely looked like the boy in Bernadette Armley's photo frame, the one who really was his half-brother, James, or Jay, the girl called him. Sean tried to understand what she'd just said about Terry and his younger brother, and it made him feel sick. He stroked her cheek and she opened her eyes as he reached for his radio. He called for an ambulance.

'And can you radio a couple of officers to come up for a suspect under arrest?'

'Don't worry,' Khan said, 'I'll be very happy to give our

lads a hand with Mr Starkey. In the middle of his back, in case he needs a bit of a push.'

'Fuck off, copper. You can't threaten me.'

'Did anyone hear any threats?' Khan twisted the cuffs hard.

'Didn't hear a thing, sir,' Sean said. 'Only a crow making a racket up there on the satellite dish.'

CHAPTER FORTY

Doncaster

Gavin Wentworth appeared at Sean's elbow as he queued in the canteen.

'Hi, Gav, sorry I lost you. I got pulled onto a job with Khan.'

'So I heard. You really must stop hanging around on the tops of tower blocks.'

'Yeah, right,' Sean reached for a plate of hot food and asked for extra peas. It was about time he started eating more healthily.

'At least you had your clothes on this time. Can I join you?'

'Sure, I'm over there with Carly.'

Sean sat down and tucked into his food. Carly was looking at him with a big grin and eventually he asked her what she was looking so pleased about.

'You, you daft bugger. I turn my back for five minutes and the next thing I know you're trying for a gallantry medal.'

He shook his head. 'Doubt it. Just there at the right time and lucky, I suppose.'

She took a breath, as if she was about to sing.

'Don't!' He waved his fork at her, complete with a pea that threatened to fly off. 'Please! Not the song.'

'What song's that?' Gav put his tray down and sat next to Carly. 'We need to sort out a new playlist for when, and if, we ever get this lad back on a normal shift.'

'Make sure it's got a bit of Kylie Minogue on,' Carly said. 'He loves that.'

Sean had his mouth too full of food to argue. Eventually he managed to speak.

'Sorry if I'm being antisocial, but I need to eat this and get upstairs. Khan's got Terry Starkey in interview room two with Rick, and Dawn's got Kamran Ahmed, the victim's brother, in room three. He wants me up there as an extra pair of hands.'

'Dawn? First name terms, is it now?' Gav said. 'Thought you couldn't stick her.'

'Can't,' he said through a mouth full of mashed potato, 'but I've still got to work with her.'

He cleared his plate and got up to go. Gavin leant over to Carly and Sean could hear him clearly as he walked away.

'I'm going to be looking for a new partner, if you ask me, this temporary secondment business has the whiff of something more permanent.'

Sean wasn't so sure. He would miss Gavin's terrible sense of humour for a start and all this excitement was starting to give him indigestion. Once he got upstairs, he was told to sit in on each interview alternately, to allow Khan to swap between the two. Rick Houghton was in the room with Starkey when he got there.

'For the benefit of the recording, PC Denton has entered the room and DCI Khan has left,' Rick said.

Rick was showing Starkey the photos from the crowd outside the burning shop and asking about Gary MacDonald.

'He was in HMP Lindholme with you, towards the end of your sentence.'

'If you say so.'

Terry refused to make eye contact.

'I do say so. The prison has confirmed you worked in the gardens on the same team.'

Terry shrugged. 'So, that's not a crime, is it?'

'What was he doing in Chasebridge? He's from over Stockport way, isn't he?'

'Helping out. Volunteering.'

'Helping you, Terry? In a number of different schemes?'

'I don't know what you mean.'

'We have information that Gary was supplying class B drugs,' Rick said, 'via the snooker hall.'

It was Sean's turn to look away. He didn't want to catch Terry's eye.

'What did you have against Mohammad Asaf?' Rick persisted. 'Was he on your patch?'

Terry shook his head. 'I don't know who you're talking about.'

'Or was it a commercial job?' Rick continued in a level tone. 'Cash on delivery? Whose idea was the half-hearted attempt at castration? Would you get paid more if you could deliver the goods, so to speak?'

'Fuck off. I'm not a fucking pervert!' Terry slammed his fist on the table.

Sean looked at him. Up on the roof of Eagle Mount Four, Chloe had spoken so quietly Starkey couldn't have heard her, but she what she said was pretty clear to Sean.

'Who's saying you are, Terry?' Sean said. 'That's a nasty thing to say about anyone and I'm sure DI Houghton didn't mean to offend you.'

Terry nodded, hooked by Sean's sympathy, but Sean hadn't finished.

'The thing is though, how would it look if we had intelligence about abuse, historic abuse, perpetrated by yourself?'

The colour drained from Terry's face. He wasn't the hard man any more.

'Sean, bro, what are you saying?'

'Call me PC Denton, please. I'm saying if you had a sexual offence added to your record, it would make your next stay inside very uncomfortable, wouldn't it?'

Rick waited for Sean to finish.

'Excuse us a minute, Mr Starkey.' Rick nodded to Sean to step outside. 'DI Houghton and PC Denton are leaving the room and I am pausing the recording.'

Out in the corridor Rick faced Sean. 'What was that about?'

'I was just pointing something out,' he said. 'Chloe, or Marilyn, said he'd been abusing Jay, his half-brother, for years. Jay was suicidal. I'm sure we could get her to testify.'

'Slow down, mate. Get him rattled, that's fine. But keep it under your hat for now.'

'But he is a fucking pervert!'

'Calm down, Sean,' Rick gripped his shoulder. 'Listen. If

it is true, and if there's a chance of the girl having a retrial, don't waste it here.'

'Have you got enough to charge him with Asaf's murder?' Sean said.

'Not yet, but we've got time,' Rick said. 'And Sean, I don't like him being so pally with you.'

Neither do I, Sean thought to himself, *neither do I*. A door opened along the corridor and Khan put his head out.

'Sean? I want you in here for a minute, I'll do a swap.'

As they passed in the corridor, Khan muttered to him: 'If I have to spend another minute in that room with that sanctimonious little shite, I might ring his neck.'

'I'm not sure what that word means, sir, but I think I feel the same about Starkey.'

He was opening the door when Sandy Schofield came bustling down the corridor.

'You got a Kamran Ahmed in there?'

Sean nodded.

'This message just came. You may want to pass it on yourself.'

'Thanks.'

She handed it over and disappeared back up the corridor.

In the second interview room, the smell of expensive cologne hit Sean immediately. Kamran Ahmed was wearing designer threads to match the fragrance. If they were genuine, Sean totted up at least six hundred quid, from shoes to collar.

'As I said to your colleague,' Kamran said, with a polite nod, 'I really have nothing to say until my solicitor gets here.'

'That would be your father's solicitor?' DS Simkins said, looking at her notes. 'A Mr Sadiq?'

'Yeah, that's him.'

'DS Simkins?' Sean cleared his throat. 'There's a message.'

He handed the piece of paper to Dawn Simkins and as she read it, another rare smile forced her mouth up at the corners.

'It says here that Mr Sadiq is unable to act on your behalf in this instance.' She and Sean both watched as Kamran's soft bottom lip hung open. 'The message is from your father,' Simkins continued. 'He's sorry, but that's all he says. For the tape, I'm handing the message to Mr Ahmed to read for himself. Would you like us to contact the duty solicitor?'

Kamran Ahmed shook his head. He sat in silence for a moment and when he spoke, his voice was controlled.

'I can look after myself. This is all a mistake. It's Terry Starkey you should be talking to, not me. Starkey is a known criminal. This has nothing to do with me.'

'But you know him?'

'I've . . . I've met him.'

'So do you know him well?' DS Simkins said. 'Are you friends?'

'No, of course not.'

'So why is he driving your car?'

'I've no idea. He must have stolen it.'

Kamran rested his hands on the table. His calmness was almost soothing, but the veins on the backs of his hands stood up.

'And you've reported it stolen, have you?'

'I haven't got round to it.'

Sean saw now why she was called 'the Rottweiler'. Her interview technique was persistent, she wasn't letting go.

Like Rick, she was playing as if they had all the time in the world. He could have sat for hours watching, but the door opened and Khan came back in.

'Denton? Can you sort out the tea run for DI Houghton and then come back here and do the same? It may be a long night.'

'DCI Khan has entered the interview room and PC Denton has left.'

He was back to being the tea boy, just when it was getting interesting. Sean sighed. He knew this could go on for a long while, but wished he could be there when Starkey broke. He knocked on the door of the first room and asked Rick what he and his interviewee wanted to drink. Starkey asked for tea with two sugars, if it wasn't too much bother. Sean thought he'd have to resist the urge to spit in it, but he kept his face set to neutral.

When he brought the drinks back, Rick was asking Starkey about gardening tools.

'If we found a knife a bit like this one, whose prints do you think we'd find on it?'

'No idea.'

'No idea, or nobody's prints?'

Starkey shrugged.

'No comment.'

'What would we find, Terry? Come on, we know you're familiar with the tool shed at Halsworth Grange, about what came in and out of it. We know that Taheera Ahmed was killed with a knife that had never been used for gardening. Are you sure you didn't help yourself to a fresh delivery when it arrived from the Garden Centre?'

'What's this got to do with me?' Terry shouted. 'I didn't do the girl and you can't say I did.'

There was a moment when no one spoke.

'Who did you "do", Terry? The young man, Mohammad?' Rick said. 'Or did you do the neat little warning cut on his younger cousin, Saleem? If not the girl, then who? They were all neat, sharp jobs, the work of someone who knows what he's doing with a knife. Is that you, Terry? Or have you got your own apprentices now?'

'Fuck off. I'm saying nowt. You're trying to mess with my head. No comment.'

It was getting late and Rick decided to transfer Starkey to the cells. Khan wanted to keep Ahmed going for a bit longer. Sean met him in the corridor.

'I just need one of them to say enough to tie it in with your recording,' Khan said, 'but at the moment, all we've got is one pack of lies against another. I don't understand why Ahmed's protecting Starkey, and until we get Lizzie's DNA tests on Taheera, we haven't got enough to prove anything.'

Sean stifled a yawn and Khan took the hint.

'You'd better get off. You've had a long day.'

'You can say that again.'

'And take tomorrow off. We owe you that.'

'OK,' Sean said, but his heart sank, he wanted to be part of it, see it through to the end. Khan was waiting for a response. Sean forced a smile. 'Thank you, sir.'

Nan was waiting up for him. She had something to show him. He wasn't sure how much to tell her, but news had already filtered down from the Chasebridge estate to The Groves.

'I'm so proud of you for saving that girl! At first I wasn't sure about her, but I went up to the library and did a bit of research. I always knew there was something about that case that didn't fit. That lass was peculiar all right, dragged up in the pub half her life, but I never had her pegged as a killer. But what about Bernadette Armley? Is it true she got carried off in an ambulance? Bit too convenient, that. I know you don't have to tell me, but I reckon that son of hers has something to do with all this, and she's been covering his back.'

He didn't have the energy to remind her what she'd originally said about Marilyn Nelson and he wasn't going to be led on the subject of Terry Starkey, he just shrugged and let her show him the printouts she'd made. He listened to her forming a campaign to get a pardon for Marilyn, until his eyes were closing. Before he went to bed, he sent Lizzie Morrison a text, but he couldn't stay awake long enough to wait for the reply.

CHAPTER FORTY-ONE

Doncaster

The New Moon Chinese restaurant was empty at lunchtime, which suited Sean fine. He was early, but he hadn't been able to settle all morning. Lizzie had promised to meet him straight from the lab. He wanted to hear it in person, no email trail, no texts. She said she understood.

He asked for a jug of water and ordered a mixed starter. A bowl of prawn crackers arrived straight away and he broke one in his fingers and let it melt on his tongue. He wasn't really hungry, but it was something to do. He checked the time on his phone. She was a minute late. There was music playing, barely audible despite the stillness in the restaurant, a high-pitched Chinese instrument full of sorrow. Then she was there, a laptop case over her shoulder, white blouse under her little black jacket, turning the corner of the stairs, the waiter showing her across the empty restaurant to where he was waiting.

'Got it,' she smiled briefly and sat down. She pulled a large, brown envelope out of the bag. 'The paperwork was a bit tricky, but I said I was trying to rule out cross-contamination. That thread of denim you gave me at the Asaf murder scene? I wrote on the notes that I couldn't be sure you hadn't touched it, so I needed to order a double-blind test for your DNA against Starkey's.'

'I hadn't touched it.'

'I know that. Now concentrate. You're on the system, obviously, but your dad's DNA was more tricky. He's not a suspect, although we could have arrested him for perverting the course of justice, but I didn't think you'd want that. Then Gavin Wentworth gave me this.'

She pulled out a clear plastic bag containing Jack Denton's baseball hat, which Sean had left in Gav's car on the night of the Clean Up Chasebridge meeting.

'It's much easier to prove or disprove a half-sibling relationship if you've got the father's DNA.'

'And?' He thought he would be sick if she didn't tell him soon.

'The good news is Starkey is not your half-brother. He has no DNA in common with you or your father.'

'Thank fuck for that.'

He wondered why she didn't smile; the papers were still in her hand.

'And the bad news?'

'Marilyn Nelson, or Chloe Toms, as she's now known, is, however, your sister. Your half-sister on your father's side.'

The Chinese music wailed gently in the background like a ghost calling him from somewhere.

'That stupid bastard. He must have been putting it about all over the fucking estate.'

'Before you were born, though. Chloe's older than you, isn't she?'

'I suppose so,' he said. Chloe Toms looked like a child, but Lizzie was right, she must be three or four years older at least. 'Who's her mother?'

'Well, the DNA doesn't tell me that, but the Internet was very helpful. I've quite enjoyed being a detective actually.'

She watched him and waited for a moment, as if she was testing how much he wanted to hear.

'Linda Nelson died in a car accident six weeks after her daughter was sent to prison. The newspaper reports said she worked behind the bar at the Chasebridge Tavern. She never married.'

'And the Tavern went up in smoke itself last year. Christ, it all turns to shit in the end, doesn't it?'

'Are you OK?' Her hand was moving across the table. He let her place it on top of his.

'Yeah. I'm OK. Funny, I always wanted a sister.'

Lizzie withdrew her hand and he wondered if he'd missed something.

'My nan went up to the library yesterday,' he said, 'did a bit of research in the old local papers they've put online. James Armley's death wasn't clear-cut. On the first day of the case the defence claimed it was planned as a double suicide, but the girl didn't have the bottle. Then she changed her plea to guilty to manslaughter on the second day, blamed herself I suppose, or just gave up fighting. Guess who the eye witness was, who said he'd seen her push James off?'

'Terry Starkey?'

'In one.'

332

'I never thought she had it in her to kill Taheera Ahmed either,' Lizzie said. 'But you know what?' She tapped the envelope. 'I don't think Starkey did it.'

'You're kidding! He had access to the weapon, the gloves, everything.'

'There was a print on her cheek, perfectly shaped like a pair of lips. The DNA from the saliva is her brother's. I think if we put it to Kamran Ahmed that he killed his sister, then kissed her goodbye as the blood drained from her throat, he might stop denying it and tell us where he disposed of her car. I've told Khan, but he says not to rush with the documents. He's enjoying making Ahmed sweat a bit.'

'I think Khan guessed he was behind it,' Sean poured a glass of water and drank it in one. 'But I'd assumed he'd got Starkey to do his dirty work and paid him with the car.'

'Looks like Starkey was just the accomplice, in Taheera's case. We still need something concrete to pin him with the Asaf murder. We know he had access to the right sort of knife, but it would be good if we could find it. I think he'll go down as an accessory with Kamran Ahmed, whichever way it falls.'

'Blue denim thread,' Sean said, wiping his mouth on the back of his hand. 'It puts Starkey at the scene of Asaf's murder.'

'And Chloe's drawing puts him at Halsworth Grange with Kamran Ahmed. Perhaps it wasn't just about supplying the weapon, perhaps Kamran needed Starkey with him to see it through.'

'Or in case Taheera put up a fight,' Sean said.

'But she didn't. I don't understand that.'

333

'Khan's furious,' Sean said. 'He hates Kamran, like it's personal.'

'Yeah, well it is personal for Sam,' she said.

The waiter arrived with four stainless steel dishes. Sean's appetite had come back and he couldn't wait to get stuck in.

'In what way?'

'The idea of honour killings. In fact he told me off for using the word "honour". He says they're inherently anti-Islamic.'

Sean shrugged. 'Fair enough, but how is that personal?'

'It's to do with Khan's parents. They had a love marriage, apparently, and got cut off from their families. It's complicated for him, I think, because he did the same, married a non-Muslim and they couldn't cope with that.'

'I didn't know he was married,' Sean helped himself to sesame prawn toast. He realised he didn't know very much at all about Khan.

'He and his wife are trying for a baby. He thinks his parents might soften if there's a grandchild,' Lizzie said, and stirred a spoon into the dish of salt and pepper chicken wings, piling some onto her plate.

'How did you get all this out of him?' Sean said. 'He doesn't strike me as the kind to share his personal life.'

She seemed to be focusing on her chopsticks and the business of transferring a piece of chicken to her mouth, so she didn't reply at first.

'It makes me realise how lucky I am,' she said, giving up with the chopsticks and using her fingers. 'My mum's a bit of a nightmare in her way, but I can't imagine her disowning me, or worse, because of a boyfriend she doesn't approve of.'

'Even if he was a Muslim?' Sean said.

She looked up sharply. 'Look, I went for dinner with him once. OK? Was I under surveillance?'

'No, in fact I had no idea, but like every guilty suspect, you've just given yourself away.' He was trying to keep it light, but he had a bad feeling he'd said the wrong thing. She was stabbing at the chicken now as if it was still alive.

'Do you mind me asking,' he said, 'when did you have this dinner with DCI Khan?'

'Couple of nights ago. I'd been a bit hard on him, and I felt guilty, if you must know. Look, I'm not in the business of stealing other people's husbands.'

'I'm sorry,' he said. 'I didn't mean to suggest you were.'

The sound of Lizzie's chopsticks and Sean's fork on the china dishes punctuated the music, but no more was said while they concentrated on their food. Sean was thinking about Terry Starkey. If Jack believed he was Terry's father, had the idea come from Terry himself, or someone else? Perhaps Bernadette Armley had believed it to be true all along. *How did you end up like Terry*, he wondered. Old man Starkey had been a drinker; then he was dead. Not much of a start in life for his son. Perhaps Terry was jealous of his younger brother, James. Perhaps that's why he wanted to hurt him. Sean had often felt sorry for himself, with his mother dead and having Jack as a dad, but now he looked at it, he realised he'd been lucky. He'd had his nan, and she was solid.

'What makes one person turn out a psychopath,' he said, 'and another person, well, I don't know, like me, I suppose?'

Lizzie didn't have an opportunity to answer before there was a commotion on the stairs and a familiar figure burst through the red curtain into the dining area.

'Get your hands off me, man!' Saleem Asaf was trying to retrieve his arm from the tight grip of the restaurant manager. 'It's the copper I've come to see and he'll want to see me, best believe.'

'It's OK,' Sean said to Mr Lee, the manager. 'Saleem. What's up?'

'I need you to arrest me.'

'Excuse me?'

The boy edged his way round the other tables. He sat down without invitation and helped himself to a plate of chicken wings.

'Got to make the most of it. I ain't going to be eating like this for a while.'

'Be my guest,' Sean said. 'Lizzie, let me introduce Saleem Asaf, Mohammad's cousin.'

'Came to tell you I burnt down the shop,' he said, as he tore the meat off a wing with his teeth.

'In that case, can I have that chicken bone when you're done?' Lizzie said.

He shrugged. 'What for?'

'DNA test.' She patted her envelope.

'No need, lady. I've come here to fess up. Then your boyfriend can arrest me.'

Sean thought this would be a bad moment to look embarrassed.

'Saleem, what's this about?' he said. 'Get to the point or I'll have to ask Mr Lee to throw you out.'

'Criminal damage, can you do me for that? I burnt down the shop, innit. My dad and my uncle are going to land at

336

Manchester Airport in three hours' time and I can't be here when they get back.'

'We've been assuming it was a racist attack.'

'Good.' Saleem's mouth was full, but he still crammed more meat in.

'But you're willing to admit to arson?'

'Mmnh, hnh.'

'Why?'

'Because I did it. And you can prove it, right?' he said, handing Lizzie the stripped wing bone.

'I think so. If your DNA matches the sample we have from the crime scene.'

'But how?' Sean said.

'I think I know,' Lizzie interrupted. 'The torchlit parade was making its way round the estate. You sent Ghazala away, telling her to keep herself safe, didn't you, Saleem? You promised to lock up. Then you waited until the protestors were outside, dropped the bottle full of petrol inside the shop, went out of the back of the building and bolted the shutters.'

Saleem looked impressed. He grabbed a handful of prawn crackers, nodding as he stuffed them in his mouth.

'But why?' Lizzie asked. 'To steal pills from the Health Centre?'

'Pills? Nah.'

'So?' Sean said.

Saleem was still for a moment. 'Are you wearing a wire?'

'For fuck's sake, Saleem, this is Doncaster, not Baltimore.' Sean said. 'No, I'm not wearing a wire. Just get on with it.'

'I'm not under arrest yet?'

'No, but you will be for wasting police time in a minute.'

Saleem flicked the tassels of the tablecloth.

'OK. I thought you'd pin it on those CUC Nazis and that would serve them right. The thing is, I didn't want to run the shop. I don't want to stay on the Chasebridge estate all my life, and with Mo gone, that was my destiny, d'you get me?'

'What about your sister?' Sean said.

Saleem hesitated.

'Surely she'd run the shop?'

'I can't stay there. She can't either. It's not safe for either of us.' He lifted his T-shirt up to show his dressing, as if that explained everything.

'Is there something you haven't told me?'

'Yeah.' He turned another chicken wing over in his fingers and put it down again. 'That other detective said you got some shoe prints from the bottom of the stairs at Eagle Mount Two. From a potential witness? Well, they're mine. Your man took my shoes away from the hospital. I know he's going to work it out sooner or later. But I never had anything to do with Mo's murder, right? I walked in on them, Starkey and his crew, and a couple of younger lads, the ones I knew. Mo was already dead, but they were cutting him, daring each other . . .'

His face twisted with the effort of trying not to revisit what he'd seen. Lizzie leant forward.

'It's OK,' she said. 'I understand. I'm sorry you had to see that.'

'Is that right?' Sean asked Lizzie. 'Do the shoes match the prints?'

'I'll have to check, they're somewhere in a backlog of

evidence, but maybe that's where the other half of my ant's got to.'

'Your what?' Saleem looked confused, but Sean decided there wasn't time to explain.

'Did your sister know who Mohammad was going to meet,' Sean said, 'the night he was killed?'

'She guessed,' Saleem said. 'Mo got a text from his girl, but it wasn't really from her, you know what I mean? Her brother took her phone. He texted Mo, pretending to be her.'

'How do you know this?'

'Because he told me. He thinks he's the big man, Kamran Ahmed, but he's just a dog.' He sucked his teeth. 'He was playing gangsters. Met up with Starkey in a club, paid him to be his chauffeur and that. Cool as a cucumber he turns up to the shop, the day after Mo's murder, talking dirty to Ghazala, calling her a slag. She's had troubles, man. Some boy hurt her, I told you this before, but it weren't her fault. It doesn't make her a slag.'

He paused for a reaction but Sean and Lizzie simply stared at him.

'So I told him what I thought of his family. You know? To return the favour. Now maybe I shouldn't have done that, but he dissed my sister. I told him that his sister was the slag, she was the one that crept upstairs, to our flat, to fuck her boyfriend. Kamran Ahmed said he knew that, and why did I think Mo was dead? Did I really think those *gora* dogs cared about him, some has-been errand boy? It was never about drugs. They killed Mo for money. Kamran's money. He told me how he set it up. He even clicked his fucking fingers to show how easy he thought it was.'

339

'Who did you see, Saleem?' Sean said. 'When you arrived at Eagle Mount Two? We need a name.'

'Starkey – it was him, with the knife, cutting down there, like—' Saleem's eyes filled up and he rubbed his knuckles into them to take away what he'd seen. 'Kamran added a bit of spice to make sure they'd go through with it. He told them Mo had raped a girl, a little white girl.'

'Was Kamran there?' Sean said.

'No.'

'And did Starkey see you?'

Saleem shook his head. 'I came in and I went back out. I wasn't hanging around. One of the other boys must have told him I'd been a lookout because Starkey didn't say nothing when he did this,' he fingered the front of his T-shirt, 'but I swear, if he knew I'd been there, he'd have finished me.'

'And when Mohammad was being chased, Starkey's mother was watching from her window. Another lookout,' said Lizzie.

'Ghazala said Mohammad was happy when he left the shop that night,' Sean said, quietly.

'She keeps saying she should have stopped him,' Saleem said. 'She used to talk to that girl. I think they became friends. My sister doesn't have many friends. And now the girl's dead too.'

Saleem was still, as if he'd finally run out of energy.

'Taheera was a virgin, Saleem,' said Lizzie. 'Whatever else they were doing upstairs, it wasn't that.'

The boy stared at his hands.

'I was so scared,' he said.

Sean took a deep breath. 'Come on Saleem, let's go round

to the police station, you can hand yourself in there for the arson. I'm not actually on duty right now, just having a nice quiet lunch with a friend. I can't promise anything, but if you can stick to this story under oath, I think we might be able to help you. You've done the right thing in telling me, Saleem. Remember that.'

'And you remember,' Saleem said, 'that you promised to look after my sister.'

Sean nodded, but he wasn't sure that Ghazala needed his help; she seemed more than able to stick up for herself.

'Right, I'd better come with you and give this to DCI Khan,' Lizzie picked up the brown envelope. 'And then, Sean, you and I need to have a bit of a talk.'

'Oh?'

'We need to talk about your sister, your new half-sister.'

CHAPTER FORTY-TWO

Doncaster

Through the glass window of the observation room, Sean and Lizzie could see Kamran Ahmed sitting back in the chair, as if this was just a casual conversation. A night in custody had done little to ruffle his appearance, only his hair sat a little flatter. He pressed his hands together, fingers straight, and nodded slowly at something his interviewer was saying.

'He's controlling his responses,' Sean said, 'look at the muscles in his forearm. Tight as anything.'

Lizzie flicked a switch and the sound of Khan's voice reached them.

'. . . at Halsworth Grange you kissed her and said goodbye. Was she still alive?'

The brown envelope containing the DNA result lay on the table between them. Kamran shook his head.

'You're indicating that she was already dead?'

The young man looked up and opened his mouth but no sound came out. His hands went to his face and he covered his mouth and nose, but it was too late; the truth was forcing its way out.

'Are you going to tell us how it happened, Kamran?'

Khan's voice was gentle. Lizzie squeezed Sean's hand and they waited.

'It will be up to the court to get to the bottom of why you did this, but I want to know for myself, so humour me,' Khan said. 'You kill your sister's boyfriend and then you kill her. Because you're jealous of her?'

'No.' It came out as a whisper. 'I couldn't stand by and let her bring shame on the family.'

'Who was bringing shame, Kamran?' Khan said. 'She'd done well. Got a degree. She was working with women who'd been in prison, helping them get back on track. What's shameful about that? It seems to me that she was doing something any parent would be proud of.'

'No!' Kamran Ahmed suddenly raised his voice. 'If she wasn't ashamed, then why all the secrecy? If she didn't know it was wrong to have sex with that piece of trash, why sneak around behind everyone's back?'

'What right do you have to call anyone trash?' Khan's voice quivered with rage. 'Mohammad Asaf was going straight, Kamran. He was doing what he could to get out of the very same culture of drugs and gangs that you were so keen to get into. How dare you sit here before me and try to defend yourself, when your own father won't send his lawyer to stick up for you.'

The room was silent and Kamran Ahmed slumped back in his chair. Sean held his breath. Lizzie stood so close to him their hips touched.

'Why did you kill her, Kamran?' Khan said. 'It's too late to pretend you didn't, because we know you did.'

The young man's eyes filled with tears.

'What was I supposed to do?' He blinked and the tears streamed down his face. 'After that boy was dead, she shut herself in her room; wouldn't speak to anyone. She wouldn't tell my parents what was wrong. And then I started to get scared. I thought they'd get it out of her sooner or later, about the boy. Or that girl in the shop would say something.'

'Go on.'

'When there was nothing on the news, I thought, I don't know, maybe Terry Starkey had cleared it up, but then there was that fire at the shop and Terry was on the TV, talking about it, like he hadn't been part of it. I had to do something and . . .'

'You panicked?'

'Yes, no . . .' Ahmed sniffed back the tears and rubbed his eyes. 'She shouldn't have been seeing that boy. Why couldn't she have waited? Been more like my other sister and let our parents choose?'

'That's a smokescreen, Kamran, and I think you know it.'

'I need a glass of water.'

Somewhere off camera they could hear water being poured and a uniformed arm reached forward to put a plastic cup down in front of Kamran Ahmed. He sipped slowly.

'He's buying time,' Lizzie said.

'Why's he bothering?' Sean said. 'He's up to his neck in it, isn't he?'

'I don't know, but it's almost as if he wants Khan's approval.'

'How did you persuade her to meet you at Halsworth

Grange?' Khan had dropped his voice to a calm, relaxed tone and it appeared to work. Kamran nodded two or three times, gathering his thoughts before he spoke.

'I told her I knew who'd killed her boyfriend and we could meet him, trick him into admitting it, then call the police. I told her he used to work up at Halsworth Grange, in the garden, and he'd be going there to pick something up.'

'I see.'

'He stayed in the car.'

'Starkey?'

'Mm. He wasn't needed. Just . . .'

'Yes?'

'He gave me the knife and the gloves. Told me what to do. She was waiting by her car.' He paused. 'I said, let's walk across the meadow. She came with me.'

'She didn't want to know why?'

Kamran shook his head. 'I asked her if she remembered it, when we used to have picnics there, when we were kids. She said, yes. Then she wanted to know what I had in my hand. I said it doesn't matter. We walked towards the edge of the field and she said she didn't want to live any more.'

'And you went ahead?'

'It was my duty.'

'No,' Khan's fist came down on the table and the crash distorted the observation room speakers. 'It is never anyone's duty to take an innocent life.'

Sean turned to Lizzie. She was biting her lip, holding back her own tears. He put his arm round her shoulder.

'Let's go.'

*　*　*

At six-twenty that evening Sean and Lizzie arrived at the hospital. A strict ward sister told them they'd have to wait until visiting started at half past. Sean decided not to show his badge to speed things up. He knew that Chloe wouldn't want any unnecessary attention. They asked a young houseman how she was, and it felt like another white lie, telling the doctor he was family, even though now it was apparently true. The doctor said she'd collapsed due to malnutrition and dehydration, but she was going to be all right. They had her on a drip and a gradual diet and she was waiting to see a psychologist. They had put her in a side room for now, to give her some peace and quiet. The doctor wanted to know if she had any history of eating disorders.

'I'm sorry, I don't know,' Sean said. 'We haven't been exactly close.'

He tried not to catch Lizzie's eye, but he could see she was trying to hide a smile.

'You're going to have to decide what to do about publicity,' she said, as they walked towards Chloe's room.

'What do you mean?'

'It's a great story. Policeman saves woman's life, only to discover she's the sister he never knew he had. You'll be on the sofa with Fern Britton before you know it.'

'I don't think so,' Sean said. 'Fern Britton doesn't do that daytime show any more. Seriously though, I'm not a fan of being on the telly and it's the last thing Chloe needs. I think we'll keep it between us, the three of us, if you don't mind.'

'Just us? What about your dad? Doesn't he deserve to know he has a daughter?'

'Maybe one day, if he ever sobers up,' Sean said. 'I'll tell Nan first. She'll know what to do.'

Chloe was awake. She turned her head on the pillow and smiled when she saw him.

'I'll leave you two for a minute,' Lizzie said and stepped outside the room, letting the door close softly behind her.

'You're the policeman, aren't you?' Chloe's face was pale and her lips barely moved.

'Yes.'

'I'm a bit rubbish at trying to kill myself, aren't I?'

'It's a good thing, really,' he said.

'People keep trying to save me.'

'Aye, well. It's my job but . . .'

'It's OK. Thank you,' she said. 'I know now, there was a reason I had to stay alive. I had to tell someone about Terry.'

'Oh?'

'Did you hear what I said, on the top of the flats?'

'Yes.'

'It was all true.' She looked up at the ceiling and took a long breath. 'Jay didn't want anyone to know, even after he was dead. Said it would destroy his mum. But you can't keep having secrets, can you?'

'No, Chloe, you can't,' Sean said. 'Or would you rather be Marilyn?'

'I was always Linnie to Jay. Then inside I got Lyn. Now I'm Chloe. I've lived all these lives, you see? Better at living then dying.' She closed her eyes and her breathing settled. He wondered if she'd fallen asleep.

'Chloe?' he said.

'Yes?' she said, but her eyes remained shut.

'They're going to review your conviction. I think there's a good chance they'll overturn it. You've got a lot of people wanting to help you.'

She opened her eyes and looked at him for a few seconds before she spoke.

'I won't get the last ten years back though.'

'No,' he said. 'You won't.'

Her eyes fluttered as if she was too tired to keep them open. The room was very warm. Sean loosened his collar.

'Who's your friend?' Chloe said. 'That woman outside?'

'That's Lizzie.'

'She's pretty.'

'Yes.' He turned towards the door. The back of Lizzie's head was visible through the window, the light catching the shine in her dark hair. 'Yes, she is.'

As he watched, a large man and a short, stout woman approached Chloe's room. The man was carrying an enormous bunch of blousy-headed flowers, wrapped in a cone of brown paper. Lizzie spoke to them and nodded towards Sean.

'You've got visitors,' he said.

Chloe raised her head to see.

'Bill,' she said. 'And Brenda.'

'Shall I tell Lizzie to let them in?'

'Not yet,' her head dropped back into the pillow. 'Is she your girlfriend?'

Sean thought about what had passed between him and Lizzie before they had arrived at the hospital. They'd sat for an hour in The Salutation pub, discussing the case, until Lizzie had said.

348

'Let's talk about us.'

'There's an "us"?' he'd said.

'I hope so'. And she'd kissed him. He was still wondering if he'd imagined it.

He took Chloe's hand.

'Yes,' he said, 'I think she is my girlfriend.'

'That's nice. And thank you, for what you did.'

'You're welcome, Chloe, you're very welcome.'

She smiled weakly and closed her eyes again.

'And welcome to my family,' Sean said quietly, but he wasn't sure if she heard him.

ACKNOWLEDGEMENTS

Many thanks to everyone who has helped me in my research, especially Ghazala Fateh, Brian Watson, Alex, Boris, The Captain, Reza Ben Gajra and Maggie Pearson. Thank you to Andy Morgan and Benedict Wallbank for their structural knowledge of ten-storey tower blocks and all my friends on social media who have answered random questions over the last eighteen months. Thank you Josh Parker for gardening advice, love and food; you have been unwavering in your support for my writing and I am eternally thankful that we found each other.

Thank you to everyone who has given me encouragement along the way, especially Carole Bromley, Lesley Glaister, Rivka Fine, Claire Malcolm and the team at New Writing North. Thank you to Laura Longrigg at MBA Literary Agents for looking after me so brilliantly and Allison & Busby; an amazing team who have made this all possible.

Thank you to Fiona Barrows, Livia Nicholson, Allison Loftfield, Chris Bridge and Eleanor Wilson for reading various drafts and versions. A huge thank you to my family for your ongoing support.

Particular thanks to the residents and colleagues at HMP Askham Grange and YOI Wetherby.